Alone

Jamar Berry

DEDICATION

In memory of a fantastic author, though the genre differs from this particular pencraft, you were my mothers favorite writer. May you rest in paradise.

Wilbur Smith - Jan 9th 1933 to Nov 13th 2021

CONTENTS

ACKNOWLEDGMENTS

R v. Shipman [2000] 1 Cr App R 350

CHAPTER 1
THE FRIENDLY DOCTOR

In the quaint town of Elderwood, life meandered at a pace dictated by nature. Cherry blossoms decorated the streets in spring, and the sound of laughter from children playing in the park filled the air. At the heart of this idyllic setting stood a modest brick building with a pristine white sign that read "Dr. Samuel Harrow, General Practitioner." For most residents, this was a sanctuary—an establishment synonymous with compassion, healing, and the comfort of familiarity.

Dr. Samuel Harrow was the kind of doctor every town dreams of having. With his warm smile and reassuring demeanor, he exuded a charm that put even the most anxious souls at ease. He took what seemed like an endless amount of time with each patient, listening intently as they spoke of their ailments, concerns, and stories of life. Yet, what truly endeared him to the town was his uncanny ability to remember the smallest details about their lives— birthdays, anniversaries, and personal struggles. For many, he wasn't just their physician; he was a confidant, a source of solace in a world that often felt indifferent.

Harrow, with his salt-and-pepper hair and kind blue eyes, was a fixture in Elderwood's community. Whether he was attending local events or volunteering at the annual fair, he made himself available to those around him. "He's a healer of both body and spirit," the townsfolk would often say, their voices laced with admiration. But unbeknownst to them, beneath his professional veneer lurked something darker.

One crisp morning, just as the sun began to rise and cast a soft glow over the town, Harrow prepped for another day in his practice. The waiting room was a comfortable blend of faded photographs and well-loved magazines, a cozy space for patients to feel at home. His nurse, a young woman named Lucy, had already brewed a fresh pot of coffee, filling the air with its rich aroma.

"Morning, Dr. Harrow!" Lucy chirped as she glanced up from the reception desk, a cheerful smile lighting her face. "Looks like another busy day ahead!"

"Good morning, Lucy," Harrow replied, his tone warm as he adjusted his tie in the mirror. "Let's hope we can help some people feel a bit better today."

As the hours passed, the waiting room filled with familiar faces—Mr. Thompson, the elderly widower; Mrs. Carpenter, the town's librarian; young Emily, the girl with the chronic cough. Harrow greeted each patient with a firm handshake and a genuine inquiry into their lives.

"Mr. Thompson! How's your garden coming along?" Harrow asked, as the old man settled into the examination chair.

"Better than ever, Doc. You should come by and see it," Mr. Thompson replied, his eyes twinkling with pride.

Harrow laughed gently, shaking his head. "I don't know if I could handle your green thumbs! But I'd love to visit."

With each encounter, Harrow's charm cast a spell that kept his patients coming back. He was their beacon of hope, a figure who seemed to carry their burdens alongside them. Little did they know, the source of his confidence and charisma was built on a precarious foundation that thrived on trust.

As the sun dipped below the horizon, bathing Elderwood in a golden glow, Harrow retreated to his office, a modest space adorned with medical diplomas and family photographs. He took a moment to breathe, his eyes scanning the framed pictures of his own family. But in the back of his mind, an unsettling thought emerged—his need to maintain control over his patients, to keep them reliant on his expertise.

That evening, he sat alone in his office, pouring over patient files while the town slowly settled into the comforting embrace of night. For him, however, the twilight brought about an unsettling sense of solitude. He had become adept at weaving a façade that captivated those around him, but within the silence, an insidious hunger stirred—a desire to retain the power he had over life and death.

And so, in the heart of Elderwood, the friendly doctor continued his work, adored by his patients, oblivious to the darkness lurking beneath the surface. For in the realm of healthcare, the line between healer and harbinger can often blur, especially when one keeps their true intentions hidden in plain sight.

The following week, the rhythm of life in Elderwood continued on, unperturbed by any foreboding clouds. The sound of laughter echoed in the streets, mingling with the gentle rustle of leaves as people went about their daily lives. Dr. Samuel Harrow, meanwhile, remained ensconced in his practice, where the line between care and control grew increasingly tenuous.

One afternoon, as the sun cast long shadows across the waiting area, a new patient entered the office. Her name was Mary Collins, an elderly woman with frail hands and a timid smile. She had recently been diagnosed with a progressive illness that left her both frightened and vulnerable. As she settled into the examination chair, Harrow took a seat across from her, his expression warm and inviting.

"Good afternoon, Mrs. Collins. How are you feeling today?" he inquired, leaning forward to signal his attention.

"Oh, Dr. Harrow, it's hard to say," Mary replied, her voice quavering with uncertainty. "Some days are better than others. I just worry about what's coming. It's all so... overwhelming."

"That's perfectly understandable," Harrow said gently, his blue eyes sparkling with reassurance. "What you're feeling is normal, and you're not alone. We'll work together to make sure you're as comfortable as possible."

With each word he spoke, Harrow wove a safety net of trust around the frail woman. He offered her a prescription for medication to manage her pain and booked her for regular check-ups, ensuring she knew he would be her pillar of support.

But as he walked her to the door, a flicker of something darker crept into his mind. The thought that Mary would become yet another one of his regulars—someone completely dependent on his care—brought an involuntary smirk to his face. It was a fleeting emotion, quickly masked by concern, but a seed had been planted, subtly intertwining his need for control with his façade of compassion.

Later that evening, Harrow sat in his office, indulging in a moment of solitude. Despite the affectionate facade he presented to the town, he felt an unsettling sense of emptiness that gnawed at him. The power over life and death that his profession granted him was intoxicating, and the more patients he'd tended to, the more a dangerous fascination grew within him. In that silence, he reflected on the days ahead.

In the weeks that followed, Mary became a frequent visitor, her ailments escalating with each appointment. Harrow administered new medications, always with a comforting tone, never revealing the truth of his intentions. To the townsfolk, he was a savior bringing relief to suffering souls; to Harrow, they represented opportunities to exercise the control he craved.

However, not everyone was enamored with Dr. Harrow. Claire Avery, a tenacious detective who recently moved back to her hometown, began to notice something amiss. She'd heard whispers of the sudden deaths of several elderly residents, all of whom had been under Harrow's care. Each death had been recorded as natural causes, yet the coincidence bothered her—so many in such a short span of time among a demographic that, until now, had not been in danger.

Claire was no stranger to the façade of charm being a cover for something sinister. As she continued her work with the local police department, her instinct told her that the friendly doctor might not be as benevolent as he appeared. Conferences with concerned family members confirmed her suspicions: a disturbing pattern had emerged, and it seemed everyone was too enamored with the doc to see the reality.

One afternoon, after discussing recent deaths with her colleagues, Claire decided to visit Harrow's practice. As she walked through the doors, feeling the warmth of the office wash over her, she made a mental note to watch his interactions closely. Perhaps by observing him firsthand, she could uncover the truth behind the charming doctor who had captured the hearts of Elderwood.

Meanwhile, the web of deceit tightened around Dr. Samuel Harrow, as the lines between healer and predator blurred ever further. With each new patient, the duality of his nature struggled for dominance, feeding his dark desires while he continued to project the image of a caring, dedicated physician. In the heart of Elderwood, the community remained blissfully unaware of the ominous shadows that lurked beneath the surface, waiting for the right moment to catch them all off guard

CHAPTER 2
THE PERFECT PERSONA

As the sun began to rise on another beautiful day in Elderwood, Dr. Samuel Harrow donned his white coat with a self-satisfied smirk. He reveled in the knowledge that he was revered in the community, a healer in every sense of the word—or so it seemed. Today would be another busy day filled with patients whom he had cultivated like flowers, tending to their needs while fostering an illusion of unwavering support.

Arriving at the practice, he could already see a line of patients waiting outside, their faces marked with anticipation and trust. Each one of them regarded Dr. Harrow with a mix of reverence and gratitude, as if he were a guardian sent to shield them from their ailments. It was a feeling he had cultivated with great care, and he intended to maintain it at all costs.

"Good morning, everyone!" he called cheerfully as he stepped through the door, his presence instantly brightening the atmosphere.

"Morning, Doc!" echoed back, a chorus of familiar voices greeting him like an old friend. He basked in the warmth of their affection, the town's adoration feeding his ego.

As he ushered the first patient, Mrs. Turner, into his office, he felt the crumbling edges of his own isolation soften. In that intimate space, he was not just a doctor; he was a confidant, a caretaker navigating the fragile terrain of his patients' lives.

"Now, Mrs. Turner," he began, his voice mellow and inviting, "how have you been feeling since our last visit?"

"Well, not great, to be honest," she replied, her brow furrowed. "Some days are better than others, but I still have that cough."

Harrow nodded sympathetically, his mind already calculating the prescriptions he might offer. "Let's take a look; I think it's time to adjust your medication. You have a strong spirit, and we'll find a way to help you feel better," he assured her, using that same persuasive charm that had won over so many patients before.

As he examined her, he felt a familiar thrill coursing through him—a sense of control over her well-being. His fingers deftly pressed against her ribs, as he listened to her breathing, but his thoughts drifted to darker territories. How easy would it be to elevate her dependence? To ensure that she needed him more than ever?

By mid-afternoon, he had seen dozens of patients—each left feeling better, revitalized, and imbued with a sense of hope. Yet, in the quiet moment that followed an overwhelming day, Harrow found himself alone once again. The waiting room was empty, and the sounds of the town faded as he reclaimed the solitude of his office. He closed his eyes for a brief moment, allowing the weight of his actions to settle around him. But instead of guilt, a sense of satisfaction filled the void.

Meanwhile, Detective Claire Avery continued to visit his practice, seated inconspicuously in the corner of the waiting room, her keen eyes observing the interactions between patients and the doctor. In the brief moments before they entered his office, she caught snippets of conversations—a desperate plea for relief, a soft cry of fear. Each encounter reinforced her growing suspicion.

Despite Harrow's warm facade, something felt off. The number of elderly patients under his care who had succumbed to sudden health crises unsettled her. Each cheerful goodbye exchanged by the doctor raised her alarm, igniting a persistent whisper in her mind: what lies behind that charming smile?

One sunny afternoon, as Claire sat watching, she noticed Mrs. Collins arrive for her appointment, her frailty more pronounced than ever. Claire's instincts kicked into high gear, fueling her curiosity about the elderly woman's frequent visits to Dr. Harrow. The detective steeled herself as she plucked up the courage to approach Mary once her check-up was complete.

"Excuse me, Mrs. Collins," Claire said softly, her voice tender yet probing, "can I ask you a question about Dr. Harrow?"

Mary blinked in surprise, her expression a mix of confusion and hesitation. "Oh, dear. Is something wrong?"

"Not at all," Claire reassured her. "I'm just curious about your visits. Dr.

Harrow is very well-liked in town, but I'm interested in how he has been helping you specifically."

"It's been… complicated," Mary replied slowly, the weight of her words hanging heavy in the air. "He's been so kind to me, but sometimes I wonder… is this really helping me?"

Claire's heart raced. "What do you mean?"

Mary looked around, as if wary of eavesdroppers. "I feel… more tired after each visit. I know he means well, but sometimes, I just don't feel right. I can't help but wonder if it's the medicine."

Claire nodded slowly, the subtle truth resonating deeply. "Thank you for sharing that with me, Mrs. Collins."

As Mary shuffled away, Claire felt the walls of Harrow's dome of trust begin to crack, revealing shadows lurking within. She had a hunch that the doctor's caring nature might mask something far more sinister.

CHAPTER 3
A GROWING DARKNESS

A few days later, Claire returned to her desk in the precinct, her thoughts racing with newly gathered information about Dr. Harrow. As a seasoned detective with a keen eye for detail, she was no stranger to the complexities of human behavior. Yet, the duality displayed by the so-called friendly doctor intrigued and unsettled her. How could someone so adored hide such unsettling truths?

Sifting through the notes she had compiled, Claire grew more convinced that there was a disturbing pattern beneath the surface of Harrow's charming facade. The records of several recent deaths—patients under his care who had either taken a sudden turn for the worse or had passed away unexpectedly—demanded further investigation. She couldn't shake the feeling that something was profoundly wrong.

"Hey, Claire!" called Officer Daniels, bringing her back to the present. He leaned on the desk, his expression casual yet curious. "You've been digging into Dr. Harrow, huh? You think there's something to the rumors?"

She nodded, her voice steady but laced with determination. "I believe so. I've talked to several families of patients who've died recently, and there are too many coincidences. It feels like he's been playing some kind of dangerous game."

Daniels raised an eyebrow, impressed. "What do you intend to do?"

"I'm going to gather more evidence," she replied, her mind already racing with a plan. "I want to see if I can obtain medical records for the patients in question—analyze the medications prescribed, and look for any inconsistencies in his practice."

With a small smile, Daniels replied, "I'll back you up. If anyone can dig this out, it's you and your instincts."

That afternoon, with a sense of purpose, Claire set out to visit some of the deceased patients' families. She hoped to gain their insights and understand their loved ones' experiences with Dr. Harrow better. After a few visits, her suspicions intensified when she learned how many patients had noted changes in their health after seeing him—concerning side effects that went unaddressed.

One such family, the Millses, had lost their grandmother, a once-vibrant woman who had begun to lose weight dramatically and developed a peculiar pallor in the weeks leading up to her death. "It was like she gave up," Mrs. Mills said, one tear rolling down her cheek. "She was fine one day and suddenly—just gone. Dr. Harrow kept saying it was just part of getting older."

Claire listened intently and took copious notes. "Did he change any of her medications during that time?"

The family exchanged worried glances. "He did," Mr. Mills admitted. "But we trusted him. He seemed to know what he was doing, and we thought the changes were for the best."

Claire's heart sank. The more she unearthed, the clearer the picture became—a pattern of neglect disguised as care. She knew the road ahead would be challenging, especially if she were to confront Harrow directly.

Later that evening, as the sun dipped below the horizon, casting long shadows in her small apartment, Claire turned on her laptop and began drafting a report. With each passing minute, her resolve solidified. She would need to tread carefully; Harrow's reputation was a double-edged sword. Telling the community about her suspicions could raise alarms that might lead him to cover his tracks.

The following day, Claire returned to the precinct, determined to get a hold of those medical records. With the support of her colleagues, she prepared to make her move. Armed with patience and cunning, she would be watching Harrow closely, waiting for any sign of the truth hidden behind the façade.

As she waited for colleagues to return with the records, Claire considered her next steps. In the back of her mind, a nagging thought persisted—was it too late for the patients she feared might still be caught in Harrow's web? And what of Mrs. Collins? She was becoming a strong link in Claire's chain of evidence, yet her frail condition made the detective uneasy.

Claire decided not to wait any longer. She had to safeguard Mary, to pry her from the clutches of Harrow's meticulous care. Just as she resolved to visit the practice, her phone buzzed with an incoming call. To her surprise, it was Lucy, Harrow's nurse.

"Detective Avery," Lucy said nervously, her voice trembling over the line. "I need to talk to you about Dr. Harrow."

CHAPTER 4
THE FIRST VICTIM

The air in the precinct felt charged with a heightened sense of urgency as Claire listened to Lucy. What could the nurse have to say about Dr. Harrow? She had always appeared trustworthy—loyal to the physician she worked for. Yet now, on the other end of the line, Claire could sense the nurse's hesitation, the fear in her voice.

"Detective Avery," Lucy said, her tone shaking, "I really need to meet with you. It's about Dr. Harrow... I'm not sure what to do."

"Of course, Lucy," Claire replied, trying to keep her voice steady. "Where can we meet?"

"Can you come to the office? Tonight after hours. Just... be discreet."

"Absolutely," Claire agreed, her heart racing. She would finally get the answers she needed. As she hung up the phone, the city of Elderwood felt more ominous than usual. She quickly gathered her things and prepared to confront whatever secrets Lucy was harboring.

Later that evening, the practice was quiet, the ambiance eerily soothing with the faint buzz of fluorescent lights overhead. Claire parked her car on the street and walked to the entrance, her heart beating with anticipation. As she pushed the door open, she was greeted by a familiar sight—the reception desk, the waiting room, and the hallways that once seemed filled with warmth now felt cloaked in shadows.

Lucy appeared from the back office, her face white as a sheet, her hands wringing nervously. "Thank you for coming," she whispered, visibly shaken.

"What's going on?" Claire asked, leaning in closer. "You sounded distressed on the phone."

"I can't take it anymore," Lucy admitted, glancing around as if she feared being overheard. "Doctor Harrow... there's something really wrong with him. I don't think he's helping his patients."

"What do you mean?" Claire pressed, her instincts kicking into high gear.

"Start from the beginning."

Lucy took a shaky breath and nodded. "At first, I thought he was just being thorough. He has this way of convincing patients to trust him completely. But then I started noticing strange things. Medications he prescribed that... well, they didn't seem necessary."

"Strange how?" Claire asked, her mind buzzing.

"Most of the older patients came in for minor ailments—coughs, small pains. But he kept increasing their dosages, prescribing multiple medications. I've never seen a doctor do that without caution. Last week, I overheard him on the phone... discussing one of those patients, Mrs. Collins. He sounded... pleased. Almost excited."

Claire's throat tightened. "Excited?"

"Yes! It was like he thrived on their conditions worsening," Lucy said, her eyes wide with terror. "I've been feeling guilty every time I see him write another prescription. But he's so charismatic... What do I do, Detective?"

"Lucy, you might be the key to stopping him," Claire said firmly. "We need to document everything you've seen. This isn't just a feeling anymore; it's evidence. I believe he is putting these people at risk."

Lucy nodded, determination breaking through her fear. "I'll help you. I'll keep a log of everything he's doing. You have to promise me that I won't get in trouble. I didn't know what was happening at first—I trusted him."

"I promise," Claire said, her resolve solidifying. "We'll protect you. But we need to move quickly. If I'm right, he could strike again."

With Lucy's help, Claire began devising a plan to gather evidence against Harrow. As they discussed strategies, the overlooked documents and patient lists in the office took on new meaning. Each name mentioned now felt like a potential lifeline to uncovering Harrow's dark intentions.

But with every word exchanged, a cold realization settled in Claire's chest—time was running out. As she prepared to leave, Claire turned to Lucy. "You must be careful. If Harrow suspects you're questioning him, it could become dangerous."

"I will," Lucy promised, her voice steadying. "I won't let him see it coming."

That night, as Claire drove home, thoughts swirled in her mind. The shadows of suspicion that had begun to close in on Dr. Samuel Harrow were now emerging into something more sinister—an understanding that with every life he controlled, the chance of discovering the truth demanded courage and cunning.

Little did they know, Harrow was always a step ahead, his ability to manipulate the trust of those around him growing more intricate with each passing day.

CHAPTER 5
MANIPULATIONS

A heavy fog rolled into Elderwood the following morning, shrouding the town in an eerie silence. Claire awoke with a sense of urgency, her mind replaying the conversations from the night before. Determined to follow through on their plan, she knew that waiting any longer would give Dr. Harrow more time to cover his tracks.

With a steaming cup of coffee in hand, Claire reviewed her notes, organizing the patient information she hoped to gather from Lucy. There was no time to waste—she needed to start compiling evidence that could tie Harrow to the suspicious deaths that had plagued the elderly community. Each name she had collected echoed in her mind, and she couldn't shake the feeling that they were fated to fall into his chilling grasp.

After dressing quickly, Claire drove to the practice, the mist lingering like a shroud around her vehicle. As she parked outside, the familiar façade of Harrow's office loomed ahead, deceptively welcoming. Spurred by determination, she stepped out, the chill of the damp air biting at her skin.

Inside, the waiting room was bustling with patients. Claire noticed Lucy working diligently behind the reception desk, a forced smile in place to appease the incoming crowd. Their eyes met briefly across the room, and Lucy nodded subtly, signaling that she would keep a close watch.

"Dr. Harrow," Claire thought as she glanced at the doctor's office door. "I need to see what kind of monster lies behind that smile."

Just as Claire contemplated her next move, she noticed a familiar face in the waiting room. It was Mary Collins, the elderly woman who had become one of Harrow's frequent visitors. Mary appeared smaller than ever, her frail body hunched and weary, giving off an air of resignation.

"Mrs. Collins!" Claire approached, her heart pounding. "How are you doing today?"

"Oh, dear, Detective," Mary replied, her voice trembling. "I'm just here for my usual check-up. I hope Dr. Harrow can help... but it's been rough lately."

Claire hesitated, an instinctive urge to protect the vulnerable woman shifting her focus. "Have you been feeling worse since your last visit?"

Mary bit her lip, her eyes glistening with unshed tears. "Yes, I've felt weaker. And I don't know… should I be taking all this medication?"

"Tell me about it," Claire urged gently, her mind racing with concern.

With shaking hands, Mary pulled out a crumpled list of medications from her purse. As Claire reviewed it, alarm bells rang in her mind. The list was extensive, with overlapping prescriptions that detailed a concerning cocktail of drugs.

"Mary, I need you to trust me," Claire murmured. "I'm going to investigate this. I want to ensure you're safe. Can you meet me after your appointment?"

"Of course, dear," Mary nodded, visibly relieved. "I just want to feel better… I don't want to be a burden."

As Mary entered Harrow's office, Claire turned back toward Lucy. "We need to act fast. I can't let Harrow keep prescribing to her like this. The medications don't feel right, and if she continues down this path…"

Just then, Claire felt a rush of dread surging through her as she caught sight of a shadow moving in the corner of the practice—a man in a dark coat, standing just outside, watching. She instinctively moved closer, straining to hear.

"He seems to have taken an interest in Mary," Lucy whispered nervously, noticing Claire's gaze.

The figure—that of a local reporter known for his penchant for gossip—had been lingering, probably sensing something was amiss in Elderwood. Claire's stomach knotted. If he connected the dots about Dr. Harrow and Mary, it could turn into a media whirlwind she wasn't prepared to face yet.

"Stay cautious, Lucy," Claire warned, watching the reporter retreat down the sidewalk, his hands tucked into his coat. "We can't let this get out—not yet."

Once Harrow's door swung open, he emerged, and Mary shuffled out behind him, looking more defeated than before. "Mrs. Collins, I'll see you next week," Harrow called with his characteristic charm, his eyes glinting in the soft light.

"Thank you, Dr. Harrow," she whispered, trying to muster a smile, but Claire could see the anxiety etched on her face.

Harrow's gaze darted to Claire with a calculated smile. "Detective Avery! Always a pleasure." The undertone of his voice sent a chill down her spine.

"Good morning, Dr. Harrow," Claire replied, her demeanor steady. "Just checking on the community."

"Good to see you are looking after everyone," he said, his eyes narrowing slightly, as if gauging her intentions. "Always vigilant, I see."

"There's a lot to watch for," Claire maintained her composure, but inside, a fire ignited. The way Harrow regarded her felt predatory, as if he could sense the unease that hung in the air between them. His charming smile did little to quell the instincts urging her to probe deeper.

"Well, if you ever need anything," he said, his tone dripping with feigned sincerity, "don't hesitate to reach out. I'm always here for the people of Elderwood."

"Of course," Claire replied, forcing a smile to match his. "Seems like you have your hands full today, Doctor."

"Just doing my duty," he responded, the satisfaction barely concealed in his voice. With a slight nod, he walked past her, retreating back into his office.

As he disappeared from view, Claire's heart raced, a mix of adrenaline and apprehension coursing through her veins. She turned to Lucy, who wore an expression that mirrored Claire's own concern. "Did you catch that?" Claire asked, lowering her voice. "He's playing with fire, and he knows it."

Lucy nodded, her face pale. "I'll keep an eye on everything he does. I'll document it carefully, just like we discussed. But I don't know how much longer I can stand working for him if this keeps up."

"Just stay vigilant and remember—trust your instincts," Claire reassured her. "I suspect he might be aware that we're watching."

As Mary Collins headed for the exit, Claire quickly moved to intercept her. "Mrs. Collins, can we talk for a moment?"

"Of course, dear. I was just heading home," Mary replied, her voice a soft quaver.

Claire led her outside, the heavy fog wrapping around them like a shroud. "We need to discuss your medications. Are you feeling worse these days? It's vital to be honest so I can help you."

Mary hesitated, her gaze flickering to the ground. "I don't want to worry anyone. Dr. Harrow has been nothing but caring to me. I feel safe with him."

"Mary, I understand, but you have to trust me, too. I've heard from other families, and I think there's something troubling about the way he's treating you. He may be enhancing your dependency on him," Claire lowered her voice, the urgency giving her a sense of purpose.

Mary's expression shifted, a dawning realization replacing her earlier trust. "You don't think he's trying to… hurt me, do you?"

"I can't say for certain yet. But I truly believe we need to act quickly," Claire urged. "I'm going to do everything I can to keep you safe. Will you help me?"

Mary's resolve seemed to strengthen. "What do I need to do?"

"Gather your medications and any notes you've made about your symptoms. Let's meet soon—preferably away from here. I'll be in touch," Claire instructed, hoping to instill a sense of security.

As they said their goodbyes, Claire couldn't shake the feeling that she was running against time. The fog was lifting, but a sense of unease clung to her like a lingering memory.

That afternoon, feeling an unsettling mixture of determination and dread, Claire returned to the precinct, ready to establish a more strategic plan of action. As she sat at her desk, ready to dig deeper, the phone rang— interrupting her thoughts. It was Lucy, her voice tinged with urgency and alarm.

"Detective, I've just watched something disturbing," Lucy said, her tone frantic. "Mary just came back into the office with Dr. Harrow. He was... he was very angry."

"What do you mean? Angry about what?" Claire pressed, a cold feeling settling in her stomach.

"He shouted at her. It looked like he was accusing her of something. I couldn't hear exactly, but his body language... he was threatening. I think he suspects she's talking to someone outside of the practice."

"Stay close, Lucy. This could escalate. What about the other patients?" Claire's heart raced as she stood up, ready to move.

"I'll watch everything. I promise," Lucy said, her voice desperate. "But Claire, I'm afraid."

"Don't worry. I'll figure this out. Just stay safe," Claire reassured her, but as she hung up the call, a sense of dread choked her.

She needed to act, and she needed to protect Mary. Time was not on their side. If Harrow was becoming aware of Claire's scrutiny, the stakes had risen significantly.

That night, Claire plotted her next steps with resolve. The web of manipulation Dr. Harrow had spun around Elderwood was becoming increasingly dangerous, and she would do whatever it took to untangle the threads before it was too late

CHAPTER 6
THE ENABLER

The next morning, the air in Elderwood felt thick with tension, the lingering shadows of the fog from the previous day now turned into a brittle clarity. Claire awoke, her mind still swirling with thoughts of Mary and the unsettling call from Lucy. Time was no longer a luxury they could afford.

After a quick breakfast, Claire drove to the precinct, determined to gather all the pertinent information regarding Dr. Harrow's patients. The office buzzed with activity, but all she could focus on was piecing the puzzle together. She needed to understand the extent of Harrow's practice, and she knew the medical records would be critical to uncovering the truth.

"Morning, Detective," Officer Daniels greeted her as he passed by her desk. "You look like you didn't sleep much last night."

"Just anxious about this case," Claire admitted, avoiding his gaze. "I'm working on something that's starting to feel bigger than I expected."

He raised an eyebrow. "You think it involves more than just routine malpractice?"

"Definitely," Claire replied, her voice low. "I believe Dr. Harrow could be endangering his patients, and we need to get our hands on the medical records to see the history of prescriptions he's issued."

Daniels nodded, sensing the weight of her conviction. "Alright, I'll help. Let's see what we can find."

Together, they dove into a deeper investigation of Dr. Harrow's patient records. Names were pulled from the database, and the deeper they delved, the clearer the disturbing patterns emerged. Increasing dosages, questionable prescriptions, and a startling number of deaths around the same time—all pointed to a queasy reality that churned in Claire's stomach.

"Look at this," Daniels said, pointing to a series of entries on the screen. "These patients—most of them are elderly. Several have been prescribed stronger medications than necessary for what they came in for."

"Exactly," Claire replied, her pulse quickening. "It's like he's experimenting with them, manipulating their bodies to ensure they come back for more."

As they sifted through the documents, the clock ticked ominously. They needed to act quickly, especially with Lucy providing insight into Harrow's increasingly erratic behavior.

Just then, Claire received a text from Lucy: Dr. Harrow is in a bad mood today. He's been on edge since Mary left the office.

"Lucy might be in danger," Claire muttered, biting back her concern. "I'm going over there."

"Wait, let me come with you," Daniels suggested, grabbing his jacket. "Two sets of eyes are better than one, especially if he's getting desperate."

As they made their way to the practice, a sense of unease gripped them both. Claire felt the weight of responsibility pressing down on her. They arrived at the office just as a patient was exiting. The woman looked frazzled, her eyes darting nervously as she hurried past them.

"Lucy!" Claire called as she stepped through the door. The hustle and bustle of the waiting area filled the small space, yet her focus honed in on the familiar figure behind the reception desk.

"Detective, I'm glad you're here," Lucy whispered, her eyes wide with anxiety. "I don't know what to do. He's been acting erratically and has been particularly harsh with the patients today."

Before Claire could respond, Dr. Harrow strode out of his office, the air around him thick with self-importance. "I see our vigilant detective has graced us with her presence again," he said, his tone dripping with feigned delight.

Claire met his gaze, forcing herself to remain calm beneath his scrutiny. "Just making sure everyone in the community is being taken care of, Dr. Harrow."

"Of course," he replied with exaggerated politeness. "It's good to know you're looking after the vulnerable. But I assure you, they're in the best hands with me."

Beneath the surface of his charm, Claire felt an unsettling menace linger. "I'm sure you think so," she replied evenly, resisting the urge to react to his thinly veiled threat.

Just then, Lucy chimed in, feigning nonchalance, "Dr. Harrow, I was just mentioning to the detective some of our patients have had concerns. This doesn't reflect positively on the practice. Shouldn't we address these issues openly?"

Harrow's eyes narrowed, the charm vanishing as swiftly as it had appeared. "Lucy, I appreciate your enthusiasm, but my patients trust me. Their well-being is my utmost priority."

"You know that trust is essential," Claire interjected, her heart racing. "If you truly care for your patients, wouldn't it be wise to ensure their voices are heard?"

For a split second, Claire saw a flicker of uncertainty cross Harrow's face. The tension hung palpably in the air, a standoff between the predator and the prey, the illusion of civility dangerously thin. His demeanor shifted; the warmth he usually exuded gave way to an icy glare that hinted at the darker side of his character.

"Detective, we both know how cherished this practice is," Harrow replied, his voice lowered to a menacing whisper. "There are things best left unspoken, wouldn't you agree?"

Claire steeled herself, refusing to back down. "I believe that every patient deserves to be heard, Dr. Harrow. Silence can breed distrust—especially in a profession built on care."

He smiled, but it was devoid of warmth, more a grimace than an expression of friendliness. "You're very good at your job, Claire. But too much curiosity can lead to unwanted repercussions. I would advise you to be careful."

With that, he turned sharply and retreated into his office, leaving Claire and Lucy exchanging worried glances. The door closed with an audible click, sealing off the dark depths within that Claire feared Harrow was hiding.

"Did you see that?" Lucy whispered, her voice quavering. "He feels cornered. I can't shake the feeling that he's becoming desperate. What if he tries to silence me?"

"Let's not jump to conclusions. Just stay vigilant and continue documenting everything. If he's aware that we're onto him, we may need to employ more than just caution," Claire urged, adrenaline surging through her.

Determined to act, Claire resolved to set a plan in motion to gather definitive evidence against Harrow without exposing Lucy or Mary to any further danger. "I need to meet with Mary again as soon as possible. We have to get her out of Harrow's grasp."

"Do you think she'll listen?" Lucy asked, concern etched on her features. "He's been her lifeline; it won't be easy for her to walk away."

"I know it won't, but I'll make her understand that her health is at risk. I need her to trust me," Claire replied, her voice firm. "If we want to confront Harrow, we need Mary on our side—and we need tangible proof of his actions."

They exchanged a hurried nod, and Claire prepared to leave when the door swung open unexpectedly. Dr. Harrow stepped out, his expression calm but unreadable. "Detective, we're not done here. I suggest you remember the importance of my role in this community."

"I won't forget, Doctor," Claire replied, meeting his gaze directly, her heart racing as she took a deep breath. "I care about these patients, and I intend to ensure their well-being."

Ignoring his smirk, Claire turned and walked briskly toward the door, the feeling of his watchful presence still weighing heavily on her.

Back in her car, Claire scoured her mental notes, mapping out the next steps in her plan. First, she needed to secure another meeting with Mary Collins. It was crucial they discussed her medications—preferably away from the practice. She pulled out her phone and quickly sent Mary a text, urging her to meet that evening.

Once she had arranged the meeting, she turned her focus back to Harrow. The unease stirred within her, a sense that he was always one step ahead, but this time, she was ready to strategize.

As the day turned to evening, Claire met Mary in a quiet corner of a nearby café, a place where they could talk without fear of being overheard. Claire arrived early, her thoughts racing as she scanned the room for any sign of danger.

When Mary arrived, Claire noticed the weary look on her face, indicating that the past few days had taken a toll. The soft lighting of the café provided a stark contrast to the ongoing gloom surrounding them.

"Mary, thank you for coming," Claire said, her voice gentle yet urgent as they settled into their seats. "I know you're scared, but I need you to trust me. We're running out of time."

"I—I don't know, Detective. What if Dr. Harrow finds out?" Mary stammered, her fingers twisting nervously in her lap. "He's done so much for me. I feel… trapped."

"Listen to me. We need to talk about your medications. Can you tell me what he's been prescribing?" Claire urged, leaning forward.

With a hesitant sigh, Mary pulled the crumpled list from her bag and slid it across the table. "I've been taking all of these. I don't even know if they're helping anymore."

Claire glanced at the list with a discerning eye. Some of the prescriptions were for medications that should not coexist, raising alarm bells in her mind. "This is too much, Mary. These combinations could be dangerous— especially for someone in your condition."

Mary looked crestfallen, the trust she had in Dr. Harrow now rapidly eroding. "But he said they would help me," she murmured, tears glistening in her eyes. "I thought he was doing what was best for me. I don't understand. How could he—?"

"Mary," Claire interjected gently, reaching across the table to squeeze her hand, "I believe he's been manipulating you. I think he wants you to rely on him completely—and these prescriptions are a way to keep you under his control. I know it's hard to believe, but he may be endangering your life instead of saving it."

Mary shook her head, confusion flooding her features. "I don't want to think that. I don't want to believe he could hurt me…"

"I understand how difficult this is," Claire replied, her heart aching for the woman sitting across from her. "But you are not alone in this. I will help you. We can confront him together, but first, we need to gather more evidence to protect you and other patients at risk."

Before Mary could respond, Claire's phone buzzed insistently on the table. She picked it up, glancing at the display—an incoming call from Lucy. A wave of unease washed over her; they were running out of time.

"Mary, just stay close to your phone. I need you to trust me, even if it feels uncomfortable. I'll be in touch soon."

Mary nodded slowly, resolve building despite her fears. "Okay, I… I'll do what you say."

Claire rushed out of the café, answering Lucy's call as she stepped into the cool night air. "What's going on?" she asked, her heart racing.

"Claire… it's about Dr. Harrow," Lucy said, her voice tremulous. "He's been acting even more paranoid. Just now, he called me into his office and demanded to know what I was discussing with you! I think he suspects that we're onto him."

"Is he still there?" Claire felt a chill creep down her spine.

"No, he left a few minutes ago, but it felt ominous, like he's watching my every move. I can't stay here; it's too risky."

Panic surged in Claire's chest. "Lucy, you need to get out of there. Go somewhere safe. Can you stay with a friend or family member?"

"I will," Lucy replied, her voice breaking. "But Claire, I don't know what he's capable of. I feel like I'm stuck in danger."

"Just don't go home tonight," Claire urged. "I'll figure something out. Stay by your phone, and call me if anything happens."

As she ended the call, Claire felt a wave of urgency wash over her. She needed to protect Lucy, protect Mary—everyone who had recently placed their faith in Harrow—and unravel the tightening knots of his web before it was too late.

With her mind racing, Claire returned to her car and drove toward the station, the night air thick with tension, each turn amplifying her growing sense of dread. She needed to solidify her case against Harrow while keeping her allies safe.

The precinct lights flickered in the distance as she parked, her heart pounding like the drums of war. Heading straight for her desk, Claire retrieved files, documents, and a flurry of notes, working quickly to assemble a cohesive argument against Harrow's practices.

Hours passed as she cross-referenced patient records, documented possible side effects of the medications Harrow prescribed, and pieced together information gleaned from her conversations with Lucy and Mary. Soon, a clear narrative emerged—one that painted a picture of manipulation and negligence, a doctor masquerading as a healer while wielding a potentially lethal influence over the most vulnerable.

Just as Claire felt a glimmer of hope, a creeping sensation climbed her spine. The shadow of danger loomed large; she could almost feel it on the edge of her senses. Taking a moment to steady her breathing, she dialed Mary's number, heart in her throat.

"Please pick up," she whispered silently, praying for a safe connection.

When Mary answered, Claire's voice carved through the thick tension. "Mary, are you alright? I need to know you're safe."

"I'm… I'm home," Mary replied hesitantly, her tone cautious. "I don't think he followed me, but I keep hearing things outside. I'm scared, Claire."

"Lock your door, and don't open it for anyone, okay? I'm almost at the station. I'll call you back in a few minutes," Claire instructed, her mind racing to formulate a plan.

"Okay," Mary whispered, and Claire could hear the fear tinged with her exhaustion.

As she prepared to leave the station, she suddenly caught sight of a figure watching from across the street. Heart dropping into her stomach, she realized with shock that it was Dr. Harrow, standing beneath the dim glow of a streetlight. The moment their eyes met, a chill raced through Claire.

He was staring directly at her, his expression inscrutable, a mix of calm and menace that sent her instincts into overdrive. Unable to shake the feeling of being hunted, Claire hurried back to her desk, her mind racing. Had he been watching her the whole time? Every nerve in her body screamed that she needed to be cautious, that he was dangerous—a wolf in sheep's clothing.

She ducked into a side hallway and paced while trying to think. Calling Lucy and warning her was crucial, but she didn't want to expose any hint of her anxiety. Instead, she decided to act as though everything was normal. She texted Lucy quickly: Stay alert. Harrow is nearby.

With every passing moment, Claire's mind was a whirlwind of thoughts. She had to protect Mary, keep Lucy safe, and build a solid case against Harrow. But right now, the most immediate concern was ensuring that Harrow didn't realize how close she was to unraveling his facade.

After a few minutes of strategizing, she slowly made her way back to the main area of the precinct, keeping her head down and focusing on her breathing. Suspicions flared at the back of her mind. If Harrow had followed her here, he might know that she was investigating him.

As she stepped out into the night, cautious yet determined, her heart continued to race. The streets were quieter now, but Claire couldn't shake the feeling that she was being watched. She glanced around but saw no sign of Harrow. Had he even been there? Or was it all a figment of her anxious mind?

Utilizing the darkness for cover, Claire drove back to Mary's house, the fluorescent lights of the station fading into the backdrop of the darkening sky. She replayed the scenario in her mind, reminding herself that she needed to stay calm and collected. She needed to protect Mary and make sure Harrow wouldn't anticipate her next move.

Upon arriving at the small cottage, Claire parked and waited a moment. She checked her phone for any new messages but only saw the text from Lucy, affirming she was staying with a family friend for the night.

Taking a deep breath, Claire approached the door and knocked gently. "Mary, it's Claire," she called softly. "Can I come in?"

Moments later, the door creaked open, revealing Mary's apprehensive face, lined with fear and uncertainty.

"Claire!" Mary exclaimed, her voice tense. "I was starting to worry. You were gone longer than I expected."

"I'm sorry, but I needed to make sure everything was clear," Claire replied, stepping inside and closing the door behind her tightly. "Let's talk quickly."

They settled in the cozy living room, and Claire wasted no time, pulling out the list of medications Mary had provided during their last meeting. "Let's go over these again. I want to know exactly what you feel after taking each one."

Mary nodded, visibly nervous. "I don't remember every effect, but I can try… The painkillers made me really drowsy. I sometimes felt like I was in a fog."

Claire's heart sank. "And did you notice if your symptoms got any better at all?" she probed.

Mary shook her head, fresh tears forming in her eyes. "Not really. I wanted so badly to believe he was helping me. I don't want to think he could hurt me."

"He might be," Claire said, her voice steady and clear. "There's a reason I'm here, and it's not just to talk about your medications. I'm here to protect you, and I need you to trust me completely."

Before Mary could respond, Claire felt an unsettling urge to check the window. She stood, instinctively moving to the curtains and peering outside. The street was empty, yet the calmness only amplified her anxiety.

"Mary, I need to know that you're not in any immediate danger. If Dr. Harrow comes here or if you see him lurking outside…"

"I'll call you immediately, I promise," Mary replied, gripping her hands together. "But I don't want him to hurt anyone. I've seen the way he can get. Maybe I should just go back and—"

"No!" Claire interrupted, her voice firm but gentle. "Going back won't change anything. You have to see that now. We'll figure this out together, but you have to keep your distance from him. I'm going to gather evidence, and once I have enough, I can take action against him."

Just as she turned back to face Mary, the lights flickered abruptly, plunging the room into semi-darkness. Claire's heart raced as she strained to hear for any sign of what might have caused it. The soft hum of the streetlights outside filtered through the window, but the encroaching darkness felt ominous.

"Mary, stay close to me," Claire whispered, instinctively positioning herself between the door and Mary, ready to spring into action if needed. Shadows danced along the walls as she paced the room, scanning for any flashes of movement outside.

"What's happening? Should we call someone?" Mary's voice trembled, conveying her fear.

Claire shook her head. "No, just stay quiet for a moment. Let's see if the lights come back on." But as she focused on controlling her breathing, the hair on the back of her neck prickled with the sense of being watched.

Just then, a loud thud reverberated from outside, followed by hushed voices. Claire's adrenaline surged. "Did you hear that?" she asked, her voice barely above a whisper.

"Yes," Mary replied, her eyes wide. "What do you think it is?"

"I don't know," Claire said, moving cautiously toward the window. "But we need to find out."

As Claire approached the curtain and gently pulled it back, the street illuminated only by the weak glow of distant lights, she caught sight of a figure lurking in the shadows at the edge of Mary's property. It was too dark to see clearly, but the silhouette was unmistakable.

"Stay here," Claire instructed softly as she ducked down, edging closer to the window to get a better look. The figure shifted, moving toward the porch with purpose—and suddenly, the feeling of foreboding turned into cold certainty. It was Dr. Harrow.

"Mary, it's him!" Claire exclaimed, her voice low but urgent. "Get back, now!"

With a quickness born of instinct, Claire moved to the door, checking through the peephole. As Harrow approached, Claire's pulse raced, fear and anger battling for dominance within her.

"Claire, what do we do?" Mary whispered, her hands clutching her arms as if to shield herself from the impending danger.

"Call 911," Claire urged, but her heart sank as she realized the line could be cut, even if they managed to call someone. "No, wait—I've got my phone. I'll text for help instead."

Mary nodded, her fear growing palpable as the shadows crept closer. Claire quickly sent a message to Lucy and another to Daniels, urging them to come to Mary's location.

Suddenly, there was a sharp knock on the door, and Harrow's voice sliced through the tension. "Mary! Open up! We need to talk."

Claire's heart raced. "He thinks you're in there alone! We can't let him in. He's been lying to you, manipulating you!"

"What?" Mary questioned, her voice a mere whisper. "Why is he here? Does he know?"

"No. He hasn't figured it out yet. Just keep quiet," Claire instructed, stepping back from the door. The knock came again, stronger this time.

"Mary, you need to let me in; I'm worried about you! I came to check on you!" Harrow's voice oozed with false concern.

"Claire," Mary breathed, trembling. "What if he gets angry?"

"No matter what he says, don't let him in." Claire felt the tension in the air thickening, aware that every second mattered. Harrow was just outside, and she needed to keep him out long enough for help to arrive.

"Let's move to the back of the house," Claire whispered urgently. "We'll find a way out if we need to."

Mary nodded, a flicker of resolve igniting within her. They slipped quietly through the small hallway connecting the living room to the kitchen. Claire held her breath, listening intently to the muffled sounds that emanated from the front door.

"Mary! I need to see you! You can't hide in there forever!" Harrow's voice was now edged with frustration—a tone that sent shivers down Claire's spine.

With every passing second, the room felt more claustrophobic, and Claire's pulse quickened, wondering if it was too late. She and Mary might be trapped if they couldn't escape.

As they reached the kitchen, Claire noticed the back door. "We should go," she urged. "Now!"

Just as they made their way toward the exit, a loud crash echoed through the house—the front door had splintered open with a brutal force.

"Mary!" Harrow called again, his voice now colder, more menacing. "I know you're in there! I just want to help you!"

"Claire, what do we do?" Mary gasped, her face pale.

"Out the back!" Claire urged as she hurried to the door, wrenching it open just enough for them to slip through. She had no intention of giving Harrow a chance to find them. As they crept outside, her heart raced, the muffled chaos behind them filling her with dread.

The night air was cool against her skin, the oppressive darkness wrapping around them like a cloak. Claire motioned for Mary to follow her as they moved with caution towards the small patch of trees that bordered the backyard. "We have to stay quiet," Claire whispered, glancing back toward the house and straining to hear any signs of Harrow.

They ducked behind a thick trunk, their breaths shallow as they peered through the foliage. The dim light inside the cottage illuminated Harrow's form, casting an exaggerated shadow against the doorframe. He stepped inside, his posture tense—alert, searching. Claire's heart sank at the sight.

"Where are you?" Harrow called out into the darkness, his voice a low, menacing growl. "You can't hide from me, Mary. It's only going to make this worse for you."

"Why does he sound like that?" Mary's voice quavered, panic evident in her eyes.

"There's something really wrong with him, Mary," Claire said softly, trying to keep her calm as she evaluated their escape route. "We need to get away from here before he knows we've left."

Taking a steadying breath, Claire led Mary further into the trees, navigating the underbrush as quietly as possible. Every snapping twig felt amplified by the oppressive silence around them, and Claire felt time slipping through her fingers like sand.

Suddenly, a rustling sound emanated from the direction of the cottage. Claire froze, pressing a finger to her lips to signal silence. Her heart hammered in her chest as she peered back, just in time to see Harrow burst through the back door, his eyes scanning the grounds with manic intensity.

"Mary!" he yelled, his voice now tinged with rage. "This is cowardly! You can't run from your doctor!"

Claire gripped Mary's arm tighter, urging her further away. "We need to move," she hissed, leading her deeper into the shadows of the trees. The darkness enveloped them, but the fear of discovery drove them on, as every instinct told Claire that Harrow was not just a man playing doctor. He was a predator hunting down his prey.

As they pushed through the underbrush, Claire's mind raced with possible escape routes. The woods stretched out into a field just beyond, where her car was parked. If they could reach it, they would have a chance to put distance between themselves and Harrow.

Suddenly, a sharp crack echoed behind them, and Claire's heart dropped. Harrow was moving closer; he continued to call out, but now his voice carried a psychotic edge. "You think you can just run away? I'm trying to help you!"

They needed to hurry. Claire glanced around, trying to gauge their options. The sound of crunching leaves reached her ears—the unmistakable approach of Harrow following them into the woods.

"Over there!" Claire pointed to a narrow path lined with trees leading toward the field. "Run!"

Taking off with renewed urgency, they sprinted down the path, the shadows swallowing them up as Claire risked a glance back. Harrow was gaining ground, his silhouette nearly visible in the faint light filtering through the trees.

"Faster!" Claire urged, adrenaline surging through her veins. They burst through the trees and onto the open field, the grass brushing against their legs like whispering phantoms.

"Claire, I can't run anymore!" Mary gasped, her frail body beginning to falter. The fear in her eyes spurred Claire's determination.

"Yes, you can! Just a little further!" Claire urged, fighting against her own panic. They raced toward the car, breathless and desperate.

At last, they reached the vehicle. Claire fumbled with the keys, her hands shaking as she unlocked the door. "Get in—quick!" she commanded, pushing Mary toward the passenger side before slipping into the driver's seat.

Just as she started the engine, they heard the loud snap of a branch behind them. "Mary!" Harrow shouted—an echoing roar that sent chills down Claire's spine.

"Go! Go! Go!" Mary screamed, looking back in terror.

Claire hit the accelerator, the tires spinning loudly as they sped away from the scene. Harrow rapidly receded in the rearview mirror, but not before Claire caught a glimpse of the fury etched onto his face. The image was burned into her mind—the realization that Dr. Harrow was not just a beloved figure, but a dangerous man driven by something darker.

Racing down the road, Claire glanced sideways at Mary, whose face was pale and trembling. "Are you okay?" she asked, concern flooding her voice.

"I... I don't know." Mary breathed, her voice shaky as she gripped the door handle tightly. "I can't believe we just ran from him! What if he finds us?"

"He won't. Not if we stay smart about this. We need to get to the station and—" Claire's words trailed off as she glanced in the rearview mirror, half-expecting to see Harrow's car in pursuit. But the road behind them remained empty, the darkness swallowing up their escape.

Relief washed over her, but it was short-lived. She felt a lingering dread in the pit of her stomach, knowing Harrow would not easily let this go. He was smart, charismatic, and determined to maintain the control he had over his patients.

"Claire, I feel like I'm going to be sick," Mary murmured, her voice cracking. "This is all too much. I thought he was helping me!"

"I know, Mary. I know," Claire replied, her tone gentle yet urgent. "But we have to stay focused. Once we get to the precinct, we'll figure out our next steps. With the evidence you have, I can build a case against him."

Mary nodded, but her face was still ashen. "What if he tries to get to me again? He knows I'm not safe now. He won't stop."

Claire reached over and placed her hand on Mary's, trying to anchor her in the moment. "He may have power over many people, but we have something he doesn't: the truth. And we won't let him intimidate us. I promise we will do everything we can to keep you safe."

As they drove on, the muted glow of streetlights illuminated the road, casting fleeting shadows across the dashboard. Claire's mind raced with strategies for the next steps, trying to formulate a solid plan.

"Once we get to the station, I'll need you to describe everything you can remember about your meetings with Dr. Harrow," Claire said, her focus shifting to the task ahead. "Every medication, any conversations that seemed unusual—everything matters."

Mary took a deep breath, trying to steady herself. "Okay, I can do that. But Claire, what if he shows up at the station? What if he finds out what we're doing?"

"That's why I'll alert the officers when we arrive. They can provide additional protection." Claire glanced at Mary, noticing the look of determination slowly creeping back into her expression. "I need you to stay strong. We are going to get through this, but you have to trust me."

As they neared the precinct, the familiar outline of the building began to loom in the distance, but Claire's heart began to race with apprehension. The night had turned dark, and she couldn't shake the feeling that danger still lingered close behind, waiting for them to drop their guard.

When they finally pulled up to the station, Claire turned off the engine and glanced at Mary. "Stay close to me, and don't speak until we're inside. We'll be safe with the officers present."

Stepping out of the car, Claire kept her hand on Mary's back, guiding her toward the entrance. Inside, the lights illuminated the busy atmosphere— the sounds of phones ringing, conversations buzzing, and officers discussing cases echoed around them.

"Detective Avery! You're back!" exclaimed Officer Daniels, spotting them. "What's going on? You look like you've seen a ghost."

"I need your help, now," Claire replied, urgency creeping into her voice. "Dr. Harrow is unstable. We need to speak about an urgent situation."

Claire quickly pulled him aside, keeping her eyes scanning the entrance. She didn't feel safe until they were both tucked inside a corner office away from the main hustle. Mary hovered nearby, her anxiety evident as she wrung her hands together.

"What's happened?" Daniels asked, his expression shifting to concern.

"Mary was under Dr. Harrow's care, and we believe he's been manipulating her health, even endangering her life," Claire explained, her voice steady but urgent. "We evaded him, but I'm worried about the consequences."

Daniels frowned, taking in the information. "I don't like the sound of this. Is he still out there?"

"I don't know," Claire replied, glancing at the entrance again. "But he was very close to finding us."

"Let's get some statements taken from both of you, and I'll alert the other officers. We need to keep this documented," Daniels said, stepping back with determination.

As Claire and Mary settled into the office, the gravity of the situation began to weigh heavily on Claire's shoulders. Every second they spent in the station brought them closer to the possibility of exposing Harrow's true nature, but the lingering fear of his retaliation gnawed at her resolve.

"Stay calm, Mary," Claire said, her voice low and soothing as she noticed the fear creeping back into Mary's eyes. "This is the right thing to do. We're going to keep you safe."

Mary nodded but didn't say anything. Instead, she shifted her gaze to the door, as if expecting it to burst open at any moment. The sound of footsteps in the hallway heightened her anxiety, and Claire wished she could shield her from the uncertainty.

Daniels returned with a notepad in hand, a serious expression on his face. "Alright, let's get started," he said, addressing both women. "I need you, Mary, to recount everything you can remember about your encounters with Dr. Harrow."

Taking a deep breath, Mary squared her shoulders. "I… I don't know where to start," she admitted. "I thought he was helping me, but now I'm not so sure."

"Just speak freely, and I'll guide you," Claire encouraged, sitting across from her to demonstrate support. "What was the first appointment like?"

Mary closed her eyes as if trying to summon the memories. "I went in for a cough. It was nothing serious, or so I thought. Dr. Harrow was very… warm. He listened patiently, and I felt comfortable talking to him. After that, he started prescribing me medications."

"Any specifics on what he prescribed?" Daniels prompted, jotting down notes.

"Yes. I remember the prescriptions—it was a mix of painkillers and antibiotics. New medications came faster than I expected. At first, I thought they were helping because I started relying on them more…" She paused, her voice wavering. "But then I began to feel worse, more confused and foggy. I thought it was just me, that I was getting old."

"Did he ever mention adjusting your medication based on your symptoms?" Claire asked, watching Mary closely for any signs of distress.

"Adjusting them? Not really. He would just tell me to keep taking them," Mary said, her brow furrowing. "There were times when I felt like he was more concerned about the numbers on the prescription pad than my actual well-being."

"See? That's crucial," Claire interjected, sharing a look with Daniels as the pieces began to come together. "This could certainly help establish a pattern of misconduct."

"Okay, what happened next?" Daniels pressed. "How did he react when you started feeling worse?"

Mary hesitated, glancing down at her trembling hands. "He seemed… irritated. Like it was a personal affront to him. Once, I went in, and he asked me why I hadn't followed his instructions. He got angry, and I felt so small."

Claire's heart sank further. "That sounds like a red flag, Mary. You were trusting him to care for you, and he twisted your concern into anger? That's manipulation."

"Yes," Mary whispered, her eyes glistening. "I just wanted to feel better. But the way he reacted scared me. That was when I started thinking something was really wrong."

"Good—keep going," Daniels said, his pen flying over the paper.

Their conversation continued as Mary recounted more about her experiences, gradually weaving together a tapestry of manipulation that painted Harrow in increasingly darker hues. As time passed, Claire felt a sense of purpose building. This was their chance to unearth the truth, but they had to be careful. The stakes were high.

Suddenly, a loud commotion erupted from outside the station. The thumping of footsteps echoed in the hallway, immediately followed by raised voices. Claire's stomach dropped, and she exchanged a fleeting glance with Mary, whose eyes were wide with fear.

"What's happening?" Claire asked, standing up and moving toward the door, tension mounting in the air around them.

Before they could even make sense of the noise, the door to the office swung open. One of the officers, clearly flustered, stepped in, his face flushed. "Detective Avery, we have a situation! Dr. Harrow is here, and he's causing a scene—demanding to see you immediately!"

"What?!" Claire exclaimed, her mind racing. "He can't be allowed in here!"

"He's threatening to escalate things if we don't let him speak to you," the officer said with urgency. "It's getting tense out there."

Claire felt her heart pound in her chest. "We need to keep Mary safe! Don't let him in!"

"I'll handle it, but we should move you both to a secure room for the time being," he replied quickly.

"Good idea," Claire said, but as she turned back to Mary, she could see the fear etched on her face. Mary was visibly trembling, her eyes wide with panic.

"Claire… what if he tries to hurt me?" Mary whispered, pressing herself against the wall as if hoping to disappear into it.

"I won't let him," Claire replied firmly. "You're safe here with us, and I'm going to make sure you stay that way."

Just then, Officer Daniels reentered the room, urgency in his demeanor. "We need to move now. He's demanding to speak with you, and his demeanor is escalating. We can't allow him to confront you here."

"Let's go." Claire gripped Mary's arm, guiding her toward the back of the office as they moved quickly but quietly through the station. They passed a group of officers huddled near the entrance, exchanging worried glances as the commotion outside grew louder.

Claire led Mary into a small conference room, pulling the door shut behind them. "Stay here and keep quiet," she instructed, her heart pounding in her chest. She heard the chaos heightening outside as Harrow's voice cut through the noise like a knife, filled with an edge of menace.

"I won't leave without her! She's in danger, and it's your responsibility to help her!" Harrow's voice thundered, echoing through the station.

"Just stay calm," Claire said, her thoughts racing. She contemplated her next move, knowing that confronting Harrow now could put them both in immediate danger. "I'll find a way to handle this."

Moments passed, but the tension in the air thickened as Claire strained to hear what was happening just outside the door. She could feel her pulse racing, anxiety clawing at her insides. Each shout from Harrow sent a cold chill down her spine, but she had to stay strong—for Mary, and for the chance to expose the truth.

Suddenly, the door flew open, and Officer Daniels burst in, his expression serious. "He's insisting on seeing you now. We can't keep him contained much longer without escalating the situation."

"Then let me handle it," Claire took a deep breath, steeling her resolve. She was tired of hiding in the shadows, and it was time to confront the monster in this story. "If he sees me, he might back down. It might defuse the situation."

"Claire, I can't let you do that. He's unstable," Daniels replied, concern etched across his face.

"Trust me," she insisted, her voice steady and unwavering. "Staying silent is no longer an option. If I can talk to him face-to-face, maybe I can buy us some time. And if he gets violent, I know you'll be right there to back me up."

Daniels hesitated but ultimately nodded, the conflict evident in his eyes. "Fine, but we'll be right there with you, ready to intervene if necessary."

With a quick nod, Claire followed Daniels back out into the main area of the precinct. As they walked, she felt the weight of the moment looming over her, the reality of what she was about to face settling heavily in her stomach.

When they reached the entrance, Claire stepped forward, adrenaline fueling her determination. Harrow stood near the desk, his back to them, animated as he spoke with another officer. His face was flushed with anger, and Claire could see the tension rippling through his body.

"Dr. Harrow!" she called out, her voice clear and authoritative.

He turned slowly, his eyes widening as they met hers. His expression morphed from surprise to anger, a mask sliding into place as he stepped closer. "You! You've been telling lies about me!" he spat, venom tinging his words. "You're ruining my life with your investigations!"

"What you've done is far worse, Dr. Harrow," Claire replied, standing her ground. She forced herself to remain calm despite the unease churning inside her. "You've endangered lives, and I'm here to ensure that those who are vulnerable are protected from you."

"They're all just sick!" he retorted, his voice rising in pitch. "I'm trying to help them! They need me!"

"No, they need someone they can truly trust," Claire countered, her voice steady. "And that's not you. You've exploited their trust, and I will make sure everyone knows the truth."

With each word, Harrow's face flushed a deeper shade of crimson, his eyes narrowing in fury. "You think you can do this? You think you'll walk away from this untouched? You don't know who you're dealing with!"

The tension in the precinct felt electric, every officer holding their breath as they prepared for potential escalation. Claire could sense it was only a matter of time before Harrow would make a move.

Suddenly, he stepped forward, invading her personal space, his voice dripping with condescension. "You don't know who you're dealing with!" he sneered, eyes flashing with a dangerous intensity. "You think you can just waltz in here and ruin my reputation? I'll make sure you regret this."

Claire stood her ground, panic threading through her veins but refusing to show it. "You're not invincible, Dr. Harrow. Your facade is cracking, and I'm committed to exposing the truth—no matter what."

Daniels stepped slightly in front of Claire, his posture protective. "This is not the time for threats, Harrow," he warned, his voice firm and commanding. "We could easily take you in for questioning if you continue with this behavior."

Harrow scoffed, his confidence faltering slightly as he glanced towards the other officers watching the exchange. "You think they believe you? You're just a troubled detective with a vendetta!" he shouted, his voice echoing in the silence of the precinct hall.

"Enough!" Claire asserted, forcing the authority she could muster into her tone. "This isn't about you or your pride. This is about the well-being of your patients, those whom you've put in harm's way. And I will do whatever it takes to protect them."

For a moment, Harrow froze, his expression wrestling with rage and uncertainty. But just as quickly, his anger erupted again, and he took a step back, shaking his head with dismissive laughter. "You think you're a hero? You're nothing but a shadow—an obstacle in my way.

"Help!" Claire shouted, turning towards the officers. "Get him out of here!"

Before they could react, Harrow spun on his heel and bolted toward the exit, desperation fueling his escape. "You'll see!" he called back. "This isn't over, Avery!"

"Stop him!" one of the officers shouted, and chaos erupted as several officers rushed to follow Harrow.

Claire's heart raced as she turned back to Mary, who was watching in wide-eyed concern. "Are you okay?"

Mary nodded, but her face was flushed with fear. "I think so. I was so scared…"

"Just hang tight. They'll catch him," Claire reassured her gently. "But now we need to document everything you've told me about your encounters with Harrow. We need this information locked in before he tries to retaliate."

As the officers were pursuing Harrow, Claire hurried to the nearest computer and began entering notes while simultaneously requesting a dedicated report about the situation. Her fingers flew across the keyboard as the information flowed from her mind to the screen, reflecting her determination to piece together the evidence against him.

"Claire, what if he comes back?" Mary asked, peering over her shoulder. Her voice was strained, caught between hope and fear.

Claire paused, glancing up from the screen. "Then we'll be ready for him. I won't let him hurt you or anyone else."

As the minutes ticked by, the tension in the room slowly dissipated with the arrival of more officers, confirming that Harrow had been apprehended not far from the station. They brought him back, his expression hardened and defiant—but Claire could see the cracks in his facade widening.

"Let's continue your statement, Mary," she said, turning to the frightened woman. "Every detail counts, and we need to make sure he can't manipulate anyone ever again."

"Okay," Mary acquiesced, her voice steadier now, though the tension still lingered.

As they began piecing together the narrative while keeping a close eye on the tension in the precinct, Claire couldn't shake the feeling that this was only the beginning. The battle ahead would be arduous, but they were ready to uncover the truth.

CHAPTER 7
SEEDS OF DOUBT

The sun rose slowly over Elderwood, casting a golden light across the town, yet within the walls of Claire's mind, shadows lingered. She sat at her desk in the precinct, replaying conversations she had with the families of Dr. Harrow's patients. Each story painted a disturbing picture of his methods, and she felt an urgency to consolidate their experiences into something actionable.

The calls had stirred something deep within her. The fear and reluctance to question their trusted physician had left many patients vulnerable to his influence. It was time to give those whispers a voice and figure out how to protect them.

Just then, the precinct door swung open, and in strode Mary Collins, her posture a mix of determination and anxiety. Claire's heart raced as she stood to greet her.

"Mary, it's good to see you! I'm glad you came." Claire gestured for her to sit.

"I want to help," Mary said, her voice steadying as she focused on Claire. "I've been thinking a lot about what you said, and after yesterday, I realize just how serious this really is."

Claire nodded, appreciating Mary's courage. "I've spoken with several families, and many have serious concerns about Harrow's treatment methods. Your experiences are crucial, and I believe we can gather more people together—create a support group of sorts."

"But what if they aren't willing to speak? What if they're too afraid?" Mary asked, biting her lip.

"We need a starting point. If we can organize a meeting where everyone can share their experiences, it could empower them to see they're not alone," Claire replied firmly. "We can plan it carefully, ensuring everyone feels safe."

Mary considered this for a moment, then slowly nodded. "I want to help. Maybe I can reach out to my neighbors—some of them have loved ones who have seen Dr. Harrow too."

"That's a great idea," Claire encouraged, feeling a spark of hope amid the darkness. "Let's meet back here tomorrow afternoon to discuss what we've gathered."

As they finished up their conversation, the door creaked open, and Officer Daniels stepped in. "What's the plan?" he asked, recognizing the seriousness etched on both their faces.

"Mary and I are organizing a meeting with affected families to discuss their experiences with Dr. Harrow and address their concerns," Claire explained.

"That's important work," Daniels said with a nod. "But we need to be careful. If word gets back to Harrow, he could retaliate against you, Mary."

Mary swallowed hard but held her ground. "I'm not going to be afraid anymore. I need to do this for my friends and neighbors. We'll be careful."

"Good. Let's make sure we have backup when you're reaching out," Daniels advised. "I'll keep an eye on things, and if we need to, we can have officers on standby during the meeting."

"I'll make sure everyone knows that the precinct is here to support them," Claire added, feeling a surge of resolve. "We're not letting fear dictate their lives any longer."

As they finalized their plans, the door swung open a little too energetically, and a familiar voice chimed in. "What are we planning behind closed doors?"

Claire's heart sank as she turned to see Dr. Harrow standing in the doorway, his expression unreadable yet charged with an unsettling energy. "I've been looking for you, Claire. I think we need to talk."

Outwardly, she maintained her composure, but the flutter of dread inside her heightened her senses. "What do you want, Dr. Harrow?" she asked, fighting the urge to step back.

"Surely you understand my position. I'm concerned about what you're telling patients. They come to me, relying on my expertise. It's a slippery slope when someone starts planting seeds of doubt."

Mary shifted uncomfortably beside Claire, the color draining from her face. "You don't get to intimidate me anymore," Mary said defiantly.

Harrow turned his gaze toward Mary, his demeanor shifting to one of false concern. "Oh, dear Mary, you've always been so sensitive. I'm only ever here to help, to guide you toward good health."

"That's not how it seems," Claire interjected, her heart racing with a mix of defiance and fear. "You're endangering these patients by dismissing their concerns."

"Endangering them?" Harrow's voice dripped with sarcasm. "How ridiculous. I have dedicated my life to healing!"

Suddenly, Officer Daniels stepped forward, a protective stance clenching his jaw. "That's enough. You have no right to threaten anyone here. This is a safe zone for them."

Harrow's facade of professionalism cracked slightly as he glared at Daniels. "This isn't over, Officer. You're all making a grave mistake," he spat, his voice low and furious. "I'll assure you, I have friends in high places. You don't know who you're dealing with!"

Claire felt the tension spike in the room, and the protective instincts surged within her. "You may have influence, but your power ends here. You will not intimidate us anymore," she declared firmly. "We're here to fight for the patients you've wronged."

Harrow took a step closer, his eyes narrowing dangerously. "Do you really believe you can win this battle, Claire? I'm not afraid of the law or your little games. I'll expose you for the fraud you are."

With that, he turned and strode out of the room, leaving an unsettling chill in his wake. Claire clenched her fists, feeling the weight of his threat. She could not allow fear to derail their plans, but the reality of his power over the community weighed heavily on her.

"Are you okay?" Mary whispered, visibly shaken.

"I'm fine," Claire replied, though her voice carried the tremor of uncertainty. "We can't back down now. He's desperate, and that makes him dangerous. But we're in the right."

"I thought I was safe in here…" Mary trailed off, staring at the door through which Harrow had just exited.

"Don't let him intimidate you. We're going to help the community see his true colors, but we need to be strategic," Claire insisted. "You're not alone in this, and together we can expose him."

As the tension in the room subsided, Claire took a deep breath, refocusing her energy on their mission. "Let's stick to the plan. We need to gather information from as many families as possible before we confront him again."

"Right," Mary said, her resolve slowly returning. "I'll make phone calls and see who else is willing to talk."

With a renewed sense of purpose, Claire and Mary began discussing their approach, brainstorming ways to ensure the meeting would empower the affected families and open their eyes to the truth of what had happened under Harrow's seemingly benevolent care.

Meanwhile, Officer Daniels reiterated his commitment to offering protection for both women, ensuring they had backup if needed, and offering to assist in the outreach where possible.

After their discussion concluded, Claire felt a flicker of hope amidst the uncertainty. Maybe they could turn the tide against Harrow, but it wouldn't come without a cost.

As the sun set over Elderwood, casting a warm glow on their plans, Claire knew that more than ever, standing together was their best chance against the darkness that lurked in the form of Dr. Samuel Harrow. She felt the weight of that darkness intensifying, a chilling reminder that their mission was critical.

CHAPTER 8
INCREASING MORTALITY

Over the course of the next week, whispers began to ripple through the community, carrying unsettling news. Reports of sudden deaths among some of Dr. Harrow's elderly patients had steadily increased, and anger mixed with confusion clouded the air as families mourned their loved ones.

Claire felt a growing urgency to act. The stories she had gathered from families echoed in her mind, each one a thread in a tapestry that woven together revealed a disturbing pattern. She organized another meeting with the families who expressed concern, urging them to come forward with any new information about their experiences under Harrow's care.

At the precinct, the air buzzed with a mix of unease and determination. Officers shuffled past her desk, exchanging hushed conversations, the rising tension palpable. Claire had reviewed their notes over and over, searching for clues that could connect the patients' sudden declines to Harrow's methods.

"Claire!" Officer Daniels interrupted, wearing a serious expression as he approached. "I just received a call from the Mills family. They're upset; their grandmother, who had been a patient of Harrow, passed away last night."

Claire's heart sank. "Another one?"

"Yeah, and they're raising doubts about whether it was natural or not. The family has been speaking with others who've lost loved ones. They believe Dr. Harrow may be responsible," he said, concern etched across his features.

"They won't be the last," Claire sighed, rubbing her temples. "The more we research, the clearer it becomes that this pattern can't be ignored. We have to mobilize their voices—create a united front against him."

Just then, the phone rang, and Claire felt a rush of anxiety as she answered. "Detective Avery speaking."

"Claire, it's Mary," she said urgently. "I've been speaking with some patients who were under Dr. Harrow's care. We need to meet again.

Something's seriously wrong."

"Mary, breathe. Tell me what's happened," Claire replied, trying to steady her rising dread.

"I talked to Mrs. Thompson and a couple of others. They've all noticed strange things happening. Patients are deteriorating faster than expected. It's like he's experimenting with them," Mary recounted, her voice trembling. "And they're scared, Claire. Very scared."

"I know. I've been hearing similar things, but we need to keep gathering evidence," Claire reassured her. "Let's meet in an hour. We can coordinate our next steps."

As she hung up, a wave of determination coursed through her. They could no longer stand by as Harrow manipulated his patients, and these families needed to work together.

An hour later, Claire sat in a small back room of the precinct, surrounded by Mary and a few of the families who had gathered. The atmosphere was thick with tension and fear.

"Thank you all for coming," Claire began, her voice steady. "It's vital that we discuss what's happening with Dr. Harrow. I understand this is difficult, but it's important we share our experiences to see the whole picture."

Mrs. Thompson spoke first, sorrow lining her features. "I've seen so many people go under his care and then suddenly decline. It doesn't make sense! I'm terrified that it could happen to others as well."

"Exactly," Mary added, her resolve strengthening. "We can't let this continue. There's power in our stories; we can capture how he's destroyed lives and families."

One of the attendees, a younger man whose grandmother had recently passed, clutched his hands tightly as he spoke. "We need to find out how many others have suffered. My grandmother was healthy until she saw him. Now, she's gone, and it feels like he just... took her away from us."

Claire nodded solemnly. "I've been gathering names and stories. But we need to act quickly. If there's a pattern, we can substantiate the claims against Dr. Harrow and possibly put a stop to his methods."

As everyone shared their stories, Claire noted the chilling similarities—prescriptions that kept multiplying, dismissive attitudes toward their concerns, and an unsettling trend of declining health leading to premature deaths. With every story told, the threads tying their experiences together became more apparent.

This was not just about one doctor's negligence; it was about a failing system that left vulnerable lives in jeopardy.

Once the meeting concluded, Claire looked around at the families, their faces a mix of anguish and renewed determination. "Let's not let fear dictate our lives any longer. We will use our voices to shine a light on the darkness that has surrounded Dr. Harrow's practice. Together, we can hold him accountable for what he has done."

Nods of agreement rippled through the group, and Claire felt a surge of hope in that moment. They were no longer isolated; they were united in their resolve to confront the sinister truth.

Mary leaned forward, her expression earnest. "What's our next step? We need to reach out to more families, get as many testimonies as possible."

"Yes," Claire replied, her thoughts racing. "I'll continue gathering the evidence at the precinct, but if we can compile a list of all the patients he's treated—all the families affected—we can create a stronger case."

The families began discussing who else they could reach out to, exchanging phone numbers and promises to spread the word. It was a powerful moment, a turning point in their collective battle against Harrow.

As they wrapped up, Claire felt a fist of anxiety grip her chest—Harrow's wrath was bound to follow them. "We need to work quickly," she said, her voice steady but urgent. "I suspect Harrow may not take kindly to having his patients voiced against him. Safety for all of you is paramount."

Just as Claire concluded the meeting, her phone buzzed in her jacket pocket. Pulling it out, she saw a text from Officer Daniels: Dr. Harrow has been spotted outside. Keeping an eye on him. Stay alert.

Her heart sank. "Everyone, we need to be cautious," Claire warned, her mind racing. "Harrow could retaliate, and his tactics are unpredictable. Don't mention anything about our plans to anyone outside this room."

As they prepared to leave, her mind spun with the implications of Harrow's presence. They were now on the brink of exposing him, but every step forward could trigger a backlash that might endanger them even more.

After saying their goodbyes, Claire decided to stay behind for a moment, the shadows of doubt swirling in her mind. She felt a strong surge of responsibility for each family member—an obligation to safeguard those who had entrusted her with their stories.

As things settled and she tidied up the room, Claire thought about her next move. She needed to confront Harrow, to let him know she was prepared to fight back. Yet, the risk of being discovered haunted her.

Meanwhile, outside, Claire noticed the waning daylight reflecting off the police cruisers stationed around the precinct. She tucked her phone away and stepped out into the crisp evening air, ready to confront whatever challenges lay ahead.

Suddenly, a cold gust of wind whipped through the streets, sending a shiver down her spine. It felt as if the very town of Elderwood was aware of the brewing storm. Looking up, she spotted Harrow standing just beyond the police line, his expression unreadable in the dim lighting.

"Claire!" he called, his voice laced with a warning tone. "You're making a grave mistake."

"What's your intention, Harrow?" Claire responded, her heart pounding as she forced herself to stand her ground. "You can't keep hiding your actions behind a mask of charm."

In that moment, she could see the predator beneath the skin of the beloved physician, and the dread that accompanied it pressed down on her like an iron weight. He stepped closer, his eyes glinting with menace.

"Do you really think you know the whole story?" Harrow said, his calm demeanor betraying a chilling undertone. "You're sowing seeds of doubt without understanding the consequences."

"You think you can intimidate me? The truth will come to light, and you'll be held accountable for your actions," Claire countered, unwavering in her conviction.

The tension between them crackled like static in the air, and as Claire prepared for the confrontation, she knew this was only the beginning. Harrow would stop at nothing to protect his secrets, and she had to remain vigilant.

As Harrow turned to leave, Claire felt a surge of determination rise within her. She was not alone in this fight, and she would rally the voices of the community against the darkness that Dr. Harrow represented.

The battle was far from over, and she knew they were now standing at the precipice of change

CHAPTER 9
THE SKEPTIC

Detective Claire Avery awoke to the sound of her alarm, its persistent ringing pulling her from a restless sleep filled with thoughts of Dr. Samuel Harrow. As the shadows of early morning spilled gently into her room, Claire rubbed her eyes and pushed herself up. The day ahead loomed not just with the promise of hope, but also with an ever-present weight of uncertainty.

It was clear to Claire that they were entangled in a web spun by Harrow, where truth and deception twisted together like strands of a guided maze. Ever since she took on the case of the suspicious deaths tied to his practice, the air in Elderwood had shifted—an unsettling murmur seeped into the community, fostering doubt and fear.

As she prepared for the day, Claire replayed the conversations she'd had with Mary and other families in her mind. Each recollection drove home the importance of their mission. They were not merely fighting for justice but for the lives of those Harrow had manipulated. Determined to protect the vulnerable, she was ready to confront the growing darkness head-on.

At the precinct, the atmosphere buzzed with anticipation. Officers moved about with purpose, but today felt different—charged with an undercurrent of tension, as the air was thick with whispers about the doctor. Everyone sensed that a confrontation was looming.

"Morning, Claire!" Officer Daniels greeted her as he stepped into her office, the morning light creating a halo around his head. "How are you feeling today?"

"Ready to get to work," Claire replied, making sure her determination shone through. "What do we have on Dr. Harrow?"

Daniels glanced around cautiously, lowering his voice. "There are rumblings among the families, and I'm starting to see a pattern that links a number of his recent patients to alarming declines in health."

Claire's heart raced at the mention of a pattern. "What specifically?"

"I've been piecing together reports about patients who experienced sudden changes in their health after treatments, several who suffered adverse reactions from combinations of medications he prescribed," he said, pulling up documents on his laptop. "It's concerning."

"Then we need to gather this evidence and look closer at his prescription practices," Claire said, feeling her resolve harden. "If he's turned potentially safe medications into a cocktail of devastation, he's a ticking time bomb."

"Exactly. I believe we need to dig deeper into his medical history. Speak to his colleagues, even his former patients if we can find them," Daniels suggested. "For now, we need to keep this under tight wraps until we can solidify our case."

"Agreed," Claire replied. "If Harrow suspects we're closing in on him, he may go underground. We must act quickly."

Throughout the day, Claire threw herself into the investigation. She scoured files, combed through reports, and reached out to colleagues of Harrow, searching for anyone who could shed light on his practices. As the afternoon wore on, she began to feel a familiar tug—a sense of skepticism that flickered deeper within her, urging her to dissect the layers of Harrow's carefully constructed façade.

Claire sat down with an officer who had previously worked with Harrow. "Tell me about your experiences with Dr. Harrow," she pressed, leaning forward.

The officer hesitated, glancing around as if cultivating words were harder than expected. "He was always charming. People loved him. But..." he trailed off, searching for the right phrase.

"But?" Claire prompted, sensing the hesitation.

"There were elements that felt off. I remember visiting his practice a few times; he seemed to have an unnatural control over the patients' concerns. If anyone questioned his methods, he'd shut them down with charm."

"Interesting," Claire noted, her analytical mind racing. "Did you ever witness him dismiss any concerns regarding a patient's health?"

The officer's eyes narrowed thoughtfully. "There were times I sensed discomfort in some families after they left his office. He had a way of belittling their concerns. I didn't question it back then, but now…"

"Now it raises a lot of questions," Claire finished for him, the weight of his words settling heavily on her. A clearing sense of doubt began to blossom further. If Harrow could manipulate not just his patients but also those around him, it made him all the more dangerous.

"Exactly," the officer said, his expression serious. "It's something I've wrestled with since the sudden deaths began to surface. I want to help, but it's hard to come to terms with something that you thought was good for the community."

"Trust your gut," Claire replied, a glimmer of resolve igniting within her. "If we band together, leverage our information, we can expose him. I need you to testify when the time comes."

After their conversation, Claire left the officer's office with a renewed sense of urgency. She had to find a way to connect the dots, to illuminate the darkness surrounding Dr. Harrow's actions that had entrapped so many.

As she walked down the bustling hallway of the precinct, Claire detected a mix of chatter among the officers—some discussing their shifts, others whispering about the latest updates on Harrow. It was clear that many were on edge, aware that the community's trust was eroding quickly.

She settled back at her desk, where a haphazard collection of patient files awaited her review. The room felt charged with anticipation as she flipped through each document, hunting for clues that could strengthen the case against Harrow.

A sudden knock at the door pulled Claire from her focus. Officer Daniels stepped in, looking more serious than usual. "Claire, you might want to see this."

"What do you have?" she asked, leaning forward.

Daniels handed her a file, labeled with the names of several deceased patients linked to Harrow. "These are the cases that have raised the most eyebrows. They've been flagged for review—multiple concerns about questionable treatments leading up to their deaths," he explained. "I thought they could help you get a clearer picture of his methods."

As she flipped through the pages, Claire's stomach churned. Each name conjured memories of the families who had shared their pain and confusion over the deaths they'd experienced. She noted the complaints about rapid health declines, adjustments to medications without explanation, and the feeling of being dismissed by Harrow.

"This is critical," Claire said, her voice low but urgent. "If we can draw a direct line from these cases to his treatment methods, we can substantiate claims against him. I need to talk to the families of these patients."

Daniels nodded, his expression grave. "Several families have already expressed their concerns about his treatment. They might be willing to come forward, but we must approach them carefully."

With renewed determination, Claire took the list of names and set out on her next mission. Each family's story could be the key to unraveling the web of deception spun by Harrow.

Her first stop was the Mills family. Claire arrived at their home, hoping the patriarch would be open to sharing their experiences. The house looked familiar, the soft light filtering through the curtains a stark contrast to the heaviness she felt.

When Mrs. Mills answered the door, Claire was struck by the sorrow in her eyes, a reflection of the weight of grief they had all been forced to carry. "Detective Avery," she said, stepping aside to let Claire in. "We've been talking about you."

"Thank you for meeting with me," Claire replied, scanning the room filled with photographs that told stories of lives well lived. "I know this is a difficult time, but I need to discuss your husband's care with Dr. Harrow."

Mrs. Mills grimaced, her shoulders sagging. "He was such a kind man until he started seeing Harrow. I thought he was in good hands."

"What happened during those last appointments?" Claire pressed gently, taking a seat across from her.

Mrs. Mills took a shuddering breath, her hands twisting together. "We started noticing changes after he changed his medications. It seemed like every visit, there were new prescriptions, and I kept asking Harrow about side effects. He would just wave it off and say it was normal for his age."

Claire noted the details, her heart heavy with empathy. "Did your husband ever voice his concerns?"

"Only to me," she admitted, tears spilling from her eyes. "But then he grew quiet. I thought it was just because he was older and tired, but I wish I'd pushed harder. I feel like I failed him."

"No, you didn't fail him," Claire said softly. "What you're doing now is what matters. If more families speak up, we can protect others from going through the same pain."

Mrs. Mills nodded, the tears flowing freely. "I'll do whatever it takes, Detective. I want to make sure no one else experiences what we went through."

Encouraged by Mrs. Mills' commitment, Claire spent the next hour documenting details and discussing the challenges they faced in challenging Harrow's authority. She felt invigorated by the fight to support the families—and one step closer to unraveling the truth.

After concluding her visit with the Mills family, Claire moved on, visiting other families, each encounter strengthening her resolve. Collectively, the stories revealed alarming patterns that pointed toward neglect, manipulation, and outright deception.

By the end of the day, Claire returned to the precinct with a dossier overflowing with testimonies, shifting the weight of grief into a rallying cry for justice. The murmurs of mistrust that had grown among the community were beginning to coalesce into a fierce resistance against Harrow.

As she looked around the precinct, Claire felt a powerful energy building—a community awakening to the reality of the threat that Dr. Harrow posed. Conversations buzzed with urgency as officers discussed the latest updates, and Claire could sense that the tide was turning. This was no longer just about isolated incidents; it was about the collective voice of a community uniting against a common enemy.

"Claire!" Daniels called out as he approached, his expression filled with anticipation. "You're not going to believe this. A few families are here, ready to talk. They've decided to band together to confront their fears."

Claire's heart raced. "Really? That's incredible! We need to get them in here, gather more stories, and solidify their support."

Daniels nodded, motioning for Claire to follow him to the main conference room. As they entered, the atmosphere was charged with palpable emotion, a mix of anxiety and determination hanging in the air. Several familiar faces turned to Claire as she walked in.

"Thank you all for coming," Claire began, her voice steady but filled with compassion. "This is about more than just individual experiences; it's about challenging the methods of Dr. Harrow and ensuring no one else suffers at his hands."

"What if he finds out we're meeting?" one woman asked, her voice trembling. "He's already shown he can retaliate."

"I understand your fears," Claire replied, her gaze firm. "But silence only empowers him. The more united we are, the stronger we stand against him. We'll ensure that everyone has protection, and if necessary, we can have officers present during your testimonies."

"It's time for the community to stand up," Mrs. Mills declared, gaining confidence as she spoke. "I won't let my husband's death be in vain."

The conversation flowed, each family sharing their experiences, and the room grew filled with a sense of solidarity. Claire listened intently as they recounted their loved ones' stories, the chilling similarities reinforcing the urgency of their mission.

"We need to take this to the local news," another family member suggested tentatively, glancing around for agreement. "Let the community hear our concerns."

Claire considered this, realizing the power of public awareness could shift the narrative in their favor. "That's a strong idea," she said. "Public scrutiny can undermine Dr. Harrow's facade and encourage more people to come forward."

As plans began to form, Claire felt a surge of hope amidst the crushing weight of the situation. They collaboratively crafted a strategy—organizing a public gathering to share their experiences, leveraging local media to amplify their voices, and inviting anyone who had encountered Harrow's methods to join in.

After hours of discussion, Claire looked at the group and felt a deep sense of pride swelling in her chest. "We're not just fighting for ourselves anymore; we're fighting for every patient who's been silenced. Together, we can expose the truth and make Elderwood a safer place."

Just as the meeting came to a close, Claire's phone buzzed with a message from Lucy: I've heard Harrow has been trying to reach out to patients. He may know something's up. Be careful!

The warning chilled Claire, confirming her growing fear of Harrow's retaliatory nature. She glanced around at the faces of the families before addressing the group once more. "We need to remain vigilant. I'll keep everyone updated and ensure we have the support we need. If Harrow tries to intimidate anyone, we stand together. We're stronger as a united front."

As the families began to disperse, Claire's mind raced with strategies for the next steps. The impending confrontation with Harrow no longer felt abstract—it was looming, inevitable. They were on the cusp of bringing his actions into the light, but the darkness that cloaked Harrow made her acutely aware of the risks involved.

That night, Claire returned home, her mind filled with swirling thoughts about the day's events. She couldn't shake the nagging feeling that Harrow would retaliate. She needed to devise a plan to ensure the safety of the families and her own. But they had sparked something powerful—a community awakening determined to reclaim their trust and safety from a predatory doctor.

The battle was on, and Claire was ready to rise to the challenge.

CHAPTER 10
WHISPERS IN THE SHADOWS

The following morning, Claire awoke with a renewed sense of purpose and a growing urgency to act. The community was awakened, but the threat of Dr. Harrow still loomed large over their collective resolve. As the first light of dawn filtered through her window, illuminating the scattered papers on her desk, she realized that time was no longer a luxury.

After a quick breakfast, Claire grabbed her phone, determined to check in with the families before heading to the precinct. She knew their courage must be bolstered in the days ahead; they needed to feel supported and invincible, especially after the stirring outcome of their meeting.

"Hi, Mrs. Mills," Claire said when the older woman answered. "I just wanted to see how you're feeling today after everything."

"Quite anxious, to be honest," Mrs. Mills admitted, her voice thick with emotion. "It's one thing to share stories, but now I'm nervous about the attention it may bring."

"I understand. But remember, you're not alone in this. We're all fighting for the same cause," Claire reassured her. "Every shared story is a step towards protecting our community."

After hanging up, Claire continued reaching out to others, her resolve strengthened by their shared determination. Each call felt like a thread weaving a larger tapestry of resistance, binding them together in this uphill battle against Harrow's manipulation.

Upon arriving at the precinct, Claire felt the weight of anxiety hanging in the air—a mixture of anticipation and fear as officers gathered to discuss the latest updates. She found Officer Daniels, whose concerned expression confirmed her suspicions.

"Claire, we need to talk," he said, motioning her to a quieter spot. "There's been a report: someone saw Dr. Harrow near the precinct earlier this morning. He was asking questions about you."

Her heart sank at the realization. "He's tracking us? Trying to intimidate me?"

"It seems so. We can't have him around here causing trouble. This investigation is delicate, and if he knows we're starting to close in, he might escalate his tactics," Daniels replied, his voice edged with concern.

Claire felt the weight of the danger—not just for herself, but for the families who had bravely spoken out. "We need to protect them. If he's targeting individuals, I have to warn each family that spoke up. He might try to scare them into silence."

"Good idea. Let's coordinate and have officers check in on them through the day," Daniels suggested. "We can also monitor Harrow's movements to prevent any overt intimidation."

As they divided their tasks, Claire felt a mixture of fear and determination swirling within her. She would not let Harrow undermine the strength of the community they were piecing together; too many lives depended on it.

That afternoon, Claire decided to visit the homes of the families who had shared their stories, checking on their safety and helping them prepare for the next steps in their collective confrontation with Harrow. As she drove through the streets of Elderwood, she felt a growing unease beneath her resolve. Something about the way the town looked—the run-down houses, the frightened faces peeking out from behind curtains—seemed to echo the dark energy that Harrow had instilled in the community.

When she reached the Thompson residence, Mrs. Thompson let her in, but Claire noticed the nervous energy in the air. "Detective, I just can't shake this feeling," Mrs. Thompson confessed as she nervously paced the living room. "What if he comes for us? I can't bear the thought of losing my husband and then being threatened by him."

Claire stepped forward, placing a reassuring hand on her shoulder. "That's why we have to stand strong together. You're not alone in this. I'll ensure you have the support you need. We'll call in backup to watch over you, and we'll organize a safety plan for everyone."

"I appreciate that," Mrs. Thompson replied, though her expression remained clouded with worry. "But even so, I don't know what to believe anymore. It feels like we're being watched."

As they talked, Claire noticed a flicker of movement outside the window. She turned, her instincts kicking in. "Did you see that?" she asked, peering through the curtains.

"See what?" Mrs. Thompson said, now nervously glancing toward the window.

"I don't know, it could just be my imagination, but I swear someone was passing by," Claire said, her heart hammering in her chest. "Let's stay cautious. I recommend we keep the doors locked and stay vigilant."

They continued discussing contingencies, reiterating the importance of reaching out to other families to inform them of potential danger when Claire's phone buzzed sharply with a new notification.

It was a message from Officer Daniels: We've received reports of increased sightings of Harrow around town. Stay alert.

The gravity of the situation struck Claire like a jolt. Dr. Harrow had always been a step ahead, but now it felt as though he was actively pursuing a confrontation. He was no longer content to manipulate from the shadows; he was brazenly drawing attention to himself.

"Mrs. Thompson, we need to go," Claire said, her voice tight with urgency. "If Harrow is around, I don't want you exposed to any potential danger. We should head to the precinct. It's safer there."

"Is that really necessary?" Mrs. Thompson asked, her eyes wide with fear. "I don't want to cause any trouble."

"This isn't about causing trouble—it's about your safety," Claire insisted gently but firmly. "We need to make sure you're protected, especially given everything that's been happening."

With a reluctant nod, Mrs. Thompson agreed. Claire quickly helped her gather a few essentials before they made their way to the car. The small town of Elderwood, which had once felt like a safe haven, now felt like a labyrinth filled with shadows and growing threats.

As they drove toward the precinct, Claire kept a watchful eye on the rearview mirror, scanning for any sign of Harrow's vehicle. The roads seemed eerily quiet, and the usual bustle of daily life felt muted, as if the town collectively held its breath in anticipation.

Once they arrived, Claire ushered Mrs. Thompson inside, where the atmosphere buzzed with activity but also a sense of purpose. Officers hustled about, their focus clearly shifting toward a response to the ongoing concerns surrounding Harrow.

"Detective Avery!" Daniels called out when he spotted her, urgency in his voice. "We've got a situation. Harrow has been spotted near the community center, and a few families are on edge. We need to ensure their safety."

Claire's heart dropped. "Do you think he's trying to intimidate them? We need to get the word out immediately," she said, her mind racing. "If he thinks he can confront them without repercussions, it'll only embolden him."

"Yes, but we'll need a plan," Daniels said, his expression serious. "Let's gather whoever we can and alert families to stay indoors until we can assess the situation."

Claire turned back to Mrs. Thompson, who was watching the exchange wide-eyed. "We need to stay alert. If he's making a scene, we can't let him disrupt the progress we're building."

As they organized a team of officers to reach out to affected families, Claire felt a surge of resolve. They wouldn't let Harrow hold the community captive with fear. It was time to regroup and reinforce their unity against the doctor who had crossed lines that no physician ever should.

Minutes later, the precinct buzzed with action as officers set out to monitor the community center, ensuring that families remained safe and secure. Claire's phone buzzed with incoming messages; she focused on keeping the families informed.

Among the messages received was another note from Officer Daniels: Harrow's near the center. Looks agitated. Stay close.

Claire's stomach knotted at the thought of Harrow potentially confronting families again. They had to act quickly. "Let's move," she told Mrs. Thompson, her determination renewed. "We need to be ready in case something escalates."

"Ready for what?" Mrs. Thompson asked, her apprehension still evident.

"We're not just going to allow him to intimidate us anymore. We're here to show him we won't be silenced, and that we'll stand up for what's right. Together, we can protect our friends and neighbors."

As they reached the community center, the atmosphere charged with tension. Claire scanned the area, spotting several families huddled together, appearing anxious. She understood that the threat of Harrow lingered heavily in their minds.

"Listen up, everyone!" Claire began, stepping into the center's main hall to capture the attention of those present. "I know it's a troubling time, but I'm here to reassure you that we are gathering support to confront Dr. Harrow's actions. Your safety is our priority."

The collective energy in the room shifted as families turned to Claire, their expressions shifting from fear to a cautious hope. "If anyone sees him, please report it to an officer immediately. We can't let him intimidate us, and we will stand together in the face of this threat."

As the families nodded, Claire felt a surge of strength—this was their moment, a chance to reclaim their power from the shadows Harrow had cast. They were no longer alone, and it was time to rise against the oppressive force that had attempted to manipulate their trust.

The gathering audience began to murmur, each family sharing their own fears and retelling their experiences. Claire could see the resolve building among them, a shared determination to stand against the darkness.

Little did they know, the confrontation with Harrow would soon come to a head, one that could either solidify their resolve or shatter it completely. The air was thick with tension as Claire paced in front of the gathered families, each of their anxious faces etched with the weight of the fear that had been ingrained in them.

"We're here to look out for one another," Claire reminded them, sensing the flickering flames of hope beginning to burn brighter. "By sharing your stories, we empower ourselves to confront the truth."

As the discussions among families continued, Claire caught sight of Officer Daniels patrolling outside, his serious demeanor reinforcing the gravity of the situation. It was a comfort to know they had backup, but the prospect of Harrow lurking nearby still filled Claire with dread.

Just then, a commotion broke out by the entrance. A heavy set of footsteps echoed across the wooden floors, and Claire's heart raced as she turned to the door to find Dr. Harrow himself standing there, his presence commanding immediate attention.

"Claire!" he called out, his voice strong yet tainted with a manic undertone. "I see you've gathered quite the crowd. But I have to wonder—what are you all so afraid of? A doctor trying to help people?"

The room fell silent, all eyes trained on him. Claire's mind raced. She hadn't expected him to confront them here, in this very moment, during their gathering. "Dr. Harrow," she said, stepping forward confidently to face him. "What you're doing is more than helping; it's putting lives at risk."

The corner of his mouth twitched in an unsettling smirk. "You're mistaken if you think you know the truth, Claire. These people need guidance, a steady hand. If they struggle, it's their own fault for not trusting me."

"Trust is built on transparency and respect, not manipulation!" Claire shot back, her voice fierce. "You've taken advantage of these families, and they have every right to question your methods."

"You're painting yourself as some kind of champion," he retorted, stepping closer with an imposing presence. "But you're merely a skeptic struggling to hold onto her doubts. When the truth comes out, when it's clear that I was simply doing my job, you will be left with nothing but shame."

Before Claire could respond, murmurs rippled through the crowd, fear and uncertainty reflected in their eyes. She knew she had to act quickly. "Listen!" she shouted, raising her voice to reclaim their attention. "This man is trying to manipulate you just as he has with your loved ones. Don't let him intimidate you."

Harrow's composure grew more volatile as the atmosphere thickened with tension. "I suggest you all reconsider your alliance with her," he said, his voice taut and laced with barely concealed anger. "Claire Avery is not your friend. She's a threat to your care and well-being. What you need is a proper doctor, not a cynical detective."

"Stay away from them!" Claire warned, stepping protectively in front of the families. Each passing second felt critical as Claire stared him down, her heart pounding in anticipation of what might unfold.

Suddenly, Officer Daniels stepped forward, his stance fierce and authoritative. "Dr. Harrow, I need you to leave the premises immediately. You've caused enough distress today."

Harrow's eyes flared with anger, but the noise of sirens approaching began to fill the air, a reminder that reinforcements were on their way. "This isn't over, Claire. I'll come back for you. You're going to regret bringing these people together," he snarled before turning abruptly and storming out of the community center.

"Is everyone alright?" Claire asked, turning back to the anxiously gathered families. She could feel the fear still lingering in the air but was resolute in her desire to bolster their courage.

"We need to stand united," one father spoke up, determination returning to his voice. "He thinks he can scare us into silence, but we'll fight back."

"Exactly," Claire agreed, emboldened by the support of the families. "We're not just names on a list; we're a community. Together, we can expose the truth about Dr. Harrow."

The gathering began to look more like a rally for justice—a shared strength fueled by a collective desire for accountability. In the wake of Harrow's threats lay a stubborn resolve to fight against the shadows he had cast over them.

As the families began to share their stories once more, Claire felt a renewed sense of hope. The confrontation with Harrow had tested their mettle, but they emerged even more united. Each shared tale was a step toward breaking the chains of fear he had crafted.

That night, Claire returned home, the weight of the day's encounters still looming large in her mind. She knew the struggle was far from over— Harrow would push back, and they'd need to be ready.

As Claire stepped into her small apartment, she felt the familiar comfort of her space envelop her, but the sense of unease wouldn't dissipate. The walls that had often cradled her thoughts now felt daunting, echoing with the challenges that lay ahead.

She tossed her bag onto a chair and walked to the window, staring out at the dimly lit streets of Elderwood. The quiet of the night contrasted starkly with the turmoil brewing in her mind. Harrow wasn't just an adversary; he was a man who thrived on power and manipulation, someone willing to do whatever it took to maintain control.

Pulling out her phone, Claire quickly typed a message to Officer Daniels: We need to stay vigilant. Harrow is not going to back down easily. We must prepare for his next move.

As she sent the message, her thoughts drifted back to the meeting and the resolve she'd witnessed in the families. Would that strength continue to carry them through the shadows, or would fear claw its way back in? The doubts of the community hung in the air like a suffocating fog, while she and the families fought valiantly to dispel them.

Feeling restless, she wandered back to her desk, where she had laid out the files she had compiled on Harrow's patients. The stories they had shared, filled with fear and confusion, ignited a fire in her—a desire to protect and to seek justice.

As she reviewed the documents, a name that had escaped her attention before caught her eye: Elizabeth Graham, an elderly woman who had been under Harrow's care. According to the report, Elizabeth had suffered a sudden heart failure shortly after being prescribed a new medication regimen.

Unease washed over Claire. She couldn't shake the feeling that there was more to Elizabeth's story. Quickly, she grabbed her phone and decided to reach out to the Graham family. They deserved to know the truth, and if there was a pattern to discover, it would be important to connect the dots.

As the phone rang, Claire felt the hours of the day slipping away, almost as if time held its breath. When the familiar voice of Mr. Graham answered, it briefly startled her—his weary tone revealing the burden of grief.

"Hello?" he asked, confusion evident in his voice.

"Mr. Graham, this is Detective Claire Avery," she introduced herself. "I'm reaching out to you regarding your late wife, Elizabeth. I wanted to talk to you about her care under Dr. Harrow."

There was a long pause, which felt charged with emotion. Finally, he replied, "You mean to tell me this is about that doctor? Why? It's too late for us."

"It's never too late to seek the truth," Claire insisted gently. "I believe there are more families who have been affected by Harrow's practices. I need to ask you a few questions to better understand what happened during Elizabeth's treatment."

His voice wavered as he replied, "I—I never felt right about the way he treated her. She went in for a minor issue, and suddenly there were all these new prescriptions. It felt like she was just another number to him."

"Did you express your concerns to Dr. Harrow?" Claire probed, feeling the weight of his anguish.

"I tried," Mr. Graham said, his voice thick with emotion. "But he had this way of dismissing me, of making me feel like I was overreacting. It became hard to know if I was the one who was losing patience or if he was truly as careless as it seemed."

Claire's heart sank. "I'm very sorry for your loss, Mr. Graham. But what you're sharing is essential for others to hear. We need to make sure no one else experiences the same pain you have. Your voice matters."

Another lengthy silence passed, filled with the echoes of grief. Finally, Mr. Graham sighed deeply. "You think it could help?"

"Yes," Claire affirmed, the conviction in her voice unwavering. "Your story could help us expose Harrow for what he really is and prevent other families from suffering."

"Alright," he relented. "I'll do what I can. It's time someone spoke up about how he treated Elizabeth."

As they concluded their conversation, Claire felt an overwhelming sense of purpose settle within her. Each voice added to the collective outcry against Harrow raised the possibility of change, a chance to expose the torment inflicted on families by his actions.

After hanging up, Claire took a moment to compose herself, her thoughts racing with ideas. They were building an alliance of strength, one that could break the cycle of manipulation and reclaim trust in their community.

The following day would be crucial; she needed to convene once more with the families who had come forward with their stories. Claire could feel the momentum building, as if every passing moment drew them closer to unveiling the truth of Dr. Harrow's practices.

Her early morning was filled with preparation. She gathered testimonies, highlighted key points in the patient files, and prepared a presentation that summarized the alarming patterns they had uncovered. Each account was a voice in a chorus that sought to challenge the very foundation of trust Harrow had built.

Arriving at the community center, Claire felt a mixture of anticipation and anxiety. She needed to empower the families, to grant them the courage to fight back. As the hour approached, more families trickled in, their faces reflecting a blend of determination and apprehension.

"Thank you all for being here again," Claire said as she stood before them, her heart pounding with urgency. "Together, we have the chance to expose Dr. Harrow and protect others from what we've experienced. Today, we'll share our stories and unite our voices."

An air of solidarity washed over the room as the families exchanged glances, their resolve palpable. Claire felt a spark of hope igniting among them, amplifying the power that lay in unity.

As she moved through the gathering, Claire encouraged family members to share their experiences, reiterating the importance of each story. The camaraderie that formed between them was beautiful to witness, a stark contrast to the isolation Harrow had instilled.

Just as the meeting gained momentum, Claire's phone buzzed in her pocket. She discreetly glanced at the screen to find a text from Officer Daniels: Heads up. We've had another death reported linked to Harrow, and it's starting to become a concern at the precinct. We need to act fast.

Claire's heart sank as she absorbed the information. It was becoming increasingly urgent to rally these families and present their experiences to the appropriate authorities.

"Everyone, I need your attention," Claire called out, cutting through the chatter as the discussions halted. "I just received news that another patient has died, and it reinforces the need for us to act swiftly. We cannot let Dr. Harrow continue to operate without accountability. We have to take our testimonies to the police and push for a thorough investigation."

Nervous murmurs rippled through the group as they processed this information. "What if he retaliates?" someone asked, glancing around the room with concern.

"We can't let fear rule us," Claire said firmly, her voice unwavering in its conviction. "We must be ready. Our safety is paramount, and I will ensure we have backup when presenting our case."

As the families began to share their thoughts, a sense of urgency settled into the gathering. This was no longer about individual stories; it was a united front against a threat that had claimed too many lives.

"I'll reach out to the local news station," Mrs. Mills suggested, her voice carrying a newfound strength. "If we can get the media involved, it could amplify our message."

"That's a powerful idea," Claire agreed. "Public awareness can shift the narrative. If we're able to expose Harrow's methods, it may compel authorities to act swiftly."

Fueled by their shared determination, the families began collaborating on further steps, drawing together their accounts into a comprehensive document of grievances against Harrow. Claire guided the discussions, ensuring each voice was heard, each testimony validated.

As the meeting progressed, Claire's heart swelled with pride watching the families find strength in each other. They were taking ownership of their fears and transforming them into action—changing the trajectory of their community together.

Just as they were finalizing their strategies, the door to the community center swung open with a loud creak. Claire turned to see Officer Daniels entering, his expression tense.

"We need to talk," he said, moving swiftly toward Claire. "There's been a development, and I think you'll want to hear this immediately."

Claire felt her pulse quicken, a mix of anticipation and dread washing over her. "What is it?"

"We've just received reports that several patients under Harrow's care have begun to speak out on social media, expressing their concerns about his treatments. It's gaining traction," Daniels said, urgency thick in his voice. "But we've also heard troubling whispers that he's aware of this and may be preparing to act defensively."

Claire's mind raced. "We have to get ahead of this before he tries to silence any more voices. We must ensure everyone feels safe enough to come forward."

Daniels nodded, the weight of the situation settling heavily around them. "We need to move quickly. If we're able to coordinate this effort, we can present a united front against him, but we need to mitigate any risk to those who are coming forward."

Claire turned back to the families, determination written across her features. "We have an urgent responsibility ahead of us. Are you all ready to stand together? I need each of you to commit to this fight."

A chorus of affirmations filled the room, voices blending into a unified declaration of resolve. Each individual person was wrestling with their fears, yet the collective energy propelled them forward, fueling a sense of purpose that cascaded through the group.

"Great," Claire said, feeling a renewed strength in their unity. "This is our chance to confront Dr. Harrow—not just for ourselves but for every individual who has suffered in silence. We urge the community to stand by us, to be the voices that expose the truth."

Mrs. Mills stepped forward, her face illuminated with determination. "Let's create a public statement that outlines our concerns. If people see that we're coming forward as a united front, they'll be less afraid to speak out."

"Absolutely," Claire agreed. "We can release a statement to local media and set up a community meeting, where we can share our experiences directly. But first, we need to gather as much evidence as we can to back our claims."

As they began to strategize, the atmosphere shifted, charged with purpose. Claire felt a surge of hope—this gathering was transforming individual tragedies into a collective rallying cry for justice.

"Let's make sure that everyone knows the meeting date," Claire instructed, her eyes scanning the room. "We need families and anyone affected by Harrow's treatment methods to join us. The more people we have standing together, the harder it will be for anyone to silence us."

Once the plans were laid out, Claire noticed a shadow pass over the doorway. She turned just in time to see Officer Daniels walking back into the room, his brows furrowed with concern.

"Claire, I need to talk to you privately," he said, his tone urgent.

"Excuse me for a moment," she said to the families before stepping aside with Daniels. "What's going on?"

"I just received word that Harrow has a few supporters among the community. He's been rallying some locals, discrediting the reports that have begun circulating about him. If this escalates, it could create a divide," Daniels explained, worry creasing his forehead.

Claire's heart sank. "So he's trying to undermine our efforts before they even begin?"

"Exactly," Daniels replied. "I think we need to be proactive. We should gather personal testimonies and document them thoroughly. This will counter any rumors he spreads."

"That makes sense," Claire agreed, her determination settling deeper within her. "We'll need to be prepared for his tactics. We can't let him frame this as paranoia or a vendetta against him."

As Claire returned to the families, she felt the weight of responsibility settle squarely on her shoulders. Harrow was formidable, and the path ahead was strewn with dangers. But they were resolute in their commitment to combat the lies and deceit that had persisted within their community.

"Listen up, everyone," Claire said, her voice rising to regain the group's attention. "We have a challenging road ahead, but we're not facing it alone. With every story shared and every voice united, we will uncover the truth behind Dr. Harrow's practices. Together, we're going to take back our community."

The families nodded, confidence rekindling in their eyes. A wave of hope surged through Claire, mingled with apprehension—but she knew they were no longer seeking justice as isolated individuals. They were stepping into the fight as a collective force, a force strong enough to combat the darkness that had plagued them for far too long.

Determined to stay one step ahead of Harrow, they quickly organized themselves, ready to face whatever challenges lay ahead. With the sun beginning to set outside the community center, painting the sky with hues of orange and purple, the families prepared to shine a light on the truth and reclaim their power.

CHAPTER 11
FAMILIAR FACES

As the early morning sun painted Elderwood in golden hues, Claire ventured into the precinct with a focused determination. The meetings from the previous days had ignited a flame within her, and now it was time to delve deeper into the web of connections surrounding Dr. Harrow and the growing list of deceased patients.

She settled at her desk, pulling up files on her computer that contained patient histories and records related to those who had passed away unexpectedly under Harrow's care. Each name sparked a mixture of sadness and urgency within her as she studied their backgrounds. The numerous families sharing their pain had become her motivation; she owed it to them to uncover the truth.

Claire sifted through documents, cross-referencing names and events, trying to spot trends, anything that could link the patients together. Her heart raced as she noticed something intriguing—several deceased patients had attended the same community events; they had socialized at the same places, mingled through the same circles. This suggested there was a network connecting them that might lead back to Harrow's influence.

As she pieced together the puzzle, she remembered the Thompsons mentioning a local charity event where many of Harrow's patients had mingled. The elderly often congregated at these gatherings, and Harrow had been known to sponsor or attend them, positioning himself as a figure of care and support to the community.

Claire decided to reach out to Mrs. Thompson, hoping that additional context might provide clarity. She dialed Mrs. Thompson's number, anxiously drumming her fingers against the desk.

"Hello, Mrs. Thompson," Claire greeted when she answered. "I wanted to follow up about the community event last month—the one sponsored by Dr. Harrow. Do you remember who was there?"

"Oh, dear!" Mrs. Thompson said, her tone brightening slightly despite the weight of their previous conversations. "Yes, I remember it well. Lots of folks came—mostly the elderly. There were games, dances, and a lovely dinner. Everyone was so happy to see each other!"

"Anyone you specifically recall who was in attendance?" Claire asked, her mind racing with the possibilities.

"Well, let's see. I know Mr. and Mrs. Mills were there. And the Grahams! And then there was Mrs. Collins. She looked so lively that evening," she shared, nostalgia coloring her voice. "It was a fun time."

Claire furrowed her brow. "And you're sure Harrow was present?"

"Absolutely! He was the one overseeing the event, making sure everyone was comfortable," Mrs. Thompson replied, a note of warmth creeping into her tone. "He even took the time to sit and chat with many of the guests."

Claire felt a shiver ripple through her. The more connections she uncovered, the more troubling the picture became.

"Thank you, Mrs. Thompson. This information is quite useful," Claire said, her voice steady despite the whirlwind of emotions inside her. "I'll be sure to keep you updated."

As they ended the call, Claire quickly compiled a list of names connected to the event, thinking that perhaps this could lead to understanding why some patients had experienced rapid declines in their health. Not only would these connections tie individuals to Harrow, but they could also reveal if he had been targeting specific patients.

With her list in hand, Claire began making calls to the families of those who had been at the charity event. She needed to draw out any shared experiences or insights related to their interactions with Harrow—anything that might strengthen the case against him.

"Hello, Mr. Mills," Claire said when she reached him later that day. "I'm following up regarding the charity event you attended with Dr. Harrow. Could you share any thoughts you have about that evening?"

Mr. Mills paused before responding, his voice slightly skeptical. "It was a pleasant evening. But it was strange—after that gathering, my wife's health seemed to change. Harrow was so attentive to her... almost too attentive."

"Too attentive?" Claire probed, eager to unravel the context.

"Yeah, he made a point to sit with her for quite some time, asking questions that didn't seem to relate to her health at all, almost like he was fishing for something," Mr. Mills said, tension lacing his words. "I thought it was a bit odd, but at the time, I chalked it up to him just being courteous."

Claire made a note of that, feeling a sense of urgency growing in her chest. "Thank you, Mr. Mills. You've provided important context—

connections I'd like to further investigate as we work to understand what's happening."

As she hung up the phone, she felt an unsettling pattern surfacing. She spoke to individual families in the days that followed, each account leading her closer to a troubling realization—something about Harrow's behavior was deeply manipulative.

By the end of the week, a clearer narrative began to emerge. Many of the patients claimed to have felt a subtle, yet disconcerting, shift in Dr. Harrow's demeanor after attending the charity event. They described how he seemed to take a peculiar interest in them, often asking probing questions that veered off-topic from their health concerns.

Claire meticulously compiled these accounts, realizing they formed a pattern—one that suggested Harrow's attentiveness was more than just professional concern. It was as if he had been carefully observing his patients, searching for vulnerabilities he could exploit to maintain control over their health.

The connections between the deceased patients and their attendance at the charity event pointed to a disturbing possibility: Harrow might have been using these social gatherings to solidify his influence, laying the foundation for manipulating those who trusted him the most.

With this growing evidence, Claire decided it was time to convene with Officer Daniels and discuss her findings. She needed to strategize on how to use the information to protect the community effectively.

As Claire walked into his office, Daniels looked up, his expression one of curiosity mixed with concern. "You seem more focused than usual. What do you have for me?"

Claire laid out her notes on the desk, pointing to the key names and incidents she had linked together. "I've been digging into connections between the deceased patients and specific events they attended with Harrow. Each account highlights a concerning shift in behavior after social interactions—questions they felt were intrusive or unrelated to their health."

Daniels scanned the notes, his expression darkening. "This is troubling. It seems like Harrow has been manipulating not just their health but their vulnerabilities too, taking advantage of their trust during these community events."

"Exactly," Claire said, her determination cementing with every word. "He's creating an environment where people feel safe sharing personal details, only to use that knowledge to control their treatment. This is bigger than just malpractice; it's psychological manipulation."

"We need to act fast," Daniels agreed, rubbing his chin thoughtfully. "If we can accumulate enough testimonials and solidify a case, we could bring this to the attention of the medical board and law enforcement. But we need more voices to open the floodgates."

Determined, Claire began mapping out their strategy. "Let's set up a town meeting. We can invite all the families who have been affected and encourage them to share their experiences in a safe environment. It's time to confront Harrow collectively and show the community what he has been doing."

"That's a solid plan," Daniels said, excitement creeping into his tone. "But we must ensure everyone involved understands the risks. Harrow will not take kindly to being exposed."

"Agreed," Claire replied, her heart racing at the thought of confrontation. "We'll need to prepare a statement that outlines their experiences while emphasizing the importance of community support. People need to feel empowered."

As they discussed logistics, Claire felt the weight of responsibility settle over her shoulders once more. The risk was real, and while they had formulated a plan, she couldn't shake the doubt creeping into her mind. Would they be able to protect the families as they stepped forward?

That evening, determined to make the community meeting a reality, Claire reached out to the families, sharing her vision for the gathering. As her phone buzzed with replies, she felt a mix of anxiety and hope; the response was overwhelmingly positive. They were ready to speak out together against Harrow.

On the day of the town meeting, the community center was filled with energy, the air thick with anticipation. Claire arrived early to set up the space, ensuring everything was in place for the families who would soon share their stories. The vibrant sunlight streaming through the windows felt like a stark contrast to the weight of the darkness represented by Harrow.

As the room filled with familiar faces, Claire took a moment to absorb the energy. She saw the strength in each family—people who had faced the unimaginable and were now standing up to reclaim their power.

"Thank you all for being here today," Claire began, stepping to the front of the room. "We are gathered not just in remembrance of those we've lost but to ensure their stories are told. Together, we will shine a light on the reality of what Dr. Harrow has done."

One by one, families began to share their experiences—raw and unfiltered. Claire watched as voices that had been shrouded in doubt blossomed into a chorus of truth. Each account strengthened their case; they were not alone in this battle against Harrow's manipulation.

As the meeting progressed, Claire felt the weight of the moment. She realized the time had come to confront the man who had instilled fear in their lives, and this was the first step toward reclaiming their community from his oppressive grasp.

But in the back of her mind, apprehension gnawed at her—Dr. Harrow would not take this lightly. The storm was gathering, and Claire braced herself for the confrontation ahead.

CHAPTER 12
UNRAVELING THREADS

The air was thick with uncertainty as Lucy, Dr. Harrow's nurse, sat in the small break room of the practice, her heart racing. The conversations from the previous days echoed in her mind, a cacophony of doubt and hesitance about her boss. Ever since the families had begun to speak out against Harrow, a chill had settled deep in Lucy's bones.

She had worked alongside Harrow for years, witnessing firsthand the charisma that drew patients in and the confidence that seemed to envelop him like a cloak. But now, as she brewed her morning coffee, doubt gnawed at her mind, and she realized the warmth she once admired had begun to chill.

The peculiar changes in Harrow's behavior had intensified; he had grown more irritable and dismissive. Gone were the days when he would patiently listen to survivors' concerns. Now, he snapped at anyone who questioned his decisions or the treatment he prescribed. The uneasiness had started to spread like wildfire through the office staff, and Lucy could feel the tension building.

As she stirred her coffee, she recalled the conversations she'd overheard—patients expressing confusion about their medications and expressing fear about the sudden declines in health experienced by their loved ones. Each revelation chipped away at her loyalty, made her question everything she thought she understood about their practice.

Just then, the door swung open, and Dr. Harrow walked in, a tense smile plastered on his face. "Morning, Lucy," he greeted, but his tone felt strained, almost forced.

"Good morning, Doctor," she replied, trying to reflect some semblance of normalcy. However, as she scrutinized his expression, the lines of stress around his eyes made her stomach turn.

"I need you to prepare for today's patients. We have a busy schedule, and I don't want any delays," he ordered, his voice tinged with an edge that sent an uneasy ripple through her.

"Of course," she said, forcing a smile despite her growing apprehension.

She began organizing the appointment files, her hands trembling slightly as she sorted through documents linked to patients' treatments.

Something was brewing beneath the surface—there was a wound within their practice that Harrow seemed desperate to hide. The more she watched him, the more she felt the shadows gathering around him, and the anxiety clung to her like a heavy fog.

As the morning progressed, Lucy observed Harrow interacting with patients, a façade of calm masking an undercurrent of agitation. His smiles felt rehearsed, and his gestures lacking the warmth they once exuded. He was confronting patients with an intensity that bordered on intimidation, dismissing their slight hesitations as frivolous concerns.

Lucy's unease grew as she documented appointments, noting discrepancies in Harrow's prescriptions that she couldn't shake off. The changes were more pronounced, and she began to question whether his motives were fuelled by a genuine desire to care or by something darker.

After a particularly tense interaction with an elderly gentleman, Harrow returned to Lucy, dismissing the patient's concerns with a wave of his hand. "Can you believe these people? They think they can question my expertise just because they read something on the internet," he scoffed, but there was an edge to his voice that made Lucy uneasy.

"Maybe we should consider their concerns, Doctor," she suggested hesitantly, her heart racing at the thought of voicing her doubts. "They are our patients, after all. Their health is our responsibility."

"Responsibility?" Harrow's laughter was hollow, echoing in the small room. "I know better than they do. Trust me, I have everything under control."

The dismissive confidence rattled her, and for the first time, Lucy found herself doubting his authority. The urge to confront him swelled within her, fueled by the whispers of discontent echoing from the patients they served.

"Doctor, I just think we need to keep an open line of communication with our patients," Lucy said, trying to stay steady. "If they feel unheard, they may be less likely to return for follow-ups."

Harrow's demeanor shifted, and he stepped closer, the air crackling with tension. "You need to understand something, Lucy—there's a lot at stake here. The moment you start questioning my treatment methods is the moment our practice will lose credibility. Do you really want to risk that?"

Cowering under his intense gaze, she felt herself retreating inward. "No, of course not," she stammered, feeling a sliver of fear twist within her. "I just think we should be cautious."

"I'm done with caution," he snapped, his voice sharp as a blade. "You don't want to be on the wrong side of this."

Lucy felt her heart race as she composed herself and managed to nod in agreement. "I understand, Doctor."

But as he walked away, a sense of foreboding washed over her. She could no longer ignore the unsettling changes in Harrow's behavior, nor the patterns of mistrust brewing among their patients. Doubts began to intertwine with the loyalty she had felt toward him as a mentor, revealing a chasm where concern for his patients had once resided.

Determined to break free of the fear gripping her, Lucy reached for her phone, her fingers hovering over the screen. She considered calling Claire, sharing her unease. Yet, she hesitated, wondering if she truly had enough evidence to justify her concerns.

"I need to take action," she whispered to herself, realizing that if she didn't act soon, the consequences could be dire—not just for her but for the patients who depended on both her and Harrow.

After ensuring the office was quiet, Lucy began documenting her observations in a private note. Each strange occurrence, every uncomfortable remark Harrow had made during patient interactions poured out of her. The discrepancies in prescriptions, the dismissive attitude toward patient grievances—everything began to unfold in a way that painted a picture she could no longer deny.

As she detailed how Harrow reacted to patients expressing concern, Lucy envisioned herself holding the notes before Claire, her words becoming tangible threads that could unravel the façade of care he had built. She realized she couldn't be complicit in his manipulation any longer.

With a newfound sense of purpose, she resolved to meet Claire later that day to share her findings. The urgency of the situation propelled her onward, and she wrapped up her shifts in the office with a focus that felt both liberating and daunting.

When Lucy finished her work for the day, she approached Claire's office at the precinct, her heart pounding with anxiety. "Claire, do you have a moment to talk?"

Claire looked up from her desk, surprise flickering in her eyes. "Of course! What's going on, Lucy?" she asked, leaning forward with concern.

"I've been observing Harrow more closely," Lucy began, her hands trembling slightly as she fought to keep her voice steady. "There's something seriously off about him, and I believe the way he interacts with patients has shifted. I think he's becoming increasingly controlling."

Claire's expression shifted to one of intense interest. "What kind of changes are you noticing?"

"After our last meeting, I noticed patients seem more intimidated and hesitant to express concerns. He brushes them off, dismissing their worries as overreactions. But that's not all—he's changed some of their medications, even adding new prescriptions without clear explanations,"

Lucy said, her voice thickening with conviction. "It feels wrong, Claire. I'm frightened of what could happen if this continues."

"Lucy, this is crucial information," Claire replied, her heart racing. "We need to utilize this information to build a stronger case against him. What you're seeing may help to break down the facade he's created."

Lucy swallowed hard, feeling the weight of responsibility settle upon her shoulders. "I hope so. I just can't shake the feeling that he's watching me too, like he knows I'm questioning him."

Claire stepped closer, determination flashing in her eyes. "Then we need to make sure you're safe. It's time we take action before Harrow can manipulate the narrative any further. We need to document everything— including your observations—so we can present it to the authorities."

Lucy nodded, the sense of urgency revitalizing her. "I'll write everything down and gather as much information as I can. We should also reach out to the families and ask them to share any changes they've noticed."

"That's an excellent idea," Claire encouraged, her resolve strengthening. "Together, we can shed light on his lies and bring forward the evidence needed to address this. We can't let fear rule our actions."

As they finalized their plans, Lucy felt the weight of dread begin to lift, replaced by a sense of empowerment. They would make their voices heard, push back against Harrow's oppressive grip, and take the first steps toward ensuring the safety of every patient.

Later that evening, armed with her notes and a deep sense of purpose, Lucy left the precinct, ready to contact families who had been under

Harrow's care. Each connection they made would strengthen their collective resolve, and Lucy was prepared to see this through—even if it meant confronting her own fears.

As she walked through the dimly lit streets of Elderwood, the shadows stretched long behind her, but she felt emboldened. They were united in their quest for truth, and with each encountered familiar face, she would advocate for accountability.

The fight was just beginning.

CHAPTER 13
CAUGHT IN THE ACT

The following day dawned with a fresh resolve, and Claire could feel the tension simmering beneath the surface of the community. She arrived at the precinct early, determined to gather the evidence necessary to confront Dr. Harrow and expose the truth behind his manipulative practices.

Fueled by the testimonies she had collected, Claire spread out the files across her desk, each document a testament to the pain the families had endured. The recurring patterns of negligence and an alarming rise in adverse reactions to medications filled her with urgency. They were not only compiling stories; they were building a case.

As she reviewed the testimonies, Claire made a plan to visit Harrow's practice that very day, needing to witness his interactions firsthand. She had received numerous reports detailing odd behaviors during patient visits, including subtle intimidation tactics aimed at silencing dissent.

"Claire!" Officer Daniels called as he approached, his expression tight with concentration. "We need to coordinate our efforts. We might have an opportunity to catch Harrow off guard if we combine our findings with your direct observations."

"I think that's an excellent approach," Claire replied, her heart racing at the thought of finally confronting Harrow. "We need to ensure we're prepared if he tries to deflect or intimidate us. I'm ready to lay everything on the line for the families—especially after the concerns expressed about his behavior."

As they planned the meeting with the officers, Claire thought back to her recent conversations with patients and their families. They were going to reveal the truth, and together, they would amplify their voices. She couldn't shake the feeling that time was running out.

"Let's head over to Harrow's practice during the late afternoon," Daniels suggested. "We can observe the interactions with patients and document anything that raises red flags."

With the plan set, Claire gathered her materials and headed for Harrow's office, adrenaline surging through her. As she stepped inside, the familiar scent of antiseptic and faint coffee permeated the air. Claire quickly took a seat in the waiting area, doing her best to appear inconspicuous while she gathered herself.

It wasn't long before Lucy arrived, her frantic energy clear as she nervously approached Claire. "I've heard more whispers from patients," she said, glancing around apprehensively. "They seem more uncomfortable, and some have mentioned that Harrow has become increasingly short with them."

"Exactly what we need to document," Claire replied, her mind racing with possible scenarios. "Let's watch for any signs of intimidation or manipulation during his appointments."

As they waited, the tension in the air heightened. Claire scanned the waiting room and spotted a few familiar faces—patients she had spoken to, each carrying the weight of uncertainty. Harrow's manipulation had extended its reach, and Claire was determined to expose it.

Inside the examination rooms, she could hear Harrow's voice carrying through the walls—a mix of authoritative tones and dismissive laughter that sent a chill down her spine.

It was during one of these appointments that the opportunity Claire had been waiting for arose. Harrow was finishing with a patient when he stepped out and began speaking to Lucy at the reception desk.

"Just remember, Lucy, if patients don't comply with the treatments or start feeling unwell, it's likely a result of their own negligence," he said, his tone condescending. "No one wants to take responsibility these days."

Claire's heart raced as she caught snippets of the conversation, her instincts driving her forward. This was it—a chance to capture his true nature.

"Lucy, can you clarify how Dr. Harrow approaches patients when they express concerns?" Claire called out from her seat, feigning innocence as she leaned casually against the receptionist area. She needed to catch Harrow off guard.

"Claire, I—" Lucy started to reply, but Harrow's gaze snapped toward her.

"What are you doing here?" he asked, his eyes narrowing, a shadow of irritation passing over his features.

"I'm just gathering some insights for the ongoing investigation regarding patient care," Claire said, meeting his glare with unwavering confidence.

"The investigation?" Harrow scoffed, dismissing her with a wave of his hand. "It's essentially frivolous. Patients come to me for help, but that means they need to trust my expertise. Dismissing that is nothing but self-serving."

"Self-serving?" Claire shot back, holding her ground. "It sounds more like you're concerned about losing control. You must know by now that many patients aren't happy."

The tension in the air thickened, and Harrow's expression transformed from irritation to thinly veiled hostility. "Careful, Claire. You might find yourself on the wrong side of this situation."

Just then, another patient exited the exam room, clearly distraught. She caught Claire's eye, and the fear radiating from her was palpable. Harrow shot her a warning glare before smiling disarmingly.

"Just need to go over some paperwork," Harrow said, his demeanor shifting back to the practiced charm everyone in the community had come to expect. He turned to the patient with feigned concern. "You're going to be alright, Mrs. Turner. Trust me; I know what I'm doing."

As Mrs. Turner ambled out with a worried look on her face, Claire seized the opportunity to press on. "Dr. Harrow, I think it's vital we establish an open dialogue with your patients. They have concerns that need to be addressed, not dismissed."

"I assure you, Claire," Harrow retorted, his tone sharp, "I am their physician, and I have their best interests at heart. You questioning this is both reckless and dangerous."

"Reckless? Or maybe it's necessary," Claire challenged, feeling adrenaline heightening her focus. "How can you ignore what the patient clearly expressed? Someone needs to hold you accountable for your methods."

The tension hung thick in the air. Harrow's expression grew more menacing as he stepped closer, invading Claire's personal space. "You think you can walk in here and disrupt my practice? You're playing a dangerous game, Avery."

"Perhaps you're the one playing games, Harrow," she countered, standing her ground. "This is about lives, and I won't let you continue manipulating those who trust you."

Before Harrow could respond, Lucy interjected, having overheard the escalating confrontation. "Doctor, patients have been voicing their concerns, and they deserve to be heard. Putting them down only exacerbates their fears."

Harrow gave Lucy a chilling smile that didn't reach his eyes. "You'd do well to remember your place, Lucy. Patients need trust, not someone undermining my authority."

"Authority doesn't justify negligence," Claire snapped back, anger surging. "We're here to protect those who can't speak for themselves."

Harrow took a step back, visibly shaken but maintaining his composure. "You think your little power play here can shake me? I am a respected member of this community, and you are, nothing more than a detective pushing an agenda."

"An agenda to protect lives," Claire shot back. "And I'll do everything necessary to ensure that others see through your facade."

The interaction hung in the air, thick with palpable tension until suddenly, the ringing of the entrance bell interrupted them. A police officer entered the practice, eyes darting to the two of them.

"Detective Avery, there's been a report of trouble near the community center. We could use your help," he said, urgency painted across his face.

Claire felt a swell of relief wash over her. "Of course, I'll be right there," she responded, turning to Harrow one last time. "This isn't over. We'll be watching you."

As she and the officer exited, she glanced back to see Harrow scowling, his hands clenched at his sides. A sense of foreboding settled over her, but now a spark of determination ignited her resolve. They were gaining ground, and more evidence was emerging from the cracks in Harrow's carefully constructed facade.

Outside, the sun shone brightly, with people moving about, unaware of the brewing storm that threatened their community. Claire followed the officer toward the community center, her mind racing. She had to leverage the momentum from the confrontation with Harrow and turn it into concrete evidence.

Upon reaching the center, she found a crowd gathering—the local residents were murmuring with concern about the rumors circulating regarding Harrow. The scene was charged with anticipation and fear, a reflection of the uncertainty that had filtered through the community.

"Claire! Over here!" Mary called, waving her arms to get Claire's attention. She looked anxious but determined, standing alongside a few other families.

"Mary, it's good to see you," Claire said, her expression turning serious. "Have you all been hearing the rumors about Harrow?"

"Everyone is worried that he might retaliate," Mary admitted, glancing around nervously. "But we want to stand with you. We won't back down."

"Good," Claire said, taking a deep breath. "We need to gather everyone's testimonials and prepare to present our findings together. The more voices we have, the harder it will be for Harrow to dismiss our claims."

Just then, a local news reporter approached them, microphone in hand. "Excuse me, I've received reports of concerns regarding Dr. Harrow from several families. Would you care to comment on this situation?"

Claire exchanged glances with Mary and the other families. This was the moment they needed. "Yes," Claire agreed, stepping forward. "We have a lot to discuss regarding the treatment methods employed by Dr. Harrow that have raised serious concerns about the health and safety of his patients."

As she began to speak, detailing the families' experiences and the growing fear surrounding Harrow's practice, Claire felt a sense of empowerment ripple through her. The energy of the crowd surged at her words; it was as if they were no longer just victims hiding in shadows but a united front ready to confront the darkness together.

"We stand here today," Claire said, her voice steady and resolute, "not just for ourselves but for every patient who has been silenced by fear, every family torn apart by the negligent treatment of Dr. Harrow. We deserve transparency, accountability, and care that prioritizes our health over arrogance."

A murmur of agreement rose from the gathering, and Claire glanced at the reporter, who appeared captivated, capturing every word on camera. "This is just the beginning," she continued, emboldened by the support. "We are sharing our stories to shed light on the truth and encourage others to come forward. Together, we can hold him accountable."

As she spoke, she noticed the expressions of the crowd—faint glimmers of hope shining through the clouds of uncertainty they had all shared. The fears that had once kept them apart now became the bond that united them.

Just then, the sound of hushed whispers swept through the crowd as someone in the back pointed toward a figure standing ominously at the edge of the gathering. Claire's heart sank as she recognized Dr. Harrow's imposing figure, the expression on his face unreadable but filled with a palpable tension.

"What a spectacle we have here," he called out, his voice dripping with sarcasm as he pushed through the crowd, forcing his way toward Claire. "Are you really going to believe these tales? It sounds like nothing more than a witch hunt."

"We're sharing the truth about what's been happening, Harrow," Claire shot back, feeling the anger and fear bubble just beneath the surface. "These families deserve to be heard, and we will not let you intimidate us any longer."

Harrow's face twisted into a smile that didn't reach his eyes. "I admire your audacity, Claire. But understand this: manipulating these families into turning on me won't end well for you. You're poking a bear."

The crowd murmured, the tension thickening as Claire stepped closer, determined to stand her ground. "The only bear being poked is you. We are here to expose the truth, and nothing you can say or do will silence us."

"Is that so?" Harrow challenged, his voice low and menacing. "You think your little performance will save them? You're all so worried about your health, yet it's your very fear that I might take action first that will do more harm than you realize."

As Harrow brandished a calm facade, Claire could feel the whispers of doubt creeping back into the crowd. "Don't let him manipulate you!" she urged, feeling the tension rise as she spoke. "We are stronger together. Your voices matter."

"We're not afraid of you!" one family member shouted, their voice cutting through the unease. Others chimed in with shouts of support, echoing a chorus fueled by their shared anger.

But Harrow remained unfazed, his demeanor cool and collected. "You're all making a big mistake. This isn't just about me; it's about your well-being. Keep pushing, and you might find out that the truth isn't as clear as you think."

With those chilling words, Harrow turned, walking away, leaving the crowd buzzing with a mix of anxiety and indignation. Claire felt the resolve of the families strengthen as they continued to voice their frustrations, rallying behind her call for transparency.

"Stay united!" Claire encouraged, raising her voice above the noise. "We must come together to support one another and find a way to bring this to light. Harrow will try to divide us, but we cannot let that happen."

As the group began to disperse, a renewed commitment flickered in their eyes. After such an intense exchange, Claire felt the weight of their collective resolve settle upon her, fortifying her spirit.

Despite Dr. Harrow's threats, Claire knew they had taken a significant step toward exposing the truth. Each story shared and each moment of support came together like intricate threads, weaving a tapestry that would create a protective barrier against Harrow's influence.

Later that evening, as Claire sat at her desk, she couldn't shake the sense of urgency that permeated through her. They needed to act quickly before Harrow could reorganize himself and push back against their united front. The gathering storm was brewing, and she was determined to face it head-on.

With her thoughts racing, Claire made a list of everything still needed for their impending confrontation. She would continue to gather evidence from families and reach out to local authorities. As the shadows of the evening deepened around her, she felt the adrenaline pulsing through her veins—a visceral reminder that this fight was far from over.

CHAPTER 14
PRECARIOUS BALANCE

In the days following the town meeting, the atmosphere in Elderwood became increasingly charged with tension and uncertainty. As families rallied behind Claire in their fight against Dr. Harrow, the doctor began to counter their efforts with insidious tactics that sent ripples of doubt throughout the community.

Harrow, ever cunning and charismatic, had launched a campaign of manipulation, portraying himself as the victim of a witch hunt. In coffee shops and grocery stores, whispers began circulating, spurred on by Harrow's carefully crafted narrative. "Have you heard what Claire Avery is doing?" people would murmur, casting furtive glances as they gossiped. "Accusing our beloved doctor of such things!"

Claire first noticed the shift at the precinct when she overheard a group of residents discussing Harrow in hushed tones, their faces etched with uncertainty. Questions of loyalty began to surface. "He's never harmed anyone," one woman insisted, her brow furrowed. "I don't believe those families; they're just trying to get attention."

As Claire navigated through the precinct hallways, she felt the growing unease ripple through the air, a reflection of the precarious balance that had begun to shift. Harrow's influence was contagious, and it was clear he was using his charm to lure people back into blind trust.

Determined not to succumb to the spreading fear, Claire met with Officer Daniels to discuss the troubling turn of events. "We need to counter Harrow's narrative," she urged, pacing the office. "If he's convincing the community that we're lying, it jeopardizes everything we're trying to accomplish."

"I've heard similar concerns," Daniels admitted, rubbing the back of his neck. "He's a master manipulator. We need to gather evidence that can expose his façade for what it truly is. There are cracks in his story—people just need the courage to see them."

"Agreed," Claire replied, her heart pounding with urgency as she rifled through the documents on her desk. "I'll try to reach out to the families again. If we can present a united front with more corroborative evidence, we can combat his influence."

Late that afternoon, Claire and Daniels decided to conduct a community canvassing effort, visiting homes to speak directly with those who had shown doubts or had fallen under Harrow's sway. They needed to empathetically address their concerns, countering Harrow's manipulative narrative with the undeniable realities of his practices.

As they traveled from house to house, Claire felt the unease hanging in the air like a thick fog. Each encounter was met with a mix of fear and curiosity, but it became clear that Harrow's influence was taking effect. Residents were hesitant, distrusting Claire and questioning her motives.

At one house, Mrs. Baker answered the door with a wary expression. "What do you want, Detective?" she asked, crossing her arms defensively.

"We're gathering information regarding Dr. Harrow," Claire explained, maintaining her composure. "We need to understand your experiences and how his methods may have impacted your health or the health of your loved ones."

Mrs. Baker's eyes narrowed. "I don't need to get involved in whatever witch hunt this is," she retorted. "Dr. Harrow has always been there for our community. You should be ashamed of yourself for going after him."

Claire felt her stomach knot. "Ma'am, I assure you I'm only here to help. I'm not trying to tear our community apart. I just want to uncover the truth."

Mrs. Baker shook her head, her expression unyielding. "You're only making things worse. People need him. He's a good man!"

Frustrated but steadfast, Claire tried to reason with her. "He may have presented himself as a good man, but I've spoken to families who have suffered due to his negligence. We need to listen to their experiences."

As Claire moved on to the next house, she felt the weight of Mrs. Baker's disbelief bearing down on her. Each door that closed left her feeling more isolated, the community falling further under Harrow's spell. It became increasingly clear that the precarious balance between trust and skepticism was tilting in Harrow's favor.

Returning to the precinct, Claire found several officers gathered around the television in the break room. Curious, she approached and turned her attention to the news broadcast filling the screen.

"—controversial health care practices have recently sparked outrage in Elderwood, as allegations against local physician Dr. Samuel Harrow have surfaced, raising concerns among many residents," the newscaster reported, an image of Harrow smiling in a previous community event flashing across the screen.

Tension hung thick in the air as the segment continued. "While some families have come forward with accusations of negligence, others claim that Dr. Harrow is an upstanding member of the community who has always put the care of his patients first."

Claire's heart sank as one of Harrow's supporters appeared on screen, passionately defending him. "Dr. Harrow has always had our best interests at heart. I've never seen him act recklessly with a patient. This is just a smear campaign to discredit a good man," the resident proclaimed, her voice filled with fiery conviction.

The officers in the break room shifted uncomfortably, eyes darting from the screen back to Claire. "Looks like he's working his charm," one of them muttered, and Claire could feel the collective doubt creeping back over the precinct.

"This isn't just gossip," Claire said, clenching her fists in frustration. "This is an orchestrated attempt to manipulate public perception and protect himself. We can't let him twist the narrative. The truth is on our side, and we have evidence to support that."

Daniels stepped closer, a look of concern etched on his face. "The community is loyal to him, Claire. They see a doctor who once saved lives, and they don't want to believe he could be responsible for harm. We need to break through that loyalty."

With her resolve solidified, Claire decided that fear wouldn't deter her. There had to be a way to counter Harrow's growing influence and suspend his hold over the patients and families he had preyed upon. The media portrayal had solidified him as a sympathetic figure, and Claire could sense anger brewing within her.

"We need to gather more testimonials from the families—focus on those who have publicly expressed doubts about Harrow's treatment methods," she said, determination hardening her voice. "We have to show that there's a serious pattern of negligence and distrust surrounding him."

Daniels nodded in agreement. "We can organize a walk rally where families can share their experiences. If we can get a larger turnout, it might shake the community's support for him and bring more voices to our side."

"Yes! That's perfect," Claire exclaimed, her mind racing with the possibilities. "We can reach out to local media again and create an event that highlights their stories. But we must act fast—before Harrow can further twist the narrative."

With renewed vigor, Claire and Daniels began to outline a plan, each detail focused on gathering evidence and giving families a platform to be heard. They set to work—contacting families and gathering stories, using the momentum from the recent news coverage as a springboard to empower and mobilize support.

As the day turned into evening, Claire found herself on the phone with family after family, weaving a narrative of hope, resistance, and solidarity. Each account brought them closer to reclaiming their community and shining a light on Harrow's troubling practices.

But then, just as her spirits began to rise, Claire noticed a familiar face at the edge of the precinct—the figure of Harrow standing outside, his expression difficult to read. He appeared to be watching her closely.

"Daniels, look," she whispered, pointing toward the window. "He's out there."

Daniels turned sharply, tension flaring as he approached the window. "We can't let him confront you again. We need to call this in."

"Wait," Claire interrupted, her mind racing with a need to confront Harrow directly. "I need to hear what he's trying to do. This could provide us with valuable insight."

"Claire, his presence is dangerous!" Daniels warned, concern flooding his voice.

"I understand, but we need to know how far he's willing to go," Claire insisted, her heart hammering in her chest. "If he's out there trying to manipulate the narrative, I have to be ready for whatever is coming next."

Despite Daniels' protests, Claire stepped outside, ready to confront the looming threat standing at the edge of her resolve. As she approached Harrow, he turned to face her, a predatory glint in his eyes.

"Detective Avery," he said, his tone dripping with calculated charm. "I was just passing by. How unfortunate that we keep running into each other. You should really reconsider the path you're on."

"This isn't a game, Harrow," Claire replied, her voice strong despite the tension thrumming between them. "You're taking advantage of these families, manipulating their trust."

His smile widened, but it felt false, a mask hiding malicious intent. "They're just scared, Claire. Fear can cloud judgment, and you should know that better than anyone."

"I know what I'm doing, Harrow. You've underestimated these families, and now they're standing up for themselves," she said, feeling a rush of adrenaline.

"Watch yourself," he warned, stepping closer, his voice dropping to a chilling whisper. "You don't want to be on my bad side. I have more influence than you realize, and I can make your life quite difficult—on both sides of the law."

Claire's heart raced as she felt his intimidating presence loom over her, but she refused to let fear control her. "I'm not afraid of you, Harrow," she said, meeting his gaze steadily. "What you're doing to these families is wrong, and I will expose you for it."

Harrow chuckled softly, a low, menacing sound that sent a shiver down Claire's spine. "You think you can take me down? I've spent years building my reputation in this community. People trust me, and they will believe my version of events over yours."

"Your reputation is built on deception and manipulation," Claire replied, her frustration boiling beneath the surface. "You may have fooled the community for a long time, but truth has a way of surfacing. Your time is running out."

Harrow's smile faded, replaced by a look of cold calculation. "You should tread carefully, Detective. There are consequences for crossing me. This isn't just about you—remember that."

With those final words, he stepped back, his facade of charm slipping away, revealing the predator lurking beneath. As he turned to walk away, Claire felt a mix of determination and disgust wash over her. She would not let him intimidate her or the families she had come to support.

Determined to gather more evidence, Claire returned to the precinct and reviewed the files on the deceased patients. She cross-referenced names with the recent testimonies, looking for any additional links or patterns. She was searching for that one crucial piece of evidence that could further solidify their case against Harrow.

Hours passed, and as dusk began to settle outside, Claire noticed an email notification pop up on her screen. It was from Officer Daniels.

Subject: Important Findings

She opened the email, her heart quickening as she read through his notes. Daniels had been speaking with local medical boards and had uncovered discrepancies in Harrow's treatment history—specifically concerning patients who had experienced inexplicable declines.

In a tight-knit community like Elderwood, the ramifications of Harrow's actions extended far beyond individuals; they threatened to unravel the very fabric of trust that had existed between citizens and their healthcare.

Claire forwarded the information to her colleagues, urging them to mobilize and work with the families to share these findings. The time to act was now; they needed to confront the mounting evidence before Harrow could dismiss or invalidate it.

Just as Claire was preparing to leave for the day, the precinct buzzed with activity. Officers gathered in small groups discussing the day's developments. She approached Daniels, who was deep in conversation with another officer.

"Any news on Harrow?" Claire asked, her heart pounding with anticipation.

"We've received multiple calls about him being seen in the area and causing uproar at local businesses, voicing his grievances against you and the families," Daniels replied, running a hand through his hair, visibly concerned. "He's trying to undermine everything we're working for."

"He knows we're closing in, and he's retaliating," Claire said, her determination hardening. "We need to act quickly before he can twist the narrative further."

With a shared understanding of the urgency, they quickly organized a response team. Armed with evidence from families and testimonies about Harrow's potentially harmful practices, they prepared to confront him in a way that would not leave room for his manipulation.

The sun dipped below the horizon, shrouding the precinct in twilight as Claire and the team geared up to pay a visit to Harrow's practice once more. The energy in the air was electric, a mix of anticipation and fear intertwining as they approached his office.

Upon arriving, Claire felt the adrenaline surging through her. "Remember, we're here to get the truth out," she reminded the team. "Stay focused, and let's ensure that Harrow knows we're not afraid."

Together, they entered the practice, the familiar scent of antiseptic greeting them. Claire felt a wave of confidence wash over her as she prepared for the inevitable confrontation; this time, they would approach it with the strength of numbers and the weight of justice behind them.

As they walked through the waiting room, Claire spotted Harrow at the reception desk, chatting casually with Lucy. The contrast between his composure and the tension radiating from Claire felt palpable, a twisted game of appearances playing out before them.

"Dr. Harrow," Claire called, stepping forward with an unwavering resolve, "we need to talk."

Harrow turned slowly, an amused smirk appearing on his face. "Well, well, if it isn't the detective and her entourage. What brings you here? Have you come to waste more time with baseless accusations?"

"Not baseless," Claire replied, her voice steady. "We have serious concerns regarding your treatment methods and the increasing number of suspicious patient deaths."

At that moment, Lucy's eyes widened in shock, her expression one of alarm as she took in the tension in the room. Harrow's smirk vanished, replaced by an irritated glare that seemed to slice through the air.

"What is the meaning of this?" he demanded, his tone sharp and challenging. "You storm in here with your badge and think you can command respect?"

"We're here to ensure accountability, Dr. Harrow," Claire asserted, her voice unwavering. "Enough is enough. The reports of mistreatment and the inexplicable rise in patient deaths cannot be ignored any longer."

Harrow leaned back slightly, his posture relaxing but his eyes narrowing. "You're making a huge mistake, Claire. You're jeopardizing your career and your credibility by framing this as anything more than a witch hunt."

Claire felt the weight of his words, but she stood firm, refusing to back down. "This isn't a witch hunt. It's a quest for truth. You've put so many lives at risk, and we're here to uncover your negligence."

From the corner of her eye, she noticed Lucy's discomfort as she stood awkwardly between them. Claire could sense the tension brewing not just between her and Harrow, but also within Lucy, who had been a loyal nurse.

"What do you really want, Claire?" Harrow asked, his voice laced with feigned innocence. "Are you trying to rally these families against me for your own crusade?"

"You know what I want," Claire countered. "And so do all these families you've manipulated. You've turned trust into coercion, and we won't let you continue to operate unchecked."

Harrow's eyes flashed dangerously as he shifted his focus to Lucy. "And you, Lucy. Are you really going to stand by her side? She's going to drag you down with her. This isn't a game, and I'm the one holding the cards here."

Harrow's words struck a nerve, causing Lucy to falter for a split second. Claire saw the vulnerability in her colleague's eyes, reminding her of the precarious balance they were all walking.

"Lucy, don't listen to him!" Claire urged, stepping closer to her. "You have firsthand knowledge of his methods. Trust your instincts. We're not trying to attack you; we're here to seek justice."

"I...I just don't want to get caught in the middle of this," Lucy stammered, her eyes darting between Claire and Harrow, the fear in her voice palpable.

Harrow seized the moment. "You see, Lucy? Even Claire recognizes the precarious nature of this situation—you're at risk. Joining her side will only prove detrimental. You know how this works, don't you?" His tone shifted to an almost conspiratorial whisper, manipulating the uncertainty in the air.

"Stop!" Claire shouted, cutting through the tension. "You are not going to turn this into a personal attack on any of us. This is about facts, about patients who have suffered under your care. The truth isn't on your side."

Harrow's smile re-emerged, though now it was colder, more calculating. "Perhaps this isn't the best setting for this discussion, then. You expect these families to trust you while you're threatening their doctor in his own practice?"

"Trust is built on honesty, not fear," Claire shot back, her voice unwavering as she felt a swell of support from the families present behind her. "The community deserves to know the truth about your methods, and we won't let you manipulate them any longer."

The atmosphere was crackling with tension as Harrow looked at Claire and then back at Lucy, a hint of uncertainty breaking through his confident demeanor. "You think this is all just going to unravel like your little crusade?"

"We're prepared to expose the truth," Claire replied, heart pounding. "If you continue to threaten and manipulate, we will ensure that the community understands what you are truly capable of."

Just then, the door to the practice swung open, and Officer Daniels entered, alerting Claire to a sudden burst of energy from outside. "We've received reports of Dr. Harrow making threats to families in the area. There's potential unrest. We need to ensure everyone's safety."

Claire turned to Harrow, her heart racing. "You'd better think carefully about your next move."

Harrow straightened, the bravado returning to his posture. "You've no idea who you're dealing with, Claire. This isn't over."

With a last lingering glance at Claire, Harrow turned and stormed out of the practice, leaving palpable tension hanging in the air.

"We need to act quickly," Claire told the team surrounding her, her voice resolute. "If he's indeed making threats, we must ensure these families are protected. We need to give them the strength to stand together."

As Claire and the officers collected their thoughts, a renewed sense of purpose propelled them forward. They were standing on the precipice of a monumental confrontation, one that had the potential to uproot the distrust that had festered within the community.

"We need to establish a plan to not just respond to Harrow's threats but to also strengthen our case against him," Claire said, her mind racing as she laid out the next steps. "I want to organize a meeting with the families again, emphasizing the importance of their safety and ensuring they know they have our support. We'll need to prepare them for the backlash."

Officer Daniels nodded in agreement. "And we need to keep patrols active around the families' homes. If Harrow is making threats, we don't want anyone to feel vulnerable."

Just then, another officer walked in, breathless and urgent. "Detective, we've received reports that Dr. Harrow is attempting to make contact with the families directly. Some say he's been visiting their homes, trying to dissuade them from sharing their stories with you."

A wave of anger washed over Claire. "That's unacceptable. He's trying to intimidate them into silence. We can't allow him to manipulate them further. We need to respond immediately."

"Let's draft up a public advisory for the families," Daniels suggested, already pulling out a notepad. "We should inform them to report any interactions with Harrow to us and remind them that they have protection."

As they began to brainstorm the advisory, Claire couldn't shake the feeling of urgency pressing down on her. This wasn't just about Harrow's threats; it was about the fragile trust families had placed in her—not only to protect them but to give them a voice in the face of adversity.

The urgency intensified as Claire set to work. She contacted the families, urging them to gather once more at the community center that evening. As word spread, she could feel the anticipation building; this meeting would serve as a reaffirmation of their collective strength.

When evening arrived, the community center buzzed with families gathering—each face somber but determined. Claire stepped forward, heart in her throat at the sight of so many gathered, each of them willing to stand up for what was right.

"Thank you all for coming again," Claire began, her voice steady but thick with emotion. "I know this has been an incredibly difficult time for many of you. Dr. Harrow is attempting to manipulate the truth and intimidate you into silence. But I want you to know—you are not alone."

The murmurs of agreement rippled through the room, and Claire continued, "We are gathering evidence against him, and your testimonies are critical to shining a light on the truth. This is our moment to reclaim our community."

As families began to share their stories, Claire felt the weight of the world melting from her shoulders. This was what they needed—courage and solidarity to confront the darkness together. The strength in their voices gradually shifted from unease to a powerful resolve.

However, just as the group began to feel emboldened, the doors of the community center swung open, and Dr. Harrow stepped inside, the unmistakable aura of confidence filling the room.

"Really, Claire?" he called out, amusement dancing in his tone. "Gathering the townsfolk against me? How quaint."

The atmosphere shifted instantly; whispered conversations died down, and palpable tension filled the air. Claire felt the urge to confront him, but she needed to keep everyone calm and focused.

"This is not a stunt or a witch hunt, Dr. Harrow," Claire retorted, stepping forward. "This is about the health and well-being of this community, a community that you have put in jeopardy with your reckless behavior."

Harrow chuckled softly, moving closer with an air of nonchalance, yet there was a cold intensity behind his eyes. "You don't understand how this works, do you? I have built trust here over many years. You think a handful of complaints will unravel my entire reputation? You're naive."

"People are waking up to the reality of your practices, Harrow," Claire said, asserting herself as she held her ground. "Your behavior is being scrutinized now, and that's not something you can easily dismiss."

"Scrutiny? Or mere hysteria?" he replied, glancing around the room with a dismissive wave. "You see, it's people like you who stir unnecessary trouble for the sake of your self-importance. My patients will stand by me."

Professionals and families stood quietly behind her, clearly uncertain about how to react. Claire felt a surge of anger at Harrow's manipulation, recognizing the precarious balance between truth and intimidation that played out in front of her.

"Your control over these families is crumbling," Claire countered boldly, her heart racing as she stood firmly. "We will ensure they are safe, and we will shine a light on your deceptive practices. You can threaten us, but that only proves you're afraid of the truth."

The air around them crackled with tension as Harrow's expression darkened. "You think you're untouchable because you wore that badge? You're nothing compared to what I've built. You may be able to scare these feeble-minded folks for a while, but they will come back to me."

"This is not about scaring anyone," Claire replied, her voice unwavering. "This is about making sure that the vulnerable don't fall victim to your manipulations. You're not just a doctor, Harrow; you're a danger to every person who trusts you."

A wave of murmured support rippled through the crowd, and Claire felt it bolster her courage. Harrow's bravado faltered slightly as the community began to rally behind her. It was a moment of reckoning, and Claire knew they had the upper hand.

"Stay away from these families, Harrow," she warned, stepping closer with fierce determination. "If you truly cared for your patients, you would want them to feel safe speaking their minds without fear of intimidation."

"I care for them in ways you cannot comprehend," he shot back, but the edge in his voice betrayed a hint of desperation. "You've already garnered attention and interest, but that doesn't change the facts: they need me to heal them, and you're just a detective looking for your next headline."

"Believe me, I've had enough of your headlines," Claire stated, her resolve firm. "And soon, everyone will know the truth. You can't manipulate their stories anymore."

Harrow's demeanor shifted as he leaned closer, a predatory glint returning to his eyes. "You'll regret this, Claire. Just remember, the shadows have their ways of revealing who the real enemy is."

With that last taunt, Harrow turned and strode out of the community center, his presence receding but leaving behind a palpable tension that hung in the air.

"Are we okay?" whispered one of the families, uncertainty clouding their faces.

Claire took a deep breath, shaking off the anger and fear that threatened to overwhelm her. "We're going to be fine," she reassured them. "What you all did today took immense courage, and now we have even more strength as a community. Harrow may try to intimidate us, but we are much stronger when we stand together."

As the families exchanged glances of concern, Claire listened to the murmurs of support building in the room. Each family member's resolve to stand against Harrow strengthened her belief that they were on the brink of exposing the duplicity that had plagued their community for far too long.

After the meeting concluded, Claire returned to her office to sift through the testimonies, trying to connect the dots between Harrow's manipulations and the health declines of his patients. The silence of the precinct felt heavy, and Claire's thoughts raced as she organized the information.

Just as she was entering new data into her files, the phone rang, pulling her attention away from her work. It was Officer Daniels. "Claire, we might have a break in the case. I've just received a tip-off that Harrow has been seen frequenting the homes of several patients, acting strangely."

"What do you mean—strangely?" Claire asked, her pulse quickening. "Is he confronting them?"

"More like lurking," Daniels replied. "It sounds like he's trying to intimidate them, possibly to ward off any further complaints. I think he's getting desperate."

Claire's mind raced as she considered the implications. "We need to act on this information. If he's threatening patients, we can't let him continue without someone holding him accountable."

"Agreed," Daniels said. "Let's set up a surveillance on his known routes. Maybe we can catch him in the act of intimidation."

"That's the plan," Claire confirmed, her determination solidifying. "The next step is to protect those families and gather evidence that could lead to action against him."

As the sun dipped away, casting long shadows through the precinct, Claire felt an unwavering sense of urgency. They were beginning to close in on Harrow, but the precarious balance between manipulation and truth hung heavily in the air. It was a game of risk—one they could not afford to lose.

With a clearer strategy forming in her mind, Claire gathered her notes and headed out, resolved to confront the sinister undercurrent flowing through Elderwood and expose Dr. Harrow for the danger he truly represented.

CHAPTER 15
THE CONFRONTATION

The atmosphere within the precinct was electric on the day of Claire's planned confrontation with Dr. Harrow. The stakes had never been higher, and Claire felt every heartbeat drum loudly in her ears as she steeled herself for what lay ahead.

After days of gathering evidence and witness testimonies, the momentum now shifted toward clarity. The families had rallied, emboldened by their shared resolve, and Claire knew that it was time to confront Harrow directly. They would no longer allow him to manipulate the narrative or instill fear in those who sought to hold him accountable.

As she prepared for the looming encounter, Officer Daniels walked into her office, concern etched on his face. "Are you sure you want to do this alone?" he asked, his tone serious. "We could have backup ready if you need it."

"I need to confront him one-on-one," Claire replied, an undercurrent of determination coursing through her. "This is a psychological battle, and I want to draw him out, to make him reveal what he's hiding. If he senses that we've brought officers along, he might try to deflect or intimidate even more."

Daniels sighed but nodded, clearly trusting her instincts. "Just be careful, Claire. He's unpredictable and knows how to play mind games."

"I will," she assured him, taking a deep breath to center her thoughts. This confrontation was not just about the evidence; it was about unraveling the psychology driving Harrow's manipulations.

Once Claire arrived at Harrow's practice, the familiar scent of antiseptic wafted through the air, reminding her of the undoing that lay hidden beneath the unassuming facade. She took a moment to gather herself outside the door, feeling the weight of every patient whose life he had impacted.

With a firm resolve, Claire strode into the waiting room, scanning for any familiar faces. Patients were scattered about, flipping through magazines or engaged in hushed conversations. At the reception desk, Harrow sat, charmingly engaging with a patient, the picture of professionalism—so oblivious to the storm that was brewing.

"Claire," he said smoothly, feigning surprise as she approached. "What a pleasure to see you here. Can I help you with something?"

"Actually, you can," Claire replied, her voice even. "We need to talk—right now."

The hint of annoyance flickered across Harrow's features before he swallowed it. "A private conversation, then? Very well."

She followed him down the hallway to his office, the sterile surroundings pressing in around them. As the door closed behind her, Claire felt the tension between them thicken like fog.

"Sit down, Claire," Harrow said, motioning toward the chair opposite his desk. His demeanor was still calm, but Claire sensed the underlying pressure in his voice.

"I prefer to stand," she replied firmly, choosing confrontation over submission. "I came to confront you about your treatment methods and the rapidly increasing number of suspicious deaths linked to your practice."

"Is that so?" he asked, leaning back in his chair with a disarming smirk. "I've heard whispers of discontent in the community, but you might want to consider the consequences of stirring the pot. You have no idea what you're getting into."

"What I know is that people are suffering and that patients are scared to speak out because of you," Claire shot back, feeling the adrenaline charge through her. "You've manipulated their health concerns, and now we've uncovered evidence of negligence that puts lives at risk."

Harrow's amusement faded, replaced by a glare that sent a chill through the air. "Evidence, you say? What exactly do you think you've uncovered? These are just disgruntled families looking for someone to blame."

Claire stepped forward, looking directly into his eyes. "Patients have reported adverse effects from your medications. They've expressed their fears about being dismissed or belittled when they speak up. And as for those who have passed away, families are linking their deaths to your negligent practices."

"What you think you've 'uncovered' is merely a combination of old age and human frailty," Harrow countered, his tone shifting to one of cold irritation. "You're trying to hold onto a thread of righteousness while tearing down a man who has dedicated his life to helping others. It's a shame."

"I'm not tearing you down; you're doing that yourself," Claire pressed on, her heart racing. "Every day you dismiss patients' legitimate concerns, you risk their lives. You may have been trusted in the past, but your time is running out. The truth will come to light, and I won't let you intimidate anyone."

"That idealism will be your downfall, Claire," Harrow warned, the heat of anger flickering in his eyes. "You think you're a protector of truth, but you're merely a shadow of the real enemy. You are playing a very dangerous game."

Claire took a deep breath, channeling her resolve despite the palpable tension in the air. "The only dangerous game being played is yours, Harrow. I'm not afraid of your threats. You may think you can manipulate this community, but together we are gathering the evidence necessary to put an end to your practices once and for all."

Harrow leaned forward slightly, his eyes narrowing as if attempting to gauge her determination. "You believe you have the support of the community. But people are quick to abandon others when the truth becomes inconvenient. You think you're the heroine of this story, but the narrative is more complex than you realize."

Claire could feel his words slithering into her mind, but she refused to let them take root. "People are standing up for what's right. You've underestimated their resilience and desire for justice. You may have them cowed for now, but we are building momentum, and the truth is already unfolding."

"And when it does," Harrow said, his voice low and dangerous, "it may not reveal what you expect. Remember, Claire, I've been in this position before. I know how to play the game, and I know how to win."

Concern bubbled within Claire as she could see the challenge lurking in his gaze. "And it appears that you're willing to resort to anything to maintain that power, even if it comes at the expense of innocent lives."

"Are you implying that my patients are innocent?" he shot back. "They are merely victims of their own poor health and choices. I am simply guided by the principles of medicine."

Claire shook her head, frustration boiling inside her. "Guided by ambition, perhaps. This isn't about healing; it's about control. You need their dependency to retain your status as the community's savior."

Harrow straightened, his smirk returning, but it was different this time—predatory. "You're playing with fire, Claire. What happens when the community realizes that you're simply a disgraced detective trying to stir dissent? They will turn on you just as easily."

"If I must stand alone, I will do that too," Claire asserted, her voice steady. "I refuse to allow you to terrorize others while you hide behind your mask."

For a moment, the air crackled with tension, an electric standoff that felt like it could snap at any moment. Claire held Harrow's gaze, willing him to see the truth of her convictions.

But he only chuckled softly, an unsettling sound. "Determination often blinds one to reality. I've seen it countless times. People think they're heroes—protectors of the weak—yet all they really do is invite their own downfall."

Just then, they were interrupted by a knock on the door. Officer Daniels entered, his expression stern. "Is everything alright in here?"

Harrow stepped back, smoothing his jacket and donning an air of feigned civility. "Of course, Officer. Just a friendly chat with the detective."

"Friendly is not the word I would use," Claire replied, her voice laced with steady frustration. "We were just discussing the complaints I've been gathering regarding Dr. Harrow's treatment of patients."

Daniels's gaze shifted between Claire and Harrow, suspicion threading through his expression. "We're here to ensure the safety of everyone involved, including you, Detective. We cannot allow intimidation tactics to create fear in this community. Not now."

"Exactly," Claire echoed, her voice firmer knowing they stood together against Harrow's manipulation. "In fact, I believe it's time for a proper investigation into Dr. Harrow's practices."

Harrow glanced at them, a mask of feigned innocence slipping back into place. "You both are wasting your time. You'll find nothing but the dedication of a committed physician."

"Then let's put that dedication to the test," Claire countered, her resolve hardening. "Let's take a closer look at your patient records; perhaps we can expose the truth where you've hidden it."

With a dismissive wave of his hand, Harrow scoffed. "This is absurd. You're grasping at straws, Claire. Today will not end the way you think it will."

"I'm counting on it," Claire said, feeling a sense of anticipation pulse through her. They were building toward the confrontation that would expose Harrow's manipulation—the cracks within his facade beginning to show.

As Claire and Daniels prepared to document the evidence and make follow-up plans, Harrow turned to leave. "You may think you're controlling the narrative now, Detective, but I assure you—these threads will unravel in ways you can't even begin to anticipate."

As he exited, Claire felt the weight of his intimidation attempt but knew they were on the cusp of change. With Daniels by her side, they were forging ahead, balance teetering toward justice while the storm of truth gathered around them.

With renewed purpose, Claire focused her thoughts on the steps ahead. The evidence was building; now all she needed was a way to solidify the complaints into a comprehensive case against Harrow. To do this, she would need to gather not only the families' testimonies but also relevant medical records that could directly connect Harrow to the adverse health outcomes they had been reporting.

Throughout the rest of the day, Claire coordinated with Officer Daniels to streamline the process for collecting evidence. They reached out to the families once more, assuring them that their voices were crucial to the unfolding investigation.

"Let's set up a meeting on Thursday," Claire suggested, pacing the precinct office. "We can consolidate all the testimonials and start preparing the evidence for the authorities. The more accounts we have, the more legitimate our case will become."

"Sounds good," Daniels agreed, jotting down notes. "And if Harrow continues to intimidate anyone, we have to take immediate action. We can't let him derail our momentum. If things escalate, I'll have officers ready to assist."

As the day melted into evening, Claire turned her attention to the existing evidence stored within the practice's medical records. Harrow's clinic had always maintained meticulous documentation, and she knew they could unearth critical information by analyzing it.

After hours of digging through testimonies and reports, Claire found herself standing in front of the records room at the precinct, a sense of determination coursing through her. She had clearance to access files—and she was about to see if the road to uncovering the truth would lead her deeper into Harrow's manipulation.

As she sorted through the patient files, the patterns of prescriptions caught her eye. Many patients had been prescribed similar combinations of drugs with confusing labels, and repeated visits showed medication adjustments that lacked clear reasoning. The warnings associated with the drugs—the potential side effects—seemed to build up like a ticking clock in the background of each patient's narrative, leading to the tragedies that had unfolded.

But it wasn't until she stumbled upon Elizabeth Graham's file that her heart dropped. The entries contained detailed notations from Harrow, alluding to "unforeseen complications" and "patient hesitation" leading up to her death. The language felt evasive—a carefully crafted narrative to obscure the truth.

Just as Claire was deep in thought, the door creaked open, interrupting her focus. It was Lucy, concern etched across her face. "Claire, have you seen Harrow again? I've heard he's been agitated and talking about you."

"No, not since our confrontation. But I'm gathering evidence against him, studying patient files, including Elizabeth's," Claire replied, gesturing toward the documents spread out before her. "This one is particularly troubling."

Lucy stepped closer, peering at the notes. "That doesn't look good at all. If he's trying to cover his tracks, he's going to put up a fight to protect himself and avoid facing the consequences."

"Exactly," Claire responded with steely determination. "But the more evidence we collect, the clearer the picture becomes. We will expose him for the manipulator he is."

Suddenly, Lucy's expression shifted to one of alarm. "Claire, you need to be careful. I don't trust Harrow. If he thinks you're investigating him, he will do whatever it takes to throw you off balance."

"I understand, Lucy," Claire said, trying to maintain her focus. "But I can't let fear control our efforts. If we're going to challenge him, we need the truth on our side."

As Claire continued to sift through the files, thoughtful uncertainty flickered in her mind. Time was running out; she could feel Harrow's presence looming, his relentless pursuit of control casting shadows over their investigation. They were on borrowed time.

Just as Claire began uncovering more connections among the deceased patients and their treatments under Harrow, a loud commotion echoed from the precinct entrance. The sound of voices raised in anger pierced the air, halting Claire in her tracks.

"Stay here," Claire instructed Lucy, her instincts kicking in. She quickly followed the noise, weaving her way through the various offices until she reached the lobby.

What she saw sent shockwaves through her. A group of residents from Elderwood stood at the entrance, visibly agitated. Among them, Dr. Harrow argued with several officers, his voice rising above the rest.

"I demand to speak to the detective!" Harrow shouted, his demeanor brimming with outrage. "This is an outrageous attack on my professional integrity!"

Claire pushed her way to the front, quickly assessing the situation. The tension in the precinct was thick as residents exchanged heated exchanges, some trying to defend Harrow, others visibly united against him.

"I will speak to Claire, and I will ensure she understands the damage her allegations are causing!" Harrow declared, his facade of calm cracking as anger flared behind his eyes.

Claire stepped forward, catching Harrow's intense gaze as she navigated between the distrustful glances of the petitioners. The atmosphere crackled with tension; she could feel the weight of the moment hanging precariously between them.

"Dr. Harrow," she said firmly, asserting her presence to silence the growing unrest, "I'll speak with you. But let's do this respectfully, away from the public eye."

Harrow's lips curled into a condescending smile. "Respect has to be earned, Claire. Right now, I'm not exactly feeling respected."

"Step into my office," Claire directed, her voice steady and authoritative. "Let's discuss this like professionals."

As they moved toward her office, she felt the stares of the residents lingering on their backs, their whispers carrying an undercurrent of uncertainty. Claire's heart raced; this confrontation was inevitable, and she was committed to unearthing the truth behind Harrow's manipulations.

Once inside her office, Claire closed the door, feeling the weight of the tension settle in the small space. "What's this about, Harrow?" she asked, crossing her arms defiantly. "You say I'm damaging your reputation, but your actions have already created distrust among the community."

"Do you think they are all so naive?" he snapped, his previous charm stripped away to reveal anger and desperation. "They believe your lies. You're making baseless accusations against a man who has devoted his life to healing!"

"Baseless?" Claire countered, her own frustration bubbling to the surface. "You've turned a blind eye to the suffering of your patients. The evidence against you is growing—the testimonies, the medical records. I assure you, this isn't just hearsay."

Harrow's face darkened, and he took a step closer, invading Claire's personal space. "You're playing a dangerous game, Detective. I won't let you turn this community against me without consequences. Do you really think you can take me down?"

"The only thing I think is that you're terrified of losing control, Harrow," Claire replied, meeting his gaze without flinching. "You thrive on their trust, and now that it's beginning to unravel, you're resorting to intimidation and deceit."

His jaw clenched, and a semblance of vulnerability flickered in his eyes, quickly masked by a wall of bravado. "You're misguided. I am the doctor these people need. You're only fanning the flames of fear."

"Fear is your weapon, not mine," Claire said, her voice steady. "You've caused harm. It's time for this community to see you for what you truly are."

Harrow leaned back slightly, examining her with a calculated expression. "I'm aware of your growing influence through the families. You think they'll stand by you when the truth unfolds? When the dust settles, you'll be left alone—disgraced, just like the others who've tried to oppose me."

"Your threats won't scare me, Harrow," Claire said, the weight of his words hanging in the air. "I have the community behind me, sharing their truths. We have a collective strength you can't break."

For a moment, it felt as though the air thickened with unspoken challenges. Claire could see the calculated chaos behind Harrow's composed facade; he was assessing how much he could control her, how deeply her resolve could be shaken.

Finally, Harrow straightened and smirked—a reflection of amusement mixed with contempt. "Very well, Detective. Let's see how far this bravery takes you. Enjoy your little crusade while it lasts."

With that, he turned abruptly and left the office, closing the door with a definitive thud. Claire could feel the simmering anger boil inside her, but she forced herself to focus on the task at hand. Harrow was clearly shaken, but his threats and arrogance would not deter her from the mission ahead.

As she emerged from her office, she found Daniels waiting outside, concern etched on his face. "What happened?" he asked, noting her expression.

"We're on the right path. Harrow's panic is showing," Claire replied, her determination reignited. "But we need to ramp up our efforts. If he retaliates, we have to be ready."

"Ready how?" Daniels asked, his brow furrowing.

"We need to keep gathering evidence and rally more families. I think Harrow's desperate enough to make mistakes, and we need to be vigilant."

Nodding in agreement, Daniels said, "I'll coordinate patrols around the homes of the families and keep an eye on any suspicious activity from Harrow. But we have to prepare them for his potential backlash."

Feeling the pull of urgency once more, Claire focused her thoughts, knowing that the confrontation had ignited a fire within her that could not be extinguished. They were building a foundation for something greater—a commitment to confronting the darkness embodied by Dr. Harrow.

Tomorrow would be pivotal. Claire knew the meeting with the families was the opportunity they needed to solidify their collective voices against Harrow and rally support from the community. She devoted the rest of the evening to preparing materials and refining her presentation, crafting it into a rallying cry for those who had been wronged.

As night settled over Elderwood, Claire sat at her dining table, surrounded by stacks of files, notes, and testimonials. The weight of the information pressed down heavily upon her, but with each passing moment, resolve gave way to clarity. She was no longer just a detective; she was a beacon of hope for those who had felt voiceless in the shadow of Dr. Harrow's charm.

Before retiring for the night, she made one more call to the families, ensuring they were prepared and aware of the details of the meeting. Each response invigorated her spirit and solidified her belief that they were forging a movement.

The next morning felt charged with purpose as Claire arrived at the community center. She observed tables being arranged for the gathering, and familiar faces greeted her with wary smiles. Each person who entered the room carried their own burdens, and Claire could sense the mix of hope and fear settling over the group.

As families trickled in, Claire took a moment to glance around the room, absorbing the palpable tension. Then, with a deep breath, she stepped forward to the center, ready to talk about the fight ahead.

"Thank you all for coming today," Claire began, her voice steady as she addressed the assembly. "We stand together not just as individuals but as a united front committed to holding Dr. Harrow accountable for the suffering he has caused. Each of you has a story that no longer needs to stay hidden in the shadows."

As various families began to share their accounts, Claire noted the reaffirmation within them. One by one, voices grew stronger, weaving a rich tapestry of raw emotions that demanded recognition. During this sacred gathering, the shared stories painted a picture of loss, despair, and ultimately, a relentless fight for the truth.

Just then, a ripple of murmurs swept through the crowd as a familiar figure appeared at the entrance—Dr. Harrow himself, standing with an air of false bravado.

"I see the circus has come to town," he sneered, his voice slicing through the gathered families. "What are you all doing? Feeling sorry for yourselves while stirring more baseless allegations?"

"Dr. Harrow," Claire called out, stepping forward, her heart quickening at the confrontation. "What you're witnessing here is a community uniting to express their legitimate concerns about your practices. This isn't a circus; this is their reality."

"We're done hiding," Mrs. Thompson shouted from the back, her voice filled with passion. "You can't silence us any longer!"

Harrow's demeanor shifted slightly, the contempt in his eyes shimmering with irritation as he took in the amassed crowd. "You are all misled if you believe you can turn against your doctor without facing consequences."

"Consequences for who? You?" Claire challenged, stepping closer and feeling the support of the families behind her. "This community deserves the truth, and we will not be intimidated by your empty threats."

Harrow's features hardened as he looked around the anxious faces before him, sensing the resolve behind them. "You think your threats and accusations will solidify a case against me? This will crumble, and you will be left to pick up the pieces of your community when they realize that you led them astray."

"You're the one who will be left in ruins," Claire asserted, her voice ringing with a strength she hadn't fully realized she possessed.

As tensions simmered high, Claire felt anger bubbling just beneath the surface. But alongside it thrummed something deeper—a sense of purpose that urged her to continue the fight. "Stand with us, families. Stand against manipulation, fear, and deceit. Together, we are so much stronger than you think."

The crowd murmured in agreement, and Claire could see the determination solidifying in their faces. Just as it felt like the tide was turning, an officer stepped forward, breaking through the suffocating tension.

"Dr. Harrow, if you do not leave immediately, I will have to escort you out," the officer asserted, authority weighing heavily in his stance.

Harrow glared, the smirk falling from his face. "This isn't over, Claire—a lurking predator is always aware of its prey."

With that, he turned on his heel and stormed out of the community center, leaving an air of tension and exhilaration in his wake.

As Claire gazed at the faces of her fellow citizens, she felt bolstered by their strength. "This is just the beginning. We will fight for justice, and we will not back down," she declared, her voice ringing with renewed intensity.

That day, they stood at the forefront of a significant turning point, prepared to draw back the curtain on the darkness that had allowed Harrow to thrive unchecked for far too long. Claire felt the surge of determination in the room as families rallied around one another, a united force against the fear that had hovered over them for so long.

As the meeting continued, Claire encouraged families to share specifics about their experiences with Harrow and to document any instances of intimidation or dubious treatment. The energy swelled as their collective stories began to weave a narrative that could no longer be ignored.

"One of the most powerful tools we have is our voice," Claire reminded them. "When we share our stories together, we paint a picture of the impact this doctor has had on our lives and the community at large."

"Today isn't just about speaking out," said Mrs. Mills, her voice steady. "It's a call to action. Together, we will challenge him and ensure he knows he can't manipulate us anymore."

With each passing moment, Claire watched as fear transformed into resolve among the families. They knew the path ahead would not be easy, and that Harrow would likely retaliate. The reality of confronting a figure as powerful as Harrow weighed heavily on them, but the shadows of their collective pasts ignited a shared belief in the possibility of change.

As the meeting concluded, Claire stood at the front, pride swelling in her chest. "Thank you all for your courage. We'll be documenting these experiences and organizing further steps to take our case forward. Together, we will shine a light on the truth."

With the families unified and emboldened, Claire felt a sense of renewal wash over her. They were now a formidable force ready to challenge the status quo.

In the days that followed, Claire and the gathering families worked closely to compile their testimonies into a comprehensive report. Every story mattered; every detail helped to cement their case against Harrow. Claire dedicated herself to this task, meticulously organizing each account to highlight patterns that were impossible to ignore.

But as the clouds thickened over Elderwood, Harrow tightened his grip on the community with counter-narratives. He used his charm to sway public perception, spinning tales that painted him as a benevolent doctor besieged by a bitter detective and a handful of disgruntled patients. Some members of the community began to turn against those speaking out, tainted by doubt.

During a casual visit to the local café, Claire overheard a group of women whispering heatedly about the unfolding situation. "I just can't believe they're trying to take down someone who has done so much good for our community," one woman exclaimed. "Dr. Harrow is a hero!"

Claire felt her heart sink as she realized how deeply entrenched Harrow's influence remained. "He has a way of convincing people that his treatment is safe," another woman replied. "But I heard he's been under scrutiny recently. Maybe it's time for some of these families to reconsider their claims."

Frustrated and determined, Claire knew she needed to counter Harrow's narrative. The families who supported her and sought justice were feeling the backlash of his manipulation, and she had to ensure they remained unwavering in their commitment.

"Let's set up an event," she suggested to the families during their next gathering, her voice cutting through their shared anxiety. "A chance to openly discuss Dr. Harrow's treatment methods and share our evidence with the community. We need to confront the doubts head-on and clarify our intentions."

The group rallied together, and with renewed resolve, they planned the event for the following weekend. The community center would host a forum where they could share their experiences, present their evidence, and invite others to join their cause.

As preparations took shape, Claire felt an invigorated sense of purpose. The rising tide of voices seeking to break free from Harrow's deceit seemed unstoppable. Yet, she couldn't ignore the shadows of danger lurking just out of reach.

Days passed as the families distributed flyers and shared the event details throughout the community. Anticipation hung heavily, mingled with an undercurrent of fear. Would Harrow retaliate? Would they find enough support to challenge him?

Claire's focus sharpened as the event day approached. Every ounce of energy was channeled into ensuring a successful forum, a chance to reclaim their power in a community that had once felt secure. The sense of urgency that she had felt when first embarking on this journey flared anew.

On the day of the event, the community center buzzed with excitement and apprehension. Families gathered, whispering among themselves, and as the time drew near, Claire took a moment to compose herself. She needed to channel every ounce of determination she had for those who came forward with their stories.

As the room filled, Claire stepped up to the front, ready to shepherd the gathering into the next phase of their fight. With her heart thumping in her chest, she knew the looming confrontation with Dr. Harrow would reveal not only his deceptive practices but also the strength of the community united against him. This was their moment to reclaim their narrative, to expose the shadows he had cast over their lives.

Taking a deep breath, Claire gazed at the familiar faces of the families seated in front of her. She saw the determination etched across their expressions, and a swell of pride washed over her. They were here to confront their fears, to share their stories, and to demand accountability.

"Thank you all for coming today," Claire began, her voice resonant in the room. "Each of your voices has power, and together we can shine a light on the truth. This isn't just about the pain caused by Dr. Harrow; it's about preventing further suffering in our community."

The crowd murmured their agreement, and Claire could feel the energy building. "I want to emphasize that your stories matter," she continued, choosing her words carefully. "Each experience you share is a thread in the tapestry of truth we are weaving together. We stand here today not just as individuals, but as a united front, demanding a reckoning."

As Claire spoke, she noticed Mary nodding in encouragement, an inspiring presence amidst their shared fears. "We've all come to realize that we can't be silenced any longer. Our loved ones deserve justice," Mary added, stepping up to the forefront alongside Claire.

The atmosphere shifted as families began to share their accounts, recounting their experiences under Harrow's care. The stories poured out—tales of illness, confusion, frustration, and fear—each one a brick in the foundation of their collective resolve.

"I was hesitant to speak out at first," Mrs. Thompson shared, tears welling in her eyes. "But after seeing my husband's deterioration, I realized I had no choice. We need to stand together and fight for those who can't speak for themselves."

"Yes, it's time to confront the reality of what he's done," another family member echoed, their voice quavering but growing stronger with each vocal affirmation from the crowd. "We won't let fear dictate our actions any longer!"

As the testimonies continued, Claire felt a rush of energy envelop the room. This community was becoming a vessel of truth, their voices a force capable of drowning out Harrow's manipulative whispers.

Just then, someone at the back of the room raised their hand. "What happens if he retaliates? He's already made threats. How do we stay safe?"

Claire nodded, fully aware of the precarious nature of their confrontation. "We have a plan in place. Each family will have officers assigned to them for protection. And I urge everyone to document any encounters with Harrow. We cannot underestimate his willingness to intimidate. But we are not alone in this; we're a community, and we will take action to keep each other safe."

With each passing moment, the families' commitment solidified. They began to share ideas on how they could further spread awareness about Harrow's practices. Flyers, social media posts, and even petitions—by the time the gathering drew to a close, Claire could see that a fire had ignited within everyone present.

As the meeting wrapped up, a palpable sense of solidarity buzzed through the air. Claire looked around, her heart swelling with pride. They were no longer scattered voices; they were a force to be reckoned with.

But as they dispersed, a nagging feeling settled in Claire's gut. Harrow was not one to back down quietly, nor would he hesitate to retaliate against those who threatened his carefully cultivated reputation.

"I need to stay vigilant," Claire whispered to herself as she watched families exit, uniting in their resolve. She felt the weight of responsibility pressing down on her, but she would not let it hinder her.

With plans for the next steps already forming in her mind, Claire took a deep breath, preparing herself for what lay ahead. The confrontation with Harrow was inevitable, and now, fueled by the support of the community, Claire was ready to face him head-on.

CHAPTER 16
DECEPTIVE CHARMS

The air in Elderwood felt charged with anticipation as Claire prepared for the inevitable confrontation with Dr. Harrow. After the successful gathering of families and their collective resolve to expose Harrow's manipulations, Claire knew that it was time to confront him directly regarding the truth behind his actions.

The day of the confrontation arrived, and Claire chose her outfit carefully, opting for professionalism—a crisp tailored blazer and a determined expression. She needed to project confidence, knowing that Harrow was a master of manipulation, capable of twisting any situation to his advantage.

As Claire arrived at Harrow's practice, she felt a knot of tension form in her stomach. The façade of normalcy at the clinic bore down on her as patients entered the waiting room, unsuspecting of the storm brewing. With each step she took toward the reception desk, she reminded herself of her purpose: to unearth the truth and to protect those who had placed their trust in her.

"Claire!" Lucy greeted her with a tight smile, but Claire could sense the nervous energy radiating from her. "Are you sure about this?"

"Absolutely," Claire replied, her voice steady. "We need to confront him. We can't let him manipulate us any longer."

Just then, the door to the office opened, and Dr. Harrow walked out, his expression shifting from surprise to smirking confidence as he spotted Claire. "Detective Avery," he remarked, feigning surprise. "What a pleasant surprise. To what do I owe this visit?"

"Dr. Harrow, I need to speak with you about your treatment methods and the recent allegations against you," Claire stated, her voice steady but authoritative.

"Allegations? What allegations? You must be mistaken," he replied, his tone deceptively smooth. "I am a well-respected physician and have devoted my life to the well-being of my patients. I find it offensive that you would come in here and challenge my credibility based on mere hearsay."

Claire faced him, refusing to back down. "This isn't mere hearsay. There is a growing body of evidence against you, and the families you've manipulated are prepared to speak out."

Harrow leaned against the reception desk, his charm radiating in waves as he regarded her. "Are you sure you want to pursue this line of questioning? You risk tarnishing your reputation in this quaint little town by attacking someone who has always been a source of pride and assurance for its residents."

"Are you really going to twist this into a personal attack?" Claire shot back, her confidence fueled by the strength of the families behind her. "This is about accountability, Harrow. People deserve to know the truth about the elderly patients who have suffered and those who have died under your care."

"But Claire," he said, stepping closer, his tone soothing yet laced with manipulation, "if you continue down this path, you'll inevitably harm the vulnerable. These families need me. You'd only create confusion and chaos in the community you claim to protect."

Claire felt a rush of frustration but fought to stay grounded. "You're the one creating chaos! By dismissing patients, undermining their concerns, and manipulating their trust, you are the source of their suffering."

For a brief moment, Claire caught a glimpse of doubt flickering across Harrow's face before his charismatic facade slipped back into place. "What you're doing is dangerous, Claire. You're questioning the foundation of care I've built here. Do you really want to be responsible for pulling it down? What will these families do without me?"

"I'll make sure they find the right care, the care they deserve—unlike what you've provided," Claire replied, even as the internal pressure of the conversation began to escalate. "You are exploiting their trust, and that's something I simply cannot stand by and allow."

Harrow's smile widened, but it held a glimmer of something sinister. "Is that what you believe? Do you think this is about care? I genuinely risk everything to ensure that my practice thrives. You're digging into something that could endanger your own career and life."

Realizing his tactics were designed to unsettle her, Claire squared her shoulders, meeting his gaze unflinchingly. "You can try to intimidate me all you want, but I won't be easily scared. The truth is a powerful weapon, and you can't silence it."

"Ah, the idealism of youth," he said, feigning a chuckle that turned dark. "You see, Claire, your relentless pursuit is admirable, but it also clouds your judgment. I suggest you reconsider what battle you are willing to fight here. You might not end up being the hero you envision."

Claire felt the surge of panic threading through her veins but pushed it aside. She needed to stick to the facts and resist the tempting allure of doubt Harrow was trying to sow within her. "The community is starting to wake up to the truth. It's only a matter of time before they see you for who you really are."

Harrow leaned in closer, invading her personal space. "And what exactly do you think will happen if they do, Claire?" His voice was low, almost conspiratorial, hinting at the harm he was capable of inflicting. "The trust they have in me is built on years of care. You think you can simply uproot that?"

"I'm not uprooting trust; I'm restoring it," Claire replied, her voice steady despite the rising intensity in the room. "They deserve better than manipulation. Every patient you've dismissed, every life lost—it's all going to be exposed."

For a moment, there was silence, and Claire could see the gears turning in Harrow's mind. He was calculating, weighing his options, and for the first time, she sensed a sliver of uncertainty in his bravado.

"You're making a mistake that many have made before, Claire," he warned, his tone hardening. "You think you're protecting these families, but you risk pushing them into chaos. Without me, patients will be lost and confused. You said it yourself—they are vulnerable."

"Vulnerable to you," Claire asserted, refusing to back down. "There's a fine line between care and control, and you've chosen the latter. I won't let you treat these people like pawns in your game."

Harrow's smile returned, but it had a sinister edge that sent chills down Claire's spine. "You're persistent, I'll give you that. But persistence does not equal truth. My reputation will withstand your efforts, and soon enough, you'll find yourself the one at risk."

Claire noticed his hand clenching into a fist at his side, his composure cracking under the pressure of the confrontation. This wasn't just a battle of wills; this was a man desperately trying to cling to power, and she could smell the fear threading through his words. His attempts to intimidate her were starting to reveal his vulnerabilities.

"I'll protect these families, and I'll expose you for what you are," Claire declared with renewed strength. "If you continue to threaten them, I will make sure the truth comes to light."

"Do you think this community will stand behind you when it becomes clear you're the one breaking them apart?" Harrow replied, his voice dangerously low. "You're teetering on the edge, Claire. Just remember... those who shout the loudest often find themselves silenced in the end."

With that, he turned on his heel and strode out of the office, his demeanor cooling into a mask of indifference, but Claire knew he was shaken. The confrontation had drawn blood, and the tension between them had reached a tipping point.

As she watched him leave, she felt a mixture of triumph and trepidation. Harrow's calculations and manipulations could backfire, but in a town where trust had been undermined, there would be no easy path forward.

Claire breathed deeply, steadying herself as fear threatened to choke her resolve. "It's not over," she whispered under her breath, determination settling within her. She collected her notes, heart pounding as she prepared to take the battle directly to the community, rallying support and ensuring the families understood what was at stake.

In the following days, she continued to work tirelessly, reaching out to families one by one, encouraging them to band together. As stories were exchanged, the true weight of Harrow's actions began to surface more profoundly—sparking anger among those who had been manipulated. Families who had previously shied away from confronting the revered doctor now found strength in each other's accounts.

One evening, Claire convened at the community center with the families again. The atmosphere was charged with frustration, yet a flickering hope filled the room.

"Thanks for coming, everyone," Claire started once more, her voice ringing clear as she surveyed the faces before her. "I know our mission is fraught with challenges, especially now that Harrow is trying to manipulate public perception against us."

The murmurs of agreement echoed, emphasizing the shared sentiment of defiance that had grown since her last meeting. "We have to remain united. We're gathering more testimonies, and if anyone faces pushback from Harrow, I want you to reach out to me or any of the officers here. We will not let him undermine you."

Families began to share tales of their struggles, and their combined momentum only fueled Claire's conviction that they were breaking through the fog of fear that Harrow had perpetrated.

With each new voice, a network of support formed, fortifying the community against the deception that had crept into their lives. And as Claire felt the fiery determination spreading among the families, she understood that they were inching closer to a breakthrough. Together, they were cultivating a force capable of shattering the facade Dr. Harrow had so carefully built, and it invigorated her spirit like nothing else could.

"I want everyone to remember that our strength lies in our numbers," Claire said, her heart swelling with pride. "By sharing our experiences, we're not just telling stories; we're building a case."

Mary raised her hand, her face alight with determination. "What can we do to make our voices even louder? We can't let him come for us anymore."

"That's the spirit, Mary," Claire responded enthusiastically. "The more we raise awareness about what's happening, the harder it will be for Harrow to manipulate the narrative. We should consider reaching out to the media once more and organizing a public event. The community needs to see that we're not backing down."

As they brainstormed ideas for the event, the families contributed insights and experiences. Some suggested bringing in local leaders, while others wanted to highlight testimonials about their loved ones who had suffered from Harrow's treatment. Each suggestion strengthened their bond, cementing the urgency of their mission.

Just as enthusiasm began to rise, Claire's phone buzzed, and she glanced at the message. It was from Officer Daniels again: We've gotten a tip that Harrow is hosting an event of his own in town. He's trying to gain back the trust of the community. We need to counteract that.

"Everyone, I have important news," Claire called out, catching the attention of each gathered family member. "Dr. Harrow is planning something—a community event to regain trust. We need to be prepared to counter his narrative before it takes hold again."

A silence enveloped the room as the families exchanged glances, the severity of the situation dawning on them. "What do we do?" one father asked, anxiety lining his voice.

"We rally together," Claire asserted, feeling a surge of determination wash over her. "We need to make sure that the community hears our stories first, so when they see Harrow trying to win people back, they have context about what he's really doing behind the scenes."

"Let's organize our own event, right before his," Mary suggested, looking around the room for support. "We can invite everyone we know and share our experiences. Make it clear that we're not afraid anymore."

That idea sparked a flurry of chatter, excitement buzzing through the room. Plans began to take shape as families discussed logistics, venues, and ways to invite the media to amplify their voices against Harrow.

As the meeting wrapped up, Claire felt a sense of hope elated with each shared vision. "Together, we can break through the wall he's built. We'll show Elderwood that manipulation won't win out over truth," she encouraged, her heart swelling with pride for the families who had found their courage.

After the event, Claire returned home, her mind racing with details, strategies, and the unprecedented level of support that had formed within the community. The storm against Harrow was brewing, and she could feel the tension tightening as they prepared for the confrontation ahead.

Just as she settled down to finalize plans, Claire received a call from Lucy. "Claire, I have something important to tell you! I think I've uncovered something about Dr. Harrow's practices that you need to know. We might have more evidence!"

Excitement tinged with anxiety filled Claire's chest. "What do you have?"

"I was reviewing some old medical records, and he's treated a lot of the elderly patients in a specific manner," Lucy explained, her voice quickening with urgency. "I found notes that suggest he changed prescriptions frequently without clear reasons—sometimes mixing medications in a way that could seriously harm them."

Claire felt the adrenaline course through her veins, realizing that this could be the breakthrough they needed. "You need to bring those records to the meeting tomorrow. If Harrow altered treatments without justification, it will only bolster our case."

"I will," Lucy confirmed, her determination palpable through the line. "But Claire, we need to be careful. He's already shown he can be vindictive."

"I know," Claire replied, steeling herself. "But we're no longer walking this path alone. With the families backing us, we can stand together against his threats."

As she hung up the phone, Claire felt a storm of emotions swirling within her—determination, fear, and exhilaration all coalescing into a single thought: they were ready to face Harrow, and together, they would force the truth into the light.

CHAPTER 17
A REVELATION IN THE SHADOWS

The sun dipped low on the horizon, casting long shadows over Elderwood as Lucy arrived at the precinct. Her heart raced as she thought about the evidence she had uncovered, a tension coiling in her stomach. The decision she faced loomed ominously in her mind, pushing her closer to the edge of a cliff from which there was no turning back.

She had spent the previous evening sifting through files in the back office, ensuring that Harrow's mechanisms of manipulation would not continue unchallenged. Every prescription and note she reviewed painted a disturbing picture, culminating in her discovery of a folder labeled "Confidential Patient Records"—a folder that was not intended for her eyes.

Inside, she found multiple entries documenting medications prescribed to several elderly patients, along with notations of their health statuses. As she delved deeper, the air felt heavy with secrets. Her heart raced when she stumbled upon a record detailing Elizabeth Graham's treatment—a timeline leading up to her untimely death. Each note was a shard of evidence revealing Harrow's negligence.

"What have you been doing?" Lucy whispered to herself, simultaneously filled with dread and exhilaration. With trembling fingers, she documented the discrepancies, realizing that this evidence could potentially expose Harrow's lies.

But now, standing at the precipice of revelation, she felt the weight of the choice before her. Should she turn this information over to Claire, solidify the case against Harrow, and risk her job and safety? Or should she remain loyal to the doctor she had worked alongside for so long, knowing that revealing the truth could bring about chaos?

Taking a deep breath, Lucy made her way to Claire's office, drumming her fingers nervously against her thigh. The tension tightened in her chest as she stepped through the door.

"Claire! You won't believe what I just found!" Lucy exclaimed, her voice a mixture of excitement and anxiety.

Claire looked up from her desk, her expression shifting from focus to immediate concern. "What is it? You look like you've seen a ghost."

"I found a folder in Harrow's records that details his treatment plans for several patients, including Elizabeth Graham," Lucy began, her breath quickening as she spoke. "The notations... they're alarming. It's clear he altered medications that led to serious complications."

Claire's eyes widened. "What do you mean? Can you show me?"

Lucy nodded, pulling out her notepad where she had carefully documented her findings. "Look at this. He prescribed multiple medications to patients without clear justification and mixed treatments that could potentially be life-threatening."

Claire took the notes, scanning them with intensity. "This is incredible, Lucy. If we present this evidence, it could be the turning point we need."

"But what if he finds out it was me who uncovered this?" Lucy's voice trembled slightly, the anxiety creeping back into her mind. "What if he retaliates?"

"That's a risk we have to take," Claire replied firmly, sensing Lucy's hesitation. "You have to see that staying silent only allows him to continue manipulating and harming others. We need to expose the truth."

Lucy felt the weight of her decision pressing down upon her, her loyalty to Harrow warring with her growing understanding of the damage he could inflict. "I don't want to lose my job, Claire. I've worked with him for too long."

"And you have to consider the harm he's done to those in our care," Claire urged, her voice steady. "You have to choose what kind of healthcare professional you want to be. Do you want to reinforce this cycle of deception, or do you want to be a part of the truth?"

The sincerity in Claire's eyes sparked something within Lucy. She felt a rising conviction boil beneath the surface, pushing her closer toward a choice she had been avoiding. "You're right," she finally admitted, her voice resolute. "I need to do something. We can't let him get away with this."

Claire smiled, relief flooding her senses. "We'll present this evidence together—immediately. With everything you've found, we can solidify the case. And if he retaliates, we'll ensure you have protection."

Once again taking her strength in hand, Lucy felt the resolve solidifying inside her. Together, they would face Harrow, and the nurses who had enabled his methods would no longer hide behind his deception.

When Claire and Lucy headed back to the precinct, the weight of their mission settled within their hearts. Lucy felt apprehensive but also liberated; she'd chosen to stand on the right side of the truth. With every step, the threads connecting their resolve to the families and their fight against the dark façade of Dr. Harrow grew stronger.

Later that evening, after presenting their accumulated evidence to Officer Daniels and strategizing on the next steps, a sense of hope flickered back to life in the precinct. Their determination was solidifying into a force potent enough to confront Harrow, and the atmosphere buzzed with newfound purpose.

As Claire sat at her desk, reviewing notes and compiling a presentation for the community that would expose Harrow's negligence, she watched as Officer Daniels spoke quietly with other officers, sharing details of their findings. The camaraderie among the officers strengthened her belief that they would soon be able to put an end to his manipulative reign.

Just then, Lucy entered the office, her expression a mix of anticipation and apprehension. "Claire, I wanted to discuss our next steps before the meeting tomorrow."

"Absolutely," Claire said, motioning for Lucy to sit down. "I think we're in a much stronger position now that we have that evidence. Having you support this initiative is crucial."

"Still, I worry about the backlash," Lucy admitted, twisting her hands nervously. "Will Harrow retaliate? He'll know we've been gathering evidence against him."

"That risk exists, but we have to proceed," Claire replied, feeling the gravity of their mission strengthen her resolve. "The more unified we are, the less chance he has to intimidate us. With the support we've built from families, it's becoming increasingly difficult for his narrative to stick."

Lucy nodded, but Claire could see the doubt still flickering in her eyes. "I just don't want anyone to get hurt because of my involvement," she whispered, her voice trembling. "If he knows I shared my findings…"

"We'll be ready for anything he tries to throw at us," Claire promised, placing a reassuring hand on Lucy's. "You've already taken a huge step by coming forward. We will support you. We're building a safety net for everyone involved."

As they finalized their plans, the sound of footsteps filled the hallway, and Claire's heart raced when she recognized the figure approaching. Harrow stood at the entrance, his presence commanding immediate attention. Dressed sharply, with an air of confidence, he wasn't hiding in shadows; he was confronting them head-on.

"Claire," he called, his voice dripping with mock sincerity, "I see you've gathered quite the audience. Is this your best attempt to undermine me?"

Lucy stiffened at the sight of him, her nervousness palpable. Claire, however, remained determined, stepping forward. "We're not being undermined, Harrow; we're uniting to confront the truth behind your actions. Your influence over our community is waning, and the families are starting to share their experiences."

"Experiences, is it?" Harrow smirked, a coldness creeping into his expression. "Do you really think these tales will hold any weight? You're merely stirring the pot, Claire. People will soon realize that you're the one creating division."

"I'm not creating division; I'm uncovering the truth," Claire shot back, unwavering in her stance. "The families deserve to know what's been happening to their loved ones under your care."

Harrow leaned in closer, his voice dropping to a near whisper. "You think you can frighten me? You know nothing of the repercussions of your actions, and it's clear you're getting quite reckless. But let's be honest, Claire—without the support of those you've rallied, your position will crumble."

The challenge hung in the air between them, charged with tension. Claire felt her pulse race, but she refused to back down. "You underestimate these families. They've suffered, and now they are ready to stand against you. You won't intimidate us."

For a moment, the silence stretched thin as Claire met Harrow's gaze, a duel of wills playing out before the gathering crowd. She sensed the fear lurking beneath his carefully constructed charm, understanding that his facade was beginning to crack under the weight of the truth.

"Your bravado is impressive," Harrow said, a hint of frustration seeping into his voice. "But you have no idea what you're up against. I will make sure you regret this little uprising."

With that, Harrow turned and strode out of the precinct, the tension lifting slightly as his figure disappeared through the doorway. Claire took a deep breath, releasing the adrenaline that had coiled tightly within her.

"Did you see that?" Lucy breathed, her eyes wide with disbelief. "He's not ready to give up."

"No, but neither are we," Claire replied, her determination hardening. "We'll continue to build our case and support those who need us. The moment we show weakness is the moment he regains control."

As they gathered their thoughts, the urgency of their mission felt more tangible than ever. With each new piece of evidence and each voice raised in support, they were constructing a foundation strong enough to push back against Harrow's manipulations—a fortress that would shield their community from his influence.

Claire's mind raced with strategies as she and Lucy moved forward with their plan. They spent the remainder of the evening drafting a public statement that would encompass the collective experiences of the families. It was crucial to present their findings clearly and effectively, ensuring that the truth resonated with the community while countering Harrow's narrative.

Late into the night, Claire sifted through personal accounts and testimonies, selecting poignant quotes and incidents to weave into their statement. The more she pieced together their stories, the more she felt the weight of responsibility. This was not just a fight for justice; it was a quest to reclaim the trust that had been so ruthlessly exploited.

The next morning, with the statement finalized and a press conference scheduled, Claire felt a mix of excitement and anxiety coursing through her. The gathering would serve as a powerful platform for the community to voice its concerns and put pressure on local authorities.

"Are you ready for this?" Lucy asked as they prepared to leave. Her eyes were filled with a blend of apprehension and determination.

"Ready or not, we're doing this," Claire replied, her mind set on their mission. "We have to be clear and confident. This is our moment to shine a light on the truth."

As they arrived at the community center, the air buzzed with anticipation. Local media reporters were already there, setting up cameras and gathering sound equipment. Claire could feel the weight of their mission pressing upon her—the stakes had never been higher.

The entrance began to fill with families, their expressions a mix of determination and nervousness. Claire greeted them, urging them to stay strong. As the crowd slowly gathered, she took a moment to absorb the collective strength surrounding her; it felt like a wave of solidarity that would soon break against the tides of manipulation.

When it was finally time to begin, Claire stepped up to the podium, the microphone adjusted to her height. She took a deep breath, meeting the gaze of the gathered families and members of the media. "Thank you for being here today. We stand together as a community that demands accountability for the health and well-being of all our residents," she began, her voice clear and resolute.

"Recent troubling events involving Dr. Harrow have raised serious concerns about the care he has provided to our families. Families that have entrusted him with their health and livelihoods. We must address these issues head-on."

As Claire spoke, she unveiled the collective stories shared by the families, recounting the alarming patterns of negligence and fear that had manifested under Harrow's care. Each shared experience echoed with raw emotion, amplifying the urgency of their plea for justice.

"I urge everyone present to listen closely," she continued, locking eyes with the gathered crowd. "No one should suffer from manipulative practices that prioritize control over patient care. This community deserves transparency and compassion, and we demand that the truth be upheld."

Just as Claire felt the momentum building within the room, a commotion erupted from the entrance. Claire turned to see Dr. Harrow standing there, flanked by a few supporters who scowled at the assembly of concerned families. He looked defiant, his posture exuding an unsettling confidence.

"Claire Avery!" Harrow called, his voice echoing through the hall and silencing the crowd. "Is this your grand show? A parade of grievances? I can't believe the community has stooped to such lows."

The gathered families bristled at his presence, their collective anger palpable as they faced the doctor. Claire stepped down from the podium, moving toward Harrow, feeling the tension heavy in the air.

"This is about justice, Dr. Harrow," Claire said, her voice unwavering. "Not just for the families you've misled but also for the community that trusted you. We will expose the truth behind your facade."

Harrow laughed, a cruel sound that sent chills up Claire's spine. "You think you can take me down with a few complaints and some emotional pleading? You're delusional. I have dedicated my career to this town, and your little show won't change that."

"You built your career on a lie," Claire shot back, anger fueling her determination. "I will ensure that you are held accountable for the lives you've affected."

"Do you really believe that? You're the one who is jeopardizing lives," Harrow retorted, stepping closer, attempting to intimidate her. "Once the dust settles, no one will remember your name."

As the tension thickened, Claire understood that patience and composure were vital. "You underestimate the resolve of this community. We will not remain silent while you continue to manipulate and exploit the trust of your patients."

Harrow's anger simmered beneath his calculated demeanor, but he quickly regained his composure, flashing a disarming smile that sent a shiver down Claire's spine. "You're clever, Claire," he said, his voice deceptively calm. "But cleverness doesn't equate to truth. You're inciting fear, and fear can be a powerful weapon"—he leaned in slightly, his tone lowering conspiratorially—"but it can also backfire."

"Fear doesn't control me, Harrow. The truth is what drives me," Claire replied, feeling a surge of resolve wash over her. "You may think you can manipulate the narrative, but we are here to hold you accountable, and nothing you say will change that."

He looked around at the gathered crowd, gathering their reactions. "The truth?" he scoffed, stepping back. "You're all listening to a detective with a personal vendetta. You think these stories hold merit? The community has trusted me for years—don't let this charade change your perception of me!"

The audience murmured, unsure of how to respond as they exchanged uncertain glances. Claire sensed their hesitance and acted quickly. "This is exactly what he wants," she warned, raising her voice to address the crowd. "Harrow is manipulating our fears and trying to cast doubt on the very people who have come forward to share their experiences. You have every right to question his methods, and together, we will reclaim that trust."

Harrow's smirk faded, replaced by irritation. "You're being reckless, Claire. Stirring up dissent won't end well for you. You might just find that this community will turn against you once they see what you've truly brought to the table."

"Or maybe they will see the truth behind your deceit," Claire persisted, her heartbeat steady despite the rising tension. "We stand united, and we won't allow your former charm and bluster to cloud our judgment any longer."

Harrow's expression darkened as he realized the crowd was beginning to lean more toward Claire's defense. "Just remember this moment," Harrow said, fixing Claire with a piercing stare that felt like an icy dagger to her spine. "When the smoke clears and the true consequences of your actions reveal themselves, I will be here while you're left to pick up the pieces."

"The only pieces I intend to leave you with are those that your victims have gathered," Claire responded defiantly.

With that, Claire could feel the tension in the room hitting a breaking point. The families around her rallied, their confidence strengthening with each exchanged word. They sought connection in shared experiences, forging a bond against the manipulative tactics of a man who had hidden in the guise of a healer for far too long.

Just then, Lucy walked in, eyes wide at the sight of the confrontation unfolding before her. "What's happening?" she asked, panic etched into her features.

"Lucy, stay close," Claire commanded, knowing they needed to present a united front. "Dr. Harrow is attempting to intimidate us, but we're not backing down."

Harrow's gaze darted toward Lucy, a calculating smile returning to his lips. "Ah, my faithful nurse. You really ought to reconsider your position," he said, drawing Lucy into the conversation with his charm. "I can assure you, Claire's accusations are nothing but wild fantasies. You've seen how patients thrive under my care, haven't you?"

Lucy's voice wavered as she stood in the crossfire. "I… I just want everyone to be safe," she said, her eyes darting between Claire and Harrow. The conflict hung heavily in the air.

"Safety?" Harrow feigned innocence. "Oh, but you won't find safety through fearmongering, Lucy. Join me, and I'll ensure you have a place that honors your dedication rather than puts you at risk."

Claire stepped forward, sensing the manipulation woven into Harrow's words. "You're trying to pit us against each other, but we won't fall for it. Lucy, we need to stay honest and focused on the truth, no matter how Harrow attempts to distract us."

Harrow's expression darkened again, a fleeting glimpse of the depths of his frustration showing through his measured decorum. "Truth? What truth, Claire? Your interpretation is hardly universal. You're gathering the discontent of a few families and constructing a narrative around it. That's not justice; that's a witch hunt!"

"That's your defense, isn't it? Dismissing the experiences of those you've harmed," Claire retorted, refusing to let his condescension infiltrate her resolve. "It's time for the community to see you for who you truly are."

"You're making a mistake," Harrow stated, his tone chilling. "You will regret this confrontation more than you realize."

As Harrow left, the tension still crackled in the aftermath of their standoff. The families stood alongside Claire, their eyes wide with a mix of fear and determination. The confrontation had laid bare the dangerous game Harrow was playing and ignited a flame of resolve among them.

Claire took a deep breath, steadying herself. "This is our moment. Harrow may have tried to intimidate us, but we've shown him that we are not backing down. We have to ensure that no one else falls victim to his manipulations."

Mary stepped forward, her shoulders squared and her voice brave. "He can try to scare us, but I won't let him control my life any longer. We have to expose the truth for all our loved ones."

A wave of agreement flowed through the crowd, families nodding in solidarity. Claire felt the strength of their combined voices—this was about more than just her fight; it was about reclaiming their community, restoring trust, and shining a light on Harrow's dark practices.

"Let's stay vigilant," Claire urged, glancing at the door through which Harrow had exited. "We need to unify our efforts and ensure everyone knows they have a place in this fight. The more of us who stand together, the harder it will be for him to silence us."

With renewed energy, the families began to exchange ideas about how best to mobilize their community. They discussed coordinated outreach efforts, creating a network that would ensure their voices were heard, and preparing for any potential backlash from Harrow.

Meanwhile, Claire returned to her desk, her heart still racing from the confrontation. She knew they had to act quickly; the longer they waited, the more time Harrow would have to regroup and spin his narrative. As she sifted through notes, an email notification appeared on her screen—an update from Officer Daniels.

Subject: Harrow's Counteractions

Claire opened the email, her pulse quickening. It detailed the growing unrest in the community, with reports of Harrow approaching families to dissuade them from speaking out. He was framing Claire as a rogue detective who was dismantling the trust between patients and their doctor, painting her as an outsider trying to tear apart the fabric of their community.

As anger bubbled up within her, Claire realized that she had to counteract Harrow's growing influence. She quickly typed a response to Daniels, suggesting they hold a meeting with the officers assigned to patrol the neighborhoods of families affected by Harrow. They needed to ensure that residents felt supported and protected from any intimidation tactics Harrow employed.

That evening, as the sky darkened over Elderwood, Claire met with Officer Daniels and the support team. "We need to put together an emergency plan for the families," Claire said, her voice urgent. "Harrow is trying to manipulate the narrative in his favor, and I won't let him silence our collective voices."

Daniels nodded, considering the implications. "We can coordinate patrols for at-risk families, but we also need a plan to address Harrow's defamation. If he's spreading lies about you to the community, we need to confront him in a way that highlights your integrity and work."

"I agree," Claire replied, beginning to pace with purpose. "What if we collect testimonials from the families about their interactions with Harrow? We can then present them as a united front, showcasing the truth against the narrative he's crafting in the community."

The officers exchanged glances, already buzzing with ideas. They began organizing outreach efforts, including setting up a community forum where families could speak openly about their experiences. The gathering would not only provide a platform for those affected but also serve as a preemptive counter to Harrow's manipulative campaign.

As they fleshed out the details, Claire felt a surge of momentum building. They were preparing to show the community the truth behind Harrow's deceptive charm—the same charm that had entangled so many.

With a clear plan in place, Claire left the meeting invigorated. They were moving forward together, ready to face the growing storm that was Dr. Harrow—and they would not back down.

The following day promised to be pivotal; the time for confrontation was on the horizon, and with every testimony gathered and each family united, they were preparing to unveil the reality that lurked beneath Harrow's polished surface. The fight was far from over, but together, they would ensure that the truth could no longer be obscured by his deceitful charms.

CHAPTER 18
PARANOIA RISING

As the sun rose on another tense day in Elderwood, Claire felt the weight of the world pressing down on her shoulders. News of the community forum had spread, and with it came whispers of discontent from Dr. Harrow's supporters. The atmosphere had shifted dramatically—what was once a quiet town now buzzed with uncertainty, a palpable fear hanging in the air.

Claire arrived at the precinct early, the fluorescent lights flickering overhead as she settled into her desk. A sense of foreboding stirred in the pit of her stomach as she reviewed the latest testimonies from families, trying to piece together their concerns about Harrow's treatment methods. Rumors had begun to circulate in coffee shops and local businesses, with some residents expressing doubt about Claire's credibility as a detective.

"Did you hear about what she's doing?" one woman whispered to another as Claire passed by. "It's just a personal vendetta against Dr. Harrow. He's the only good doctor we've got!"

"Right? It's so exhilarating to take down someone who's helped so many!" said the other, laughing nervously.

Claire forced herself to remain focused, but the murmurings only deepened her resolve to uncover the truth. She had to confront Harrow's manipulation head-on; it was more vital than ever to gather solid evidence and support from the families.

Later that morning, Officer Daniels knocked on her office door, concern etched across his face as he stepped inside. "Claire," he started, his voice low, "I think we need to talk. The backlash is getting worse. I've heard complaints about you and your methods coming from Harrow's supporters—some families are beginning to distance themselves."

Claire felt a sharp pang of anxiety at his words. "Seriously? After everything we've done together?"

"Yeah. Some people think you're on a witch hunt, and they're worried about the backlash it could bring if they align with you. Harrow is crafty; he's turning the narrative against you," Daniels replied, shifting uncomfortably.

Her heart sank. "I didn't anticipate this level of blowback. I only wanted to seek justice for those who've suffered. How can they turn against us?"

"They may not see it that way," Daniels said, trying to gauge her reaction. "It's an uphill battle, and you're not alone. Just be cautious. We may need to arrange increased safety measures for you and the families who've come forward."

As Claire considered his words, a tight knot formed in her stomach. She understood the delicate balance they had to maintain; every move they made required careful consideration. "We can't let fear dictate our actions. If Harrow can manipulate the community into believing that we're the enemy, we have to expose him before he fully regains control."

Just then, the door swung open, and Lucy stepped in, her face pale and apprehensive. "Claire, you won't believe this. I just overheard Dr. Harrow talking to a few residents outside the office. He's rallying support against you—the very families we were counting on to bring forth complaints!"

Claire's heart sank. "This is exactly what I was afraid of. He's working to undermine our efforts, and we need to regroup before this spirals further."

"We could hold a private meeting with the families," Lucy suggested, her voice trembling with urgency. "We need to remind them of our purpose and take action while we still can."

"I agree, but we have to be cautious," Claire replied, feeling the pressure mount. "If Harrow is out there convincing people to turn against us, it could jeopardize everything we're working toward."

As the day wore on, Claire immersed herself completely in gathering evidence. She talked to families again, reinforcing a sense of urgency and solidarity, but the repercussions of Harrow's manipulation hung over each interaction like a storm cloud.

After a tense afternoon, Lucy approached Claire with a worried look on her face. "I don't know how much longer I can balance this. Harrow's paranoia is starting to affect me, too. People have seen him lurking outside my house, and it's making me uncomfortable."

"We'll make sure you have added protection," Claire reassured her, but she could sense Lucy's uncertainty. "You're doing important work here. If you feel unsafe, we can create a plan to keep you shielded from Harrow's tactics."

"I just keep thinking about the families," Lucy said, her voice wavering. "What's going to happen if he targets them because of us? I'm terrified that pushing forward may put them at risk."

"I understand your fears," Claire replied softly. "But we've come too far to let intimidation rule us. The truth will ultimately protect them more than silence ever will. We must face this together, and they need you as part of that strength."

As night fell, Claire returned home, the grip of anxiety tightening around her like a vise. The streets of Elderwood, now cloaked in darkness, felt eerie and still, every shadow seeming to loom larger than it should. She locked the door behind her, the click of the latch echoing ominously in the silence.

The memories of the day's events clung to her; the rumors, the whispers of doubt, and Harrow's alarming manipulation festered in her mind. Alone in her apartment, she felt the weight of the world squarely on her shoulders. Her efforts to protect the community were under threat, and it stirred a sense of urgency she couldn't shake.

Sitting at her kitchen table, Claire spread out the various files she had accumulated—patient records, testimonies, and notes of her conversations. A stack of evidence was slowly forming, but the threat that lingered in the air felt more formidable than ever.

As she flipped through the pages, she couldn't help but feel the tension building within her. The more she delved into the details, the more daunting Harrow's manipulation seemed. His power over the community grew more pronounced, like an ominous shadow creeping across the lives of those she sought to protect.

After hours of reviewing material, Claire leaned back in her chair, closing her eyes. Images of the families who had come forward danced in her mind—faces filled with fear and frustration, yet also courage. They had entrusted her with their stories, and she needed to uphold that trust, no matter the personal cost.

Suddenly, her phone buzzed, breaking the silence. Claire picked it up eagerly, hoping for a message from Lucy or Officer Daniels, but instead, it was an unexpected text from an unknown number.

"I know what you're trying to do. Leave Dr. Harrow alone, or you'll regret it."

Her heart raced as she read the message, the chill of fear coursing through her veins. Was this a threat? Was Harrow already retaliating? As the implications of the message sank in, the walls of her apartment felt constricting, shadows creeping closer as paranoia surged.

Quickly, she responded, typing with trembling fingers. "Who is this?"

Moments passed, and there was no reply. Anxiety twisted her stomach as she contemplated the implications. This wasn't just about her investigation anymore; this was personal. Harrow was sending a message—a declaration of war against her efforts.

Claire knew she couldn't let fear dictate her actions, so she took a deep breath to quell her racing heart. She needed to share this development with Daniels and Lucy, but she couldn't afford to be reckless. If Harrow was watching her, she needed to tread carefully.

Resolving to confront the threat head-on, Claire decided to head back to the precinct, feeling an urgency that outweighed her trepidation. She slipped on her coat and grabbed her keys, glancing one last time at her phone before leaving.

The drive to the precinct felt excruciatingly long, her mind swirling with thoughts. Would Harrow escalate his intimidation tactics now that she was directly challenging him? As she approached the precinct, her lips pressed into a thin line of determination.

Once inside, she spotted Officer Daniels speaking with a colleague. "Claire, you're back," he said, surprised but pleased to see her. "What do you have?"

"Harrow just sent me a threatening message from an unknown number. I think he's trying to intimidate me or warn me off the investigation," she said, forcing the tremor from her voice. "He's aware of the momentum we've built, and I believe he's getting desperate."

Daniels nodded soberly, concern growing in his expression. "We need to take this seriously. If he's threatening you, that puts you—and the families—at risk. Let's see if we can trace the message."

"Do we have resources for that?" Claire asked, praying for a quick solution.

"We can run it through our system, but I think we need to keep this under wraps for now," he replied. "We can't let Harrow know we're catching on to his tactics."

Claire felt a surge of frustration but held it at bay. "You're right. We need to be cautious and strategic. He's a master manipulator, and if we show any sign of fear, he'll exploit that."

With a plan forming, Claire and Daniels turned their attention to the task at hand. They worked through the evidence Claire had gathered, strategizing on how best to present their findings to the community, ensuring they remained vigilant against Harrow's retaliation.

As the hours slipped by, Claire couldn't shake her sense of urgency. The shadows felt weightier, the tension ever-present, but she knew they were on the precipice of something significant. Together, they would confront Dr. Harrow and expose the truth before his manipulative grip could tighten further around their community.

CHAPTER 19
THE BREAKING POINT

The days turned into a whirlwind as the community prepared for the impending showdown with Dr. Harrow. As the evening of the forum approached, Lucy felt the pressure mount. The weight of her decision to testify against Harrow hung heavily on her shoulders, gnawing at her resolve.

She spent hours going over her notes, replaying the disturbing incidents she had witnessed in her mind, the nagging worry of how Harrow would respond echoing louder with each passing moment. The act of coming forward meant stepping into the spotlight, and that spotlight brought with it a veil of danger.

Late one night, under the flickering lights of her apartment, Lucy paced back and forth, anxiety consuming her. She had spoken with Claire earlier, voicing her fears about what might happen if Harrow discovered her intentions. They had strategized on methods of protection, but deep down, Lucy felt an unsettling fear creeping into her heart.

Just as she started to calm down, her phone buzzed on the table, the sudden sound jolting her from her thoughts. She picked it up to read the message, her heart sinking as she recognized the familiar taunt.

"You're making a grave mistake, Lucy. Stay quiet, or you'll regret it."

The message sent a shiver down her spine. She glanced out the window, feeling the weight of Harrow's impending presence in her life. The moment of indecision she had been grappling with intensified.

With shaking hands, Lucy dialed Claire, determined to seek reassurance. "Claire, I just received another message from Harrow. He's threatening me."

"Lucy, we need to take this seriously," Claire replied immediately, her voice urgent. "Where are you? Are you alone?"

"I'm home, but I can't shake this feeling of dread," Lucy admitted, fear creeping into her voice. "What if he comes after me? I'm terrified."

"Stay where you are. I'll come to you," Claire said, immediately grabbing her coat and keys. "We'll work together to ensure you're safe and that Harrow knows we're not afraid."

As Claire sped through the dimly lit streets, her mind raced with worry. Harrow had become increasingly desperate, and Lucy was in the crosshairs of his manipulation. She knew that if Lucy was threatened, it could unravel the entire case they were building against Harrow.

Arriving at Lucy's apartment, Claire knocked quickly and assured that she was inside and locked the door. "Lucy, it's me!" she called.

"Thank goodness," Lucy breathed as she opened the door, relief flooding her features. "I'm scared, Claire. I don't know if I can do this anymore."

"We'll make sure you're safe," Claire replied, entering the apartment and securing the locks behind her. "You're stronger than you realize, and this moment is crucial. If you testify, we can finally hold Harrow accountable."

Lucy shook her head, her voice trembling. "But what if he retaliates? I can't live in fear every day!"

"Living in fear means he wins," Claire said, her voice steady and reassuring. "If you come forward and share your experiences, we can expose him for what he truly is. Remember, you're not alone. We're all in this together, and we'll protect each other."

As they spoke, Lucy felt a flicker of courage rekindle deep within her. But just as she was beginning to feel hopeful, the atmosphere shifted. A loud noise sounded from the hallway—a crash, followed by hurried footsteps.

"Did you hear that?" Lucy whispered, her eyes wide with terror.

Claire nodded, her instincts kicking into high gear. "Stay here," she instructed, moving toward the door carefully. "I'll check to see what's going on."

Heart pounding, Claire crept toward the door and peered through the peephole. In the dim hallway, she finally glimpsed a shadow—the unmistakable figure of Dr. Harrow, standing just outside Lucy's apartment. His posture was rigid, anger radiating from him.

"This is it," Claire murmured to herself, realizing the stakes had escalated tremendously. "I have to protect Lucy."

"Claire!" Lucy whispered urgently from behind her, panic creeping into her voice. "What are we going to do? We can't let him in!"

"Stay quiet," Claire ordered, her mind racing as she formed a plan. "If he tries to break in, we need to alert the officers immediately."

The sounds of Harrow's agitation reverberated outside the door, each thud of his fist against the wood echoing like a dull drumbeat of intimidation. "Lucy! I know you're in there! Open the door!" he barked, his voice rising with fury.

Claire could feel Lucy's fear mounting behind her. "We can't go back to the way things were," Claire whispered. "We have to confront him. He needs to understand that his intimidation won't work any longer."

"Are you sure that's the right move?" Lucy's voice quaked with uncertainty. "What if he gets angry? What if he does something drastic?"

"Even if he gets angry, we won't allow him to control us," Claire replied, determination mixing with resolve. "We've already come too far to back down now. I can't let him continue to take advantage of you or any other families."

With a nod of understanding and a deep breath, Claire moved away from the door and picked up her phone, pressing down on the speed dial for Officer Daniels. Lucy watched, anxiety evident in her expression.

"Claire, please be careful," she said, her voice barely above a whisper. "What if he hears you?"

"He'll hear me, regardless. But we need to be ready," Claire replied, her focus narrowing. The beeping sound of dialing echoed through the tense air as the line connected, but her heart sank when a voice on the other end answered.

"Officer Daniels, what's going on?" came the calm voice. Claire could hear the background noise of the precinct, a comforting sound against the anxiety radiating from the hallway.

"Daniels, it's Claire. Harrow is at Lucy's apartment, and he's been trying to get in. We need backup," she said, keeping her voice low but resolute.

"Got it. We're sending units over now. Try to keep the situation calm," Daniels instructed, quickly snapping into action. "We'll be there in just a few minutes."

Claire hung up and turned to Lucy, feeling a mixture of relief and urgency. "Help is on the way. We just need to hold our ground until they arrive."

"I'm scared, Claire," Lucy admitted, tears glistening in her eyes. "What if he tries to force his way in?"

"We'll be ready," Claire reassured her, moving closer as she positioned herself protectively in front of Lucy. "Just stay close to me, and don't make any noise. We'll confront him together if we have to."

The pounding on the door intensified, the violence of Harrow's aggression reverberating through the thin walls. "Lucy! Enough games! Open the door and stop acting foolishly!" he shouted, his voice laced with fury.

"Don't listen to him!" Claire urged, her heart racing as she gripped Lucy's arm. "Stay calm; we won't let him get to you."

Then, with a resounding crash, Harrow slammed his fist against the door with force, causing Lucy to flinch. "You think you can hide from me? I'm not just going to stand by while you spiral into paranoia!"

The door shook in its frame, and Claire's resolve hardened. "This ends now, Harrow! You can't intimidate us," she yelled, her voice steady and unwavering despite the turmoil.

"Let's see how brave you are when I reveal everything I know about you," he countered, the storm brewing behind his words. "I could easily ruin you, Claire. You're far from invincible in this town."

Just then, the sound of footsteps echoed down the hallway, a welcomed relief. Claire turned to Lucy, who was blinking away tears, her fear mingling with a flicker of hope.

"Stay back," Claire instructed, moving closer to the door, knowing they were moments away from a standoff that would shape their future.

The footsteps grew louder, and Officer Daniels rushed around the corner alongside a few other officers, just as Harrow slammed his fist against the door again. "I'm giving you one last chance to open up, Lucy! Or I will make this very difficult for you!"

"Police! Step away from the door!" Officer Daniels shouted, his voice cutting through the tension like a knife.

Harrow's eyes flashed with fury, but he hesitated, caught between the rising danger and his desire to maintain control. "You can't do this!" he yelled, dropping the mask of cool composure. "These families are misguided!"

"Enough!" Officer Daniels commanded as they moved swiftly to the door. "If you don't step back, we will have to breach."

Lucy's hand trembled in Claire's grasp, and Claire could feel her fear intensifying. But with the officers behind her, a renewed strength surged forth. "You're done Harrow! This ends now."

As the officers prepared to force the door open, Claire felt a sense of impending confrontation fill the air. The moment had arrived; the truth about Harrow would soon come crumbling down, and it would change everything for the community of Elderwood.

The door burst open, and Claire braced herself for the chaos that would undoubtedly ensue.

CHAPTER 20
CHASE THROUGH THE NIGHT

The moment the door burst open, chaos erupted. Officer Daniels and the other officers rushed into the hallway, their demeanor firm and ready to confront Dr. Harrow. Claire stepped back, bracing herself as she pointed toward the retreating figure of Harrow, who was already making a hasty exit down the corridor.

"Stop him!" Claire shouted, adrenaline coursing through her veins as she darted after Harrow, her instincts kicking into high gear. He was moving quickly, his footsteps reverberating as he rushed toward the back exit. "We can't let him get away!"

The officers were quick to respond. Two officers sprinted toward the back entrance while Claire and Daniels pursued Harrow through the maze of the precinct. As they pushed through the various hallways, Claire felt the urgency of the moment grip her. Harrow had to be stopped; she couldn't let him escape, not when lives were at stake.

"Where do you think you're going, Harrow?" Claire called out, her breath heavy with the exertion of the chase. "You can't run from this!"

Harrow glanced back, his face a mask of anger and desperation. "You'll regret this, Claire!" he shouted, his voice echoing through the hallway.

As they barreled down the corridor, Claire felt the adrenaline heighten her senses, every instinct focusing on the climax of their confrontation. They pushed through the double doors leading outside, the night air crisp against their skin, but she could see Harrow's figure already ahead of them, moving swiftly toward the parking lot.

"Get a car ready!" Claire yelled over her shoulder to the officers as they emerged into the open air. The sound of sirens wailed in the distance, but Claire knew they had to catch him first.

Harrow scurried toward his vehicle, a sleek sedan parked not far from the entrance. "Claire!" he called out, though his voice trembled with the fear of being caught. "You can't win this fight. You're throwing your life away!"

Ignoring his taunts, Claire pushed herself harder, sprinting after him. As she closed the distance, she could feel her heart pounding in her chest, fueled by both fear and resolve. Harrow reached his car, fumbled with the keys, and finally jerked the door open.

"Stop!" Claire shouted as she barreled forward.

He glanced back, panic flashing across his features. In a moment of desperation, he slammed his car door shut and hit the ignition, spraying gravel as he attempted to speed away.

"No!" Claire cried, her instincts taking over as she dashed toward the vehicle. She had to stop him before he could escape, not just for her safety but for the safety of every family he had manipulated.

In a split-second decision, Claire turned and spotted a police cruiser parked nearby, officers scrambling to respond to the chaos. She bolted toward it, adrenaline surging as she reached for the door handle, her heart racing.

Daniels, catching up beside her, shouted, "Get in! I'll drive!"

With no time to waste, Claire jumped into the passenger seat as he slid into the driver's side, instantly kicking into gear as they revved toward Harrow's escape. The car lurched forward, tires screeching against the asphalt, giving Claire a momentary rush of hope.

"Where is he?" Claire asked, peering over her shoulder as they sped through the parking lot.

"There!" Daniels said, pointing ahead as he caught sight of Harrow's car racing away from the precinct. "Hold on!"

With the cruiser set firmly on a chase, the world outside became a blur as they tore through the streets of Elderwood, the distance between them and Harrow closing with every turn. Claire's heart raced with each moment, frustration mingling with fierce determination.

"Stay on him!" Claire urged, adrenaline coursing through her as she watched Harrow's sedan dodge through traffic. "He can't get away!"

Daniels maneuvered with precision, skillfully weaving through the streets. As they approached the outskirts of town, Harrow accelerated, seemingly desperate to lose them.

"Where is he taking us?" Claire wondered aloud, squinting into the night, searching for any signs of escape. "We have to cut him off!"

"He's heading into the industrial district," Daniels noted, keeping the cruiser within a safe distance. "Let's see if we can anticipate his route."

Just as they turned onto a narrow road lined with abandoned warehouses, Claire noticed Harrow veering toward a particularly dark area. "He's going to try and lose us in there!" she exclaimed, recognizing the potential for danger.

Daniels pressed down on the accelerator, his jaw set in concentration. "I see it. Hang on!"

They followed Harrow into the darkness, the headlights of the cruiser illuminating the shadows as the chase intensified. With every corner, Claire felt her pulse quicken—this was no ordinary pursuit. The stakes had been raised, and every moment felt charged with urgency and the potential for confrontation.

"Hang in there!" Daniels shouted over the roar of the engine, weaving through the maze of abandoned warehouses. Harrow's vehicle was now just a few car lengths ahead, darting through the dimly lit lot.

"Watch your speed! He might try something reckless!" Claire warned, her mind racing as they navigated the twisting maze of industrial structures. The looming shadows created an atmosphere of unease, and Claire couldn't shake the feeling that the darkness held secrets just waiting to be uncovered.

Suddenly, Harrow veered sharply, taking a hard left toward an area littered with old shipping containers. "He's trying to lose us!" Claire exclaimed, feeling a surge of adrenaline as Daniels followed suit, not willing to let him slip away.

They turned the corner just in time to see Harrow's brake lights flash, skidding to a stop amidst the containers. The cruiser slid to a halt behind him, the tires screeching in protest as Claire's heart raced with apprehension.

"Get ready," Daniels instructed, his eyes scanning the area for any sign of Harrow making a move. "We need to approach cautiously. He'll know we're right behind him."

Claire nodded, her mind focused, knowing that one misstep could lead to disaster. The abandoned lot felt eerily quiet, the only sound the faint tapping of metal against metal in the wind. "Let's flank him. If he tries to escape, we'll cut him off."

Both officers stepped out of the cruiser, drawing their firearms cautiously as Claire positioned herself near the driver's side door. "Dr. Harrow! Step out of the vehicle with your hands up!" she shouted, her voice echoing amid the towering shipping containers.

Silence settled around them, but just as Claire was about to call out again, Harrow flung open his door and darted out, sprinting toward a gap between two containers. "He's running!" Claire yelled, bolting after him.

"Cover me!" Daniels called as he pursued Harrow through the narrow, dimly lit space between the containers, the challenge of navigating the cramped alleyway becoming increasingly difficult in the fading light.

Claire followed closely, her heart pounding in her chest as they navigated the tight confines. She could hear Harrow's heavy footsteps echoing ahead, his laughter cutting through the air with a manic edge. "You can't catch me!" he called out, his voice filled with a desperate bravado.

"Stop!" Claire shouted, adrenaline surging as they picked up speed. The tension electrified the air—a desperate determination fueled her every step. Harrow had to be stopped; they were running out of time.

Just as they reached the end of the long row of shipping containers, Harrow made a sharp right, heading back toward the open space of the lot. Claire could feel the distance closing, and her instincts kicked into overdrive.

"Officer!" she yelled, signaling Daniels, who was close behind. They angled toward Harrow, using every bit of speed they could muster. "We have to corner him!"

But Harrow was quicker than they anticipated. He spotted an opportunity on the opposite side of the lot and barreled toward the edge of the property, where a fence stood—high and daunting.

"No!" Claire shouted, knowing he could escape if he made it over. With a final burst of energy, she lunged forward, disregarding the pain in her legs as she pushed past the encroaching metal.

Harrow reached the top of the fence just as Claire launched herself forward. "You won't get away with this, Harrow!" she shouted, desperately reaching for him, fingers just grazing the fabric of his coat.

In that moment, he hurled himself over the fence with surprising agility, landing on the other side and disappearing into the shadows of the alleyway beyond. Claire slid to a stop, panting as she stared at the gap he had slipped through. She could hear Harrow's fading footsteps retreat into the darkness beyond.

"Claire!" Daniels called as he reached her, his expression filled with concern. "Did you see where he went?"

"Just over the fence!" Claire gasped, frustration and adrenaline coursing through her. "We can't let him slip away again!"

Daniels called for backup over the radio, ensuring that officers spread out to surround the area. "Stay close," he instructed, as they moved toward the fence to determine the best way to pursue him.

"Should we split up?" Claire asked, determined not to lose sight of Harrow.

"No, we'll stay together. We'll cover more ground that way," Daniels replied, the urgency in his voice palpable.

They climbed over the fence, anxiety gripping Claire at the thought of losing Dr. Harrow in the labyrinth of alleys beyond. As they landed on the other side, she took a deep breath, her senses heightened by the adrenaline coursing through her veins. The slipping shadows between the buildings beckoned with a sense of dread, yet she couldn't let fear dictate her actions.

"Which way did he go?" Claire asked, scanning their surroundings for any signs of movement.

"I think he headed right," Daniels replied, glancing toward a narrow alley that branched off in that direction. "We need to move quickly before he can escape us completely."

Nodding vigorously, Claire and Daniels darted down the dimly lit alley, their footsteps echoing off the brick walls. The narrow space felt oppressive, a claustrophobic reminder of the uncertainty lurking around every corner. They could hear their own breaths, rhythmically punctuated by the sound of distant sirens, reminding them that assistance was on standby, but they needed to apprehend Harrow before he disappeared entirely.

As they reached the end of the alley, they paused, straining to listen for any sounds that would indicate which direction Harrow had headed. It was then that they heard it—the unmistakable sound of footsteps skimming through a nearby parking lot.

"Over there," Claire whispered, pointing toward the sound. They edged cautiously toward the parking lot entrance, adrenaline flowing through them.

They entered the lot, where the dim light overhead barely illuminated the rows of parked cars. But just as Claire turned her head to scan for Harrow, a familiar silhouette emerged from behind one of the vehicles—a flicker of a coat, a flash of fear in his eyes.

"There he is!" Claire shouted, taking off after him as he bolted toward the far exit, scrambling for concealment among the cars.

"Don't lose sight of him!" Daniels yelled, sprinting close behind as they both charged into the fray. Harrow was fast, but the officers were fueled by the urgency of their mission. They could not allow him to slip away again.

Harrow dashed across the lot, narrowly avoiding several parked vehicles, and made a hard turn into another alley. Claire and Daniels followed, their hearts pounding as they chased him through the twisting passage.

"Stop! Police!" Claire shouted, her voice ringing out with authority. But Harrow didn't pause. Instead, he surged ahead with renewed energy, desperation fueling his escape.

The chase felt endless, weaving through alleys and side streets, when suddenly Harrow stumbled, momentarily losing his balance. Claire seized the opportunity, pushing herself to close the gap. She could see him ahead, his face twisted with frustration and panic.

"Claire! Watch out!" Daniels shouted, but it was too late.

Harrow spun around, slamming into Claire with surprising force. She collided with a brick wall, pain shooting through her as she tried to regain her footing. "Get off me!" she shouted, grappling with his solid grip as he attempted to shove her aside and break free.

"Your meddling ends now, Claire!" Harrow hissed, his eyes wild with fervor. He pushed against her with his full weight, shoving her back.

In that instant, Claire realized his desperation; even with his bravado, the facade of control was wavering. "You can't intimidate me anymore!" she yelled, using every ounce of strength to push back against him.

Finally, as he staggered backward, Claire grabbed his arm, twisting it to force him against the wall, pinning him in place. "You're done, Harrow! This ends now!"

Before Claire could gather herself to maintain control, Daniels arrived, catching Harrow off guard as he surged forward and easily grabbed Harrow's other arm, ready to secure him. "You're under arrest for intimidation and misconduct!" he declared, using handcuffs to bind Harrow's wrists behind his back.

"Do you know who you're dealing with?" Harrow growled, the desperation in his voice giving way to anger. "I'll have you both removed from your positions. You'll regret this!"

But Claire stood firm, breathing heavily as she recovered from the struggle. "You're not invincible, Harrow. The truth is far more powerful than your threats."

As they ushered him toward the awaiting police car, Claire felt the weight of victory envelop her. The families had rallied their strength, and together, they had countered Harrow's manipulations.

But as she secured the area and prepared to address the community once more, Claire felt a flicker of apprehension nestled deep within her—a reminder that while this confrontation was a pivotal moment, the battle against Harrow and the shadows he cast was far from over.

There had been cogs set in motion, mechanisms of revenge that Harrow could unleash. And Claire knew instinctively that she needed to be prepared for the inevitable backlash, standing resolute in the face of whatever darkness lay ahead.

CHAPTER 21
THE DARK PAST REVEALED

The air was thick with tension as the precinct settled into a hushed quiet, the aftermath of Claire's confrontation with Harrow leaving an unsettling echo in its wake. With Harrow now in custody, Claire's determination to expose the truth felt stronger than ever, but a sense of unease lingered in her mind. She knew that to fully confront him, they needed to understand what had shaped his dark motivations.

That evening, after the dust had settled from the chaos, Claire returned to her apartment. She poured herself a cup of coffee, trying to shake off the anxiety that gripped her. While she was grateful for the progress made, the question of Harrow's origins nagged at her—a haunting mystery begging to be unraveled.

Sitting at her kitchen table, she closed her eyes, allowing her mind to drift back to the information gathered from his history—a patchwork of whispers and rumors that hinted at a troubled past. Dr. Samuel Harrow was not just a doctor; he had once been a young man entangled in a world that had shaped him in ways others could scarcely fathom.

As she settled into her thoughts, flashbacks began to unfold, illuminating the dimly lit corridors of Harrow's past.

Scene Change:

Claire envisioned young Samuel Harrow, a boy of about ten, sitting on the steps of a small house, his eyes cast down as tears streamed down his face. His mother, a nurse, rushed to him, her face etched with worry. "Sammy, what's wrong?" she asked, kneeling beside him.

"Kids at school said I'm not good enough," he whispered, the hurt visible in his expression. "They said I'll never make it as a doctor like you."

His mother wrapped her arms around him, a gentle smile touching her lips. "You have to believe in yourself, sweetheart. You can achieve anything if you work hard. They don't know what you're capable of."

Scene Change:

The scene shifted to a few years later—Samuel, now a teenager, was sitting in a dimly lit kitchen filled with the aroma of burnt toast. His father sat at the table, a shadow of disappointment creeping into his features. "You're wasting your time, Sam. You'll never make it to medical school with those grades. You need to toughen up."

"Dad, I'm trying," young Harrow pleaded, desperation rising in his voice. "I want to help people like you did. I just need a little more time."

His father shook his head, the frustration boiling over. "A little more time? You need to learn what real life is about! No one cares about your dreams!"

Scene Change:

Claire's vision shifted again, revealing a more unsettling tableau. Adult Samuel stood in a hospital hallway, his eyes scanning the chaotic environment, a look of dread pooling in his expression. As he walked through the ward, he heard the hushed cries of patients and the frantic conversations of doctors.

In the breakroom, he overheard a conversation between two colleagues. "We can't keep covering up the mistakes happening with these patients," one said. "Someone's going to pay for this negligence."

Samuel's eyes widened with fear; he had made mistakes, experienced pressures and failures that clawed at him each day. He had witnessed suffering and uncertainty, yet he had never anticipated that his decisions could determine life or death.

Scene Change:

In a dimly lit room, Samuel stood before a mirror, his reflection revealing the toll that years of pressure had taken on him. He rubbed his temples, filled with a swirling clash of ambition and despair. He had lost patients due to negligence—his own mistakes. The weight of each loss pressed heavily upon his conscience, and with every failure came a burgeoning rage against the system he felt was out to destroy him.

"You have to be perfect, Sam," came a whisper—a memory of his mother's voice reminding him of the pressure that lay ahead. He was determined to prove his worth, yet his fear of failure morphed into an insatiable need for control and admiration.

Scene Change:

The flashback shifted once more, revealing a decisive moment in Harrow's career. Standing before the medical board, he defended his practices, his face flushed with anger and defiance. "I am dedicated to my patients! I know what is best for them!" His fists clenched as he spoke, a mix of pride and desperation cascading through him.

The board members evaluated him with skepticism, their uncertainty lingering in the air. "Your treatment methods have been called into question, Dr. Harrow," one board member replied, the calmness laced with authority. "You cannot dismiss concerns that have been raised. We have a duty to protect our patients."

Frustration bubbled beneath the surface as Samuel's world started crumbling around him, plunging him into darkness. "They just don't understand! They only care about rules and regulations. Patients only need a strong hand, someone who knows how to make the hard decisions!" His voice rose, echoing off the sterile hospital walls, desperation tinging each word.

The board members exchanged glances, their expressions a mixture of concern and disapproval. "Doctor, we understand that you want to help, but helping shouldn't come at the cost of patient safety," one of them replied, attempting to reason with him.

"Safety?" he spat, emotion clouding his judgement. "What about their trust? I've saved them! How can you question that?" The anger he felt seethed through him, and he stormed out of the meeting, vowing never to allow anyone to question his authority again.

Scene Change:

Returning to the present, Claire broke free from the memory, her breath coming in short gasps. The pieces of Harrow's past lay strewn before her like a fractured puzzle, each fragment revealing how ambition had twisted into a desperate grasp for control. The idealistic dreams of a boy seeking to help others had soured into the manipulative, dangerous tactics she was now fighting against.

She pulled herself together, shaking off the echoes of Harrow's past. Those memories provided the clarity she needed; they illuminated the path forward. Understanding the underpinning motives behind Harrow's actions could be the key to dismantling the influence he wielded over the community.

That evening, Claire gathered her files and made her way to the community center, determined to share her findings with the families. They needed to understand what had turned Harrow from a hopeful doctor into a man driven by a need for control and superiority.

As families began to trickle in, Claire felt the familiar rush of urgency. The space was charged with anticipation; they were gathered to reclaim their narratives and confront the darkness together.

"Thank you all for coming," Claire said, stepping to the front of the room. "I want to share something I uncovered regarding Dr. Harrow. I've been exploring his past, seeking to understand how he developed the troubling patterns we've witnessed. What I discovered is critical—it shows how his rise to power has shaped the vulnerabilities we're now facing."

Curiosity rippled through the crowd. "Dr. Harrow was once dedicated to healing, but as the pressures of his profession mounted, so did his need for control. He has been driven by fear of failure, leading him to manipulate those he should have protected," Claire explained, her voice steady yet filled with urgency.

"I don't want to excuse his actions, but I believe understanding his past is crucial to seeing how we can stop him now. We are dealing with a man who has built his reputation on fear and intimidation, and it's time we stand united against it."

As she finished speaking, the emotions in the room shifted from curiosity to resolve. Families exchanged glances, their expressions filled with a sense of empowerment.

"If he's willing to weaponize his past against us, then we have to understand that we can disarm him by refusing to stay silent," one father interjected, his voice offering a rallying cry. "We can take back our community!"

"That's right! We have powerful stories!" another family member echoed, the energy in the room rising.

Encouraged by the response, Claire felt the warmth of solidarity surround her. With the families committed to standing together, it felt like the tide was finally shifting against Harrow.

As they began to brainstorm additional strategies, Claire felt a flicker of hope amidst the darkness they were confronting. She had gathered enough evidence to confront Harrow decisively, but it was clear that they needed to prepare for the looming retaliation he would undoubtedly unleash.

Later that night, Claire returned home, feelings of uncertainty still gnawing at her. She knew their battle was just beginning, and with Harrow's manipulative grip still tight around the community, the fight for justice would require both courage and unwavering resolve.

But as the moonlight streamed through her window, illuminating the stacks of files before her, Claire felt a reconnection to her mission. They would bend the arc of justice back toward truth, no matter how dark the path would be. Together, they would confront the shadow that had held so many captive—and they would not back down.

CHAPTER 22
THE FINAL MOVE

As dawn broke over Elderwood, the quiet streets felt deceptively peaceful, a sharp contrast to the storm brewing beneath the surface. Claire awoke with a sense of urgency, fully aware that Dr. Harrow's desperation would likely lead to increasingly destructive actions. The families rallied behind her were brimming with courage, but Claire knew Harrow would not go down without a fight.

Determined to stay one step ahead, she gathered her notes and reviewed the latest evidence collected from families, piecing together a narrative that would expose the truth. But as she prepared for the meeting at the community center later that day, a chilling realization gripped her: Harrow was cornered, and cornered animals often lash out unpredictably.

In the early morning hours, Claire received a call from Officer Daniels. "Claire, we need to talk," he said, his voice urgent and strained. "We've had some unsettling reports."

"What do you mean?" Claire's stomach dropped, sensing danger on the horizon.

"It seems there have been several suspicious activities reported around the homes of families aligned with your investigation against Harrow. Instances of strangers lurking outside, unusual vehicles repeatedly parking nearby—it's concerning," he explained.

"Damn it," Claire muttered, frustration twisting in her gut. "He's trying to intimidate them. We have to make sure everyone feels safe. Can we increase patrols?"

"Already on it. But tonight, I want to hold a meeting with the families to warn them about potential repercussions. We need to ensure they know to report anything suspicious immediately," Daniels replied.

"That's a great idea. I'll coordinate with the families and make sure they understand the situation," Claire said, her mind racing with the urgency of the moment. "We can't let Harrow shake our resolve."

Throughout the day, Claire reached out to the families, gathering them for an urgent meeting that evening. With each conversation, the sense of unease escalated. She reinforced the importance of vigilance, making clear that Harrow's actions were becoming more desperate and dangerous.

As night fell, the community center buzzed with voices filled with anxiety and determination, families returning to rally together once more. Claire stood at the front, pacing as the families gathered, their expressions reflecting determination, yet underlined with a fear of Harrow's presence.

"Thank you all for coming tonight," Claire began, her voice steady. "I know circumstances have escalated, and there are whispers of intimidation that have surfaced. We must remain vigilant and united. Dr. Harrow is trying to undermine your courage. He sees the strength in us, and it frightens him."

Lucy stepped forward, her commitment palpable. "We must protect each other. If you see anything strange or suspicious, do not hesitate to contact law enforcement—not just about Harrow, but about anyone who may seem to be working on his behalf."

Claire could see the families nodding in support, the tension slowly melting into a shared determination. "Together, we've begun to shed light on the truth. But make no mistake; Harrow is a cunning adversary. He will try to manipulate the situation to his advantage."

"Let's call a meeting with the media again," a family member suggested from the back, clenching their fists. "We can't let him control the narrative any longer."

"That's an excellent idea," Claire agreed. A plan was forming, one that could potentially expose Harrow's actions to the wider community, shifting their narrative completely.

Just as they were setting final plans in motion, Claire's phone buzzed with a notification, pulling her attention for just a moment. She glanced down to see a text from Officer Daniels: Suspicious activity reported outside the Thompson residence. Harrow's been spotted again.

"Everyone, we need to stay on high alert," Claire announced, barely containing her urgency. "Harrow is up to something, and if he knows we're planning to expose him, he may attempt to eliminate the threats around him. It's time to ensure safety measures are in place."

As the families exchanged apprehensive looks, Claire felt their determination waver for just a moment. "This is the time to come together and demonstrate our resolve. We will face whatever comes next with unity," she urged, feeling an electricity in the air.

Later that night, as Claire prepared for bed, the anxiety crept back into a familiar knot in her stomach. She could sense the storm gathering; Harrow was not simply a man she could confront with words alone. His next move would be desperate, and she needed to anticipate it.

Just then, her phone rang, shattering the silence of the night. Startled, Claire answered quickly. "Hello?"

"Claire!" Lucy's voice came through, panicked and breathless. "You need to come to my apartment right away. Harrow is here! He's trying to intimidate me!"

Claire's heart dropped. "Stay calm, Lucy! I'm on my way!"

She bolted from her apartment, adrenaline surging through her. The drive felt like an eternity, each second stretching into a moment filled with dread. The thought of Harrow confronting Lucy alone ignited a fire of urgency in Claire's chest. If Harrow was resorting to intimidation, he was clearly becoming desperate.

As she navigated through the dark streets of Elderwood, Claire's mind raced with solutions. Would Harrow try to harm Lucy, or was it all just another mental game to control and intimidate? Either way, Claire needed to be there, to protect the nurse who had bravely chosen to stand by her.

Arriving at Lucy's apartment complex, Claire parked hastily and sprinted toward the entrance, her heart pounding as she climbed the stairs two at a time. She reached Lucy's door and knocked hard. "Lucy! Open up!"

"Claire, hurry!" Lucy's voice came muffled from the other side, panic dripping through her words. "He's here—I'm scared!"

"Lucy, I'm right here. I won't let him hurt you!" Claire shouted, her own heart racing as fear pushed her to act quickly.

"Just a second!" Lucy called, and Claire could hear something shift inside, the sound of hurried movements. Then, finally, the door creaked open, and Lucy stood in the doorway, her face pale and shaken.

Claire pushed past her, scanning the apartment for any sign of Harrow. "Where is he?" she demanded, her senses on high alert.

"He—I think he left just before you got here," Lucy gasped, visibly trembling. "He was at my window, Claire! I don't know how he found me! He kept asking me questions, trying to intimidate me to keep quiet about everything!"

"Did he threaten you?" Claire asked, her voice steady but urgent, needing to gauge the severity of the situation.

"Yes! He said I would regret it if I spoke out," Lucy stammered, her eyes wide with fear. "And he said something about knowing things that could ruin me. Claire, he looked furious."

Claire's mind raced with thoughts of Harrow's escalating intimidation tactics. "He cannot silence you. We'll report this, and I will ensure you're protected."

"Yet it feels like I'm walking into a minefield. Every time we think we're making progress, he strikes back harder," Lucy said, her voice thick with anxiety.

Claire took a steadying breath, looking directly into Lucy's eyes. "We've come too far to let him intimidate us into silence. You're not alone in this; we are fighting for the truth."

Just as she spoke, Claire's phone rang again, interrupting their conversation. The caller ID showed it was Officer Daniels. "Claire," he said as soon as she answered, urgency clear in his tone. "We received a call from one of the families. Harrow has been seen lingering around their homes again."

"Which family?" Claire asked, alarmed.

"The Mills," he replied grimly. "They reported seeing him near their house, acting suspiciously. Everyone is on edge over here. We need to send units to ensure their safety."

"Let them know I'm heading there with Lucy," Claire said, her heart racing. "We can't give Harrow the chance to intimidate them. He's becoming increasingly desperate."

"Got it. I'll have backup ready," Daniels assured her before hanging up.

"Claire, what's happening?" Lucy asked, sensing the shift in Claire's demeanor.

"Dr. Harrow's been spotted near the Mills' home. We need to go there now," Claire said, urgency propelling her movements. "If he's escalating his tactics, he could put them in danger."

Lucy nodded, determination returning to her eyes despite her lingering fear. "Let's go. We can't let him do this to anyone else."

Together, they rushed to Claire's car, the tension palpable as they drove through the darkening streets. As they approached the Mills' residence, Claire felt the weight of dread settle over her. They were running into a potential confrontation with Harrow, and they needed to be ready for anything.

Reaching the neighborhood, Claire spotted a police cruiser parked outside the Mills' home, lights flashing softly as officers conversed with Mr. Mills. Relief washed over her; backup had already arrived.

Claire and Lucy exited the car and rushed toward the scene, their urgency fueling their steps. "Mr. Mills!" Claire called out as they approached. "Are you okay? What happened?"

Mr. Mills turned, concern etched across his face. "He was here again. I saw him lurking near the windows, and it freaked me out. I'm glad you're here."

"We need to keep everyone safe," Claire assured him, scanning the area. "The more eyes we have, the better."

Just then, a voice pierced the air with a chilling clarity. "So, you've all decided to play the hero, have you?"

Claire turned sharply to see Dr. Harrow stepping out from the shadows at the edge of the street, his posture relaxed yet menacing, an unsettling smile creeping across his face. The night seemed darker in his presence, the oppressive weight of his aura bending the atmosphere around him.

"What are you doing here, Harrow?" Claire demanded, anger coursing through her veins at his audacity. "You have no right to intimidate these families any longer."

Harrow's gaze flickered over the gathered officers and families, a glimmer of wicked amusement lighting his eyes. "Intimidate? No, no, Claire. You misunderstood me entirely. I'm here to ensure they don't fall prey to empty accusations. You see, a physician's reputation is precious, built over years of trust, and you're trying to tear it down with flimsy claims."

"Flimsy claims?" Claire scoffed, stepping forward, fueled by indignation. "Patients have lost their lives under your care, and the patterns are clear. This is not about your reputation; it's about justice!"

"Oh, justice," Harrow repeated mockingly, his voice melodramatic as he rolled his eyes. "You would think a detective such as yourself would understand what happens when someone tries to disrupt the natural order of things. You're meddling in affairs you don't fully comprehend."

The tension in the air was palpable. Families huddled closer together, their expressions filled with a mixture of fear and defiance. Harrow was attempting to manipulate the situation yet again, and Claire could feel the resolve of the families around her, like a shield against his charm.

"You think you have control, but you're wrong, Harrow," Claire said, her voice cutting through the intimidation. "The community is starting to see you for what you really are—nothing more than a predator hiding behind a white coat."

He took a step closer, forcing his confidence onto her. "And what will you do if the community decides to side with me? Your little crusade could cost you everything. The last thing they want is to be caught in a metaphorical crossfire between a disgruntled detective and their trusted doctor."

Claire felt a tightening in her chest, but instead of caving to his manipulation, she leaned into her strength. "If they choose to remain blind, it will only demonstrate their own fear. And fear is not a reason to silence the truth."

With each word, Claire stepped closer to Harrow, willing him to understand that his intimidation tactics would no longer work.

"Ah, I see," he replied, feigning realization while maintaining his condescending tone. "You're truly convinced you're leading a noble crusade. But tell me, what about the consequences? What about the collateral damage? People get hurt in fights like this."

Claire narrowed her eyes, assessing the danger in his words. "The only people who are getting hurt are the patients you've taken advantage of, and that stops now."

Behind her, the officers bristled at Harrow's presence, readying themselves but waiting for Claire to take charge. She could feel their support tightening around her like an armor.

"Do you really think you can hold onto this power forever?" Claire pressed, pushing through the tension that had settled in the air. "Eventually, the truth will prevail, and you will be exposed for who you really are."

The smile on Harrow's face faded, replaced by a flicker of anger that sent a shiver down Claire's spine. He stepped back slightly, recalibrating, and nodded slowly. "You're a brave woman, Claire Avery. But bravery without caution is just recklessness. And recklessness leads to mistakes."

Claire straightened herself, unwavering in her resolve. "And cowardice perpetuates harm."

Suddenly, Harrow's calm facade cracked, and he sneered. "This isn't over. I will make sure to demonstrate how misguided you and your little coalition truly are."

With that, he turned abruptly and began walking away, his silhouette blending into the shadows as he retreated. Claire felt a mix of relief and tension, knowing that the confrontation had revealed the unsettling reality of Harrow's character.

"Are you alright?" Officer Daniels asked, stepping closer and gauging her expression.

"Yeah," Claire sighed, shaking off the adrenaline. "I'm just frustrated. He thinks he can sweep this under the rug, and we both know that truth will eventually triumph. We have to stay vigilant and prepare for whatever tricks he has up his sleeve."

As the families began to express their support and concern, Claire turned her focus back to them, drawing strength from their presence. This confrontation had not only strengthened her resolve but also reaffirmed the determination within the community.

"We will not stand idle while he tries to manipulate us into silence," Claire declared, her voice ringing with conviction. The families around her nodded, bolstered by her words and the fierce determination that was beginning to take root in the hearts of everyone present.

"We have been too quiet for too long," Mary chimed in, standing beside Claire. "It's time we reclaim our voices and demand the respect we deserve."

"Exactly," Claire continued, feeling the energy of the room shift as unity blossomed. "This community has faced enough pain. Together, we can expose what's been happening and ensure that Harrow is held accountable for his actions."

The crowd murmured in agreement, the collective anxiety transforming into an empowered resolve. Claire could feel the momentum building— each voice added to the chorus declaring enough was enough.

"We need to make a plan for the upcoming forum," Lucy suggested, her tone filled with optimism. "If we can present our evidence clearly and with conviction, we can draw the attention of not only the police but also the media."

"Let's make sure we gather everything we need to present our case," Claire replied, her mind racing with possibilities. "We should prepare testimonials, documents, and any evidence of manipulation that highlights the impact Harrow has had on his patients."

The families began brainstorming ideas for the forum, discussing strategies for presenting their stories compellingly. Claire felt a swell of pride as they worked together, each individual in the room stepping up, eager to contribute to their cause.

"We can also invite local leaders and influential community members," Mrs. Mills suggested. "Their presence could amplify our message even further, showing that this isn't just a problem for the families involved but for the entire community."

"Yes!" Claire affirmed, excitement coursing through her. "The more support we have, the stronger we'll be. Let's not only shine a light on Harrow's actions but also foster a conversation about the importance of transparency in our healthcare."

As they continued to strategize, the room hummed with energy, the dark cloud of doubt that had previously loomed overhead slowly lifting. Families exchanged stories, their laughter ringing through the air, momentarily brightening the seriousness of their mission.

But as the meeting drew to a close, an unsettling feeling began to settle in Claire's gut. Harrow's words from their confrontation echoed in her mind: "Bravery without caution is just recklessness." She knew he wouldn't remain passive for long; he would retaliate, and the backlash would be inevitable.

That night, Claire returned home feeling a mix of empowerment and impending dread. As she prepared for bed, her phone buzzed with a new message—this time from Officer Daniels.

"Meeting at the precinct tomorrow. Urgent updates on Harrow's behavior. Possible escalation. Be prepared."

Claire's heart raced, knowing the weight of those words. Harrow was becoming unpredictable, and the potential for danger loomed large. She needed to be ready for anything he could initiate.

The following day, Claire arrived at the precinct, her heart pounding with both anxiety and determination. She joined Officer Daniels and the other officers gathered in a huddle, their expressions serious and focused.

"Thanks for coming, Claire," Daniels said gravely. "We may need to devise a more protective strategy for the families who've spoken out. Harrow has been seen lurking around their homes again, and we suspect he's attempting to intimidate them into silence."

"Intimidation tactics can mean he's more desperate than we thought," Claire replied, feeling a sense of urgency swarm around her. "We need to ensure we have officers stationed near their homes and continue monitoring Harrow's movements."

Just then, the lead officer in charge of the surveillance team spoke up. "We've been alerted to an unexpected gathering that Harrow is planning—something big. If he intends to rally impressive support, it could escalate significantly. We need to be prepared for a potential confrontation."

Claire's heart raced. "We must do everything we can to protect the families. If he's trying to regain control, we'll be ready."

As they strategized, Claire felt the pressure mounting. In the days ahead, they would need to solidify their alliance and stand firm in their resolve, regardless of how Harrow chose to retaliate.

But the stakes were high, and Claire understood that the confrontation would soon reach a breaking point, one that would determine the fate of all they had worked for. And this time, they would not allow Harrow to manipulate his way out of the consequences of his actions.

As the meeting concluded, Claire felt the weight of the impending confrontation pressing heavily on her. Harrow's dark influence had reached a tipping point, and they were poised to challenge it at its source. United, they would expose the truth, and together they would ensure justice would prevail.

CHAPTER 23
THE TRAP

The day of the community rally dawned bright and clear, but beneath the sunny facade, Claire felt a storm brewing. It was the moment they had been preparing for, and tensions ran high. She and her allies were finally ready to expose Dr. Harrow's manipulative practices, but they needed concrete evidence to ensure their voices carried weight.

In the early hours of the morning, Claire met with Officer Daniels and a few other trusted officers at the precinct to finalize the details of their sting operation. They understood the risks involved; Harrow was cunning, and if he suspected anything, he would exploit their every move.

"Alright, here's the plan," Claire started, laying out a series of diagrams on the table. "We've set up surveillance around the community center, where the rally will be held. Harrow is known for attending these types of events, and we believe he might show up to either defend himself or intimidate the families."

Daniels nodded, studying the layout. "We'll have officers positioned at all exits, ready to respond if he tries to evade us. Our goal is to catch him in the act of attempting to manipulate the audience or intimidate any of the families."

"Exactly," Claire agreed. "We'll also have a few undercover officers mingling in the crowd to monitor his interactions closely. If families feel threatened or if he starts making dubious claims, we'll be poised to intervene."

As they prepared, excitement mingled with anxiety in the air. The rally was not just a platform to share experiences; it was a pivotal moment when they would attempt to draw out Harrow and expose the truth.

"Remember," Claire continued, "this is about keeping our families safe and revealing Harrow's true nature. The more witnesses we have, the stronger our case becomes. They'll be supported by families, friends, and colleagues in attendance."

As midday rolled around, the community center began filling with families and supporters, the air charged with anticipation. Claire paced nervously, her heart pounding as she greeted attendees, ensuring they felt safe and supported. The heartbeat of unity beat strong within the room, a stark contrast to the isolation that had once plagued so many.

Just as the rally was set to begin, Claire received a frantic message from Lucy: Harrow has been spotted outside the center. He's trying to blend in with the crowd.

Claire's heart raced. "He's here," she announced to the officers, catching Daniels's eye. "Let's get into position."

The atmosphere shifted dramatically as the event commenced. Claire stepped up to the podium, her voice filled with purpose as she addressed the crowd. "Thank you all for coming here today! We stand united against manipulation and deceit. Together, we can reclaim our narrative and force Dr. Harrow to face the consequences of his actions."

From the corner of her eye, Claire spotted Harrow standing near the back, strategically positioned yet hidden within the crowd. He was scanning the room, eyes sharp, and Claire could feel the tension build as the moment of truth drew closer.

The rally continued, family after family stepping forward to share their experiences, each account drawing on the potency of their collective strength. Claire stayed poised at the front, her eyes flickering back to Harrow, who seemed to grow more agitated with every story shared.

Just then, as a family member spoke about their experiences, Harrow's demeanor shifted. Claire watched as he leaned to the left, whispering something to a surrogate supporter of his who stood nearby. It was a telltale sign he was preparing to intervene.

"Keep going," Claire whispered to the speaker, her heart racing as she prepared for the fallout. She needed to keep the momentum moving to draw out Harrow's predatory nature.

Finally, Harrow stepped forward, pushing through the crowd with a fake smile plastered on his face. "I believe we need to clear up some misunderstandings, don't we?" he exclaimed, his voice ringing through the hall.

Claire seized the moment, stepping back toward the podium, ready to confront him. "What misunderstandings are you referring to, Dr. Harrow?"

"You see," he began, his tone laced with a deceptive charm, "these families seem to forget that I've devoted my life to their wellbeing. It's easy to misconstrue care for manipulation, especially when you're facing unwanted scrutiny."

"Manipulation is precisely what I see in your actions," Claire shot back, her heart pounding as she engaged him directly. "You cannot simply deny the experiences of those you've harmed. They have seen their loved ones suffer under your care."

He scoffed at her, but Claire noticed the nervousness beneath his bravado. "These are just misguided notions from a few disgruntled families," he said, attempting to dismiss them. "You'll see that soon enough. The truth will always come out in the wash, as they say."

That was the moment Claire had been waiting for. Harrow's dismissive remarks played directly into the scheme she and the officers had orchestrated. As he continued to belittle the families gathered, she tightened her grip on the podium, steeling herself for the confrontation that lay ahead.

"You're wrong, Harrow," she declared, her voice ringing with conviction. "The truth has already begun to surface, and we are here to ensure that it becomes undeniable. You're not just a trusted physician anymore; you're a danger to this community."

The sensation in the room shifted, a palpable tension enveloping everyone as they absorbed Claire's words. Families stirred with newfound courage, bolstered by her determination. Harrow glanced around, his confident facade beginning to crack under the weight of scrutiny.

"Is this what you want to do?" Harrow shot back, his composure starting to falter. "Ruin lives for your own agenda? You really think I'm the monster here?"

"Yes," Claire replied, her heart steadying. "You've manipulated trust and caused suffering. And today, we gather not just to share our stories but to expose you for who you truly are."

Just then, a commotion erupted at the back of the crowd as Officer Daniels signaled to his team. Several undercover officers began to move quietly through the crowd, ensuring that they were ready to intervene if necessary.

"You think this will protect you?" Harrow sneered, glancing at the officers. "You surround yourselves with police, thinking it will shield you from the truth. This is merely a desperate act."

"The only desperate acts happening here are yours," Claire replied, her voice steady despite the tension. "Every word you speak today only further validates our claims. If you were truly innocent, you wouldn't be here trying to intimidate us."

Harrow glared at her, his frustration palpable as he took a step forward. "You have no idea who you're dealing with. I will ensure you pay the price for this insurrection."

Before Claire could respond, one of the officers in plain clothes stepped forward, speaking directly to Harrow. "Enough of this! We're here to ensure the safety of the families and the investigation into your practices. You need to leave."

"Leave?" Harrow scoffed, his arrogance flaring up again. "This is my community. I've built my entire career here, and you think you can chase me out with mere accusations?"

But as he continued to rant, Claire realized they had exposed a crack in his armor. The crowd was visibly uneasy, whispering amongst themselves, weighing the truth against his manipulative tactics.

"Dr. Harrow," Claire interjected, her voice cutting through the noise, "the people of this community deserve the truth. They deserve protection. And your actions today only confirm what many have feared—your attempts to intimidate will not work."

"Working to intimidate them? You're twisting my words!" Harrow shouted, growing increasingly agitated. "They are misguided. I am the one who has cared for them, who has saved their lives!"

"You may have started your career with good intentions, Harrow, but your desperation has turned you into the manipulator you claim to hate," Claire retorted, her voice rising with intensity. "You've exploited the trust these families placed in you, and it's time for that to end."

In that moment, Claire felt the tide of the room shift dramatically. The families began to murmur their agreement, voices rising in support of her words. "We are all tired of being ignored!" Mrs. Thompson shouted. "It's time for you to answer for your actions!"

Harrow scanned the crowd, the realization hitting him. The victims he had once controlled were now uniting against him. "You'll all regret this. I will not be silenced, and I will not allow you to destroy my reputation," he hissed, retreating a step that was laced with desperation.

As he turned to leave, Officer Daniels stepped in front of him, blocking his path. "You need to come with us, Dr. Harrow. We have grounds to question you regarding your treatment practices and any accusations presented today."

The atmosphere in the room shifted, a thunderous applause breaking out among the families as they watched Harrow's bravado finally falter.

Claire felt a rush of exhilaration, the culmination of their efforts manifesting before her eyes. Harrow's facade was crumbling, and justice was inching closer to reality.

As the officers moved to apprehend him, Harrow shot Claire one last piercing glare, a mix of fury and disbelief swirling in his eyes. "You may think you've won today, but this is far from over, Claire. I won't just disappear; you will face the consequences of your interference."

With that, he was led away, anger woven tightly within him.

As the families erupted in cheers of triumph, Claire felt a mix of relief and adrenaline coursing through her. The moment they had worked tirelessly toward had finally come to fruition; they had exposed Dr. Harrow's true nature in front of the community. Yet, amidst the celebration, a flicker of apprehension lingered in Claire's mind.

This confrontation was only one battle in an ongoing war. She had witnessed firsthand how desperate people could become when cornered, and Harrow's wrath would likely be swift and ruthless. The air crackled with tension, and Claire knew they had to stay vigilant—this was an opening, not a resolution.

"Thank you all for your courage," Claire said, raising her hands to quiet the crowd. "This victory is a testament to the strength we have when we stand together. But we must remember that Harrow is still out there. His threat to our community has not vanished."

Mary nodded, her expression a mix of determination and concern. "What do we do now, Claire? We can't let our guard down."

"We will regroup and formulate a plan to ensure the safety of everyone who has spoken out," Claire replied, glancing around at the rallying families. "And it's crucial that we continue to document any suspicious behavior from Harrow or his associates. We need to be prepared for his possible retaliation."

The murmurs of agreement rippled through the crowd, their shared conviction reflected in every determined face. The families began to exchange plans for how they would stay connected and report any suspicious activity they noticed in the coming days.

Just then, Claire's phone buzzed with an incoming message, pulling her focus. She glanced down to see it was a text from Officer Daniels: We've received word that Harrow is making desperate calls, trying to rally support from those who still trust him. Be careful.

"Everyone, we need to remain cautious," Claire announced, feeling a wave of urgency wash over her. "Harrow is trying to rebuild his influence, and we can't let him turn this community against us again. Keep your phones handy and report anything unusual."

As the families began to disperse, Claire felt the weight of responsibility settle once more upon her shoulders. She worked tirelessly to support these families, but despite their victory today, she sensed an imminent threat lurking just beyond the shadows.

Later that night, Claire sat at her kitchen table, piecing together their next steps. She dug into more research on Harrow, hoping to uncover any more evidence that could support their accusations. The television played softly in the background as images of today's rally played out. The news anchors shared the story of the community standing against Harrow, showcasing snippets of Claire standing at the forefront.

But just as Claire was wrapping up her notes, her phone rang. It was a number she didn't recognize, but gut instinct told her to answer. "Hello?"

"Detective Avery," came a voice on the other end—smooth and eerily calm. "You've been making quite a stir in our little town."

Claire's heart raced as she recognized the voice. "Dr. Harrow."

"You really should consider the consequences of your actions before you go any further with your little crusade," he warned, a hint of menace lurking beneath his congenial tone. "I have friends who don't take kindly to threats against their—" he paused, weighing his words carefully, "—business interests."

"What do you want, Harrow?" she demanded, her resolve hardening. "Your manipulation ends now. The truth will come to light, regardless of your threats."

He laughed softly, a chilling sound that sent a shiver down her spine. "Oh, Claire. You truly believe you're sitting in the seat of power, don't you? The truth can be a fickle thing, and it often comes at a cost. Remember, those who chase after it can find themselves caught in the act—just like you."

With that, he hung up, leaving Claire staring at her phone in shock. The subtle threat loomed large, planting seeds of doubt in her mind. She needed to fortify not just her strategy, but also her own defenses. Harrow was no longer just an adversary; he was a predator, and she needed to be ready for whatever tactics he might employ next.

That night, Claire gathered her notes and reached out to Officer Daniels, emphasizing the need for even greater safety measures for the families. She could feel the urgency mounting within her, but she was prepared to protect the community at all costs.

The confrontation with Harrow had revealed more than just his manipulations; it had exposed the vulnerabilities that she needed to guard against. Though they had seized a small victory, the war was far from over. Tomorrow would bring new challenges, but Claire felt emboldened by the strength of the families. Together, they would face the darkness with unwavering resolve.

CHAPTER 24
DESCENT INTO MADNESS

As the sun rose over Elderwood, casting long shadows across the streets, Dr. Samuel Harrow sat in his office, a storm of anxiety swirling within him. The confrontation with Claire and the subsequent rally in the community center replayed in his mind like a broken record, each image heightening his sense of paranoia.

He could still hear the accusations ringing in his ears, the defiance of the families unifying against him. How dare they question his authority? The weight of their collective gaze haunted him, and the looming threat of exposure tightened its grip around his heart, inching him toward the precipice of madness.

Every flicker of movement outside his office window intensified his feelings of dread. He had always prided himself on being the leader—the doctor people trusted without question. Yet now, every whisper he overheard made him feel like a marked man, surrounded by enemies. He could feel the walls closing in, fraying his mental state.

"What am I going to do?" he muttered to himself, running his hands through his hair in frustration. "They don't understand what's at stake. They don't know how much I've sacrificed for this community!"

As he stared at the shelf lined with patient accolades and photographs of smiling families, rage bubbled beneath the surface. Each award felt like a mockery of his current reality. The accolades he once cherished now seemed like chains binding him to a façade that was falling apart.

Just then, the phone rang, jarring him from his spiraling thoughts. He answered, his voice taut. "Harrow here."

It was one of his supporters, a man who had been vocally opposed to the families accusing him. "Doc, the townsfolk are getting restless. They're rallying, and I've overheard whispers of more families coming forward. You can't let this continue!"

"Don't you think I know that?" Harrow snapped, feeling the temperature rise around him. He could hear the concern in the man's voice, and it only fueled his growing paranoia. "What do you suggest? We need to crush this dissent once and for all."

"Perhaps a show of force?" the supporter suggested tentatively. "We need to remind them who they're dealing with. Undermine their confidence."

Harrow paused, contemplating the idea, each word dragging him further into the abyss of his own mind. "I won't let them defeat me. They've turned my kindness into a weapon. I'll show them what they've unleashed," he said, a dangerous resolve solidifying within him.

With that, he hung up and sat in silence, his thoughts racing. He would gather his supporters and create a spectacle—something to regain control. He needed to remind everyone just how powerful he could be when threatened.

That evening, Harrow began contacting a few loyal supporters, drawing them into a scheme that felt increasingly desperate. They discussed his ideas over drinks, inflating the notion of their shared loyalty while whispering about the families that dared to defy him. In their minds, this was a fight for their community, but it was clear that the lines between protectiveness and tyranny were becoming blurred.

As the hours passed and they mapped out a course of intimidation, Harrow felt an unsettling yet exhilarating sense of power begin to unfurl within him—he was prepared to do what was necessary to keep his status intact.

Meanwhile, Claire and the families were busy organizing final details for the upcoming forum, a gathering intended to unify the community against Harrow. She could feel the anticipation and the weight of their resolve blossoming; they were ready, but the tightening grip of fear clung to the edges of their determination.

In the days leading up to the forum, Claire noticed elements of discord surfacing in the community. Families were torn; some expressed fears about Harrow's possible retaliation, and others began to waver in their commitment, intimidated by the backlash. Claire's heart sank each time she encountered hesitation; she understood the toll Harrow could inflict.

On the day of the forum, as the sun dipped toward the horizon, casting a warm glow over the community center, the atmosphere felt electric yet tense. Families gathered, their eyes filled with uncertainty, but Claire was determined to push through that fear.

She took to the front of the room, her resolve firm. "Thank you for all being here tonight," she began, her voice steady. "Today we're taking a stand against the intimidation and manipulation that has plagued us for too long."

But in the back of the room, she noticed Dr. Harrow entering—his presence an unwelcome shadow that sent a shiver through the crowd. The glares of his supporters flared alongside him, their allegiance clear as they fanned out amongst the crowd.

Claire's heart raced as she spotted Harrow's cold gaze sweeping over the gathered families, calculating the atmosphere. It felt as if a dark storm was brewing, and she could sense the tension building, the scales of safety teetering on the brink.

The families shifted uneasily in their seats, their determination momentarily overshadowed by the presence of Harrow. Claire swallowed hard, realizing that their unity would be tested tonight more than ever.

"Today is about empowerment," Claire continued, pushing through her rising anxiety. "It's about us standing together and reclaiming our voices against manipulation and fear."

Harrow stepped forward, a smirk on his face, and the crowd fell silent, attention shifting toward him. "Empowerment?" he scoffed. "What a lovely way to spin your little gathering, Claire. Do you really think that people will believe your stories over mine? I am the respected doctor in this community."

The murmurs of the families grew louder, plenty hesitant that Harrow might sway the narrative. Claire recognized the fear creeping into their expressions, and she had to act quickly to regain control of the room.

Dr. Harrow's posture oozed smugness, and as he continued to address the crowd with practiced charm, Claire felt a surge of determination well up inside her. "What the community needs is clarity," she asserted, stepping forward to meet his gaze. "They need to hear the truth about the conditions under which they've been treated."

"Truth is often subjective, dear Claire," he replied, his voice almost silk-like, but the sharpness beneath it was undeniable. "What is your truth, exactly? That I've cared for my patients? Or that you're attempting to cut down someone who has dedicated their life to healing?"

"Your idea of 'care' is manipulation, and the evidence is piling up," Claire pushed back, feeling the adrenaline rush through her. She glanced at the families, seeing the shift in their faces as they began to rally behind her, reigniting their courage.

"Is that so?" Harrow returned, his expression shifting slightly. "You think your little gathering will deter me? You believe my reputation can be crushed by a few disgruntled patients? You underestimate my influence, Claire."

"It's not just disgruntled patients," Claire shot back. "It's families who have lost loved ones under your care, and we will not remain silent any longer!"

Harrow's eyes narrowed, and Claire noticed the subtle shift in his demeanor as he became more agitated. He was losing control of the narrative, and it was clear he could feel it. The families began to murmur in solidarity, empowered by Claire's words.

"Tension alone cannot build your case, Claire," he warned, his voice lowering to a threatening tone. "You've seen the consequences of standing against me. You've pushed me to my limits, and you will regret underestimating the lengths I will go to for those I care about—whether they are my patients or my allies."

At that moment, Claire knew she needed to expose Harrow's manipulative tendencies. "You've coerced families into silence and distrust," she said, her voice swelling with emotion. "That's not the practice of a trusted physician; that's the behavior of someone terrified of losing power."

The crowd watched in rapt attention, absorbing the tension mounting like a tidal wave. As Claire pressed forward, she could feel the collective strength of the families at her back.

"Faced with your own failures, you've turned to intimidation and deception instead of accountability!" Claire declared, taking a step closer. "You cannot control this community any longer, and your days of manipulation are numbered."

For the first time, Harrow's confident facade showed signs of cracking. His eyes flickered with an array of emotions—anger, desperation, and something darker. "You're a fool," he spat, words dripping with venom.

"We'll see who the fool is when the truth comes out," Claire retorted, feeling the momentum swing firmly in her favor.

Suddenly, Harrow turned to address the crowd, feigning sincerity. "Do you really want to believe this attack? I've only ever wanted to help you!"

His smooth words fell flat in the face of the growing resolve from the gathered families. They had come too far, and the tide of fear was finally shifting against him.

"To help us?" one voice called out from the back, a father speaking for families who had suffered losses. "You think we don't see what you've done? You've misled us, and we want accountability!"

With that, Harrow's expression hardened, panic beginning to seep through his carefully orchestrated calm. "You have no idea what you're inviting into your lives," he threatened, his voice low and dangerous. "This is not just a game. I will make sure you regret this."

As the air charged with tension, Claire sensed the flirtation of finality. They were on the brink of something significant—a climactic confrontation that could either seal their victory or plunge them deeper into the shadows cast by Dr. Harrow's influence.

The families stood united, their resolve hardening in the face of Harrow's threats. Claire felt the collective strength radiating from them, each individual bolstering the other in a shared purpose. She could see it in their faces—the determination to break free from the cycle of manipulation that had plagued them for far too long.

With a calmness that contrasted with the storm raging within, Claire stepped even closer to Harrow, unflinching in the face of his fury. "Your reign of terror ends here, Harrow. You may have tried to intimidate us, but we won't be silenced any longer."

Harrow took a step back, his expression shifting from anger to a calculating demeanor. "You think you know the whole story, but you're playing a dangerous game. The truth can be a fickle friend. You're risking your career, your reputation, all for what? A handful of emotional stories?"

Claire didn't waver. "These stories are lives, Harrow. They are evidence of your negligence and manipulation. And I am standing here to ensure that those who have suffered are finally heard."

With a quick glance back at the families, Claire was struck by the fear that still lingered in the eyes of some. They were fighting not just against Harrow, but against their own doubts and the anxiety he had instilled. "This isn't just about us," Claire reminded them. "It's about making sure that future patients are protected from the same harm. In unity, we can reclaim our strength."

Harrow's jaw tightened, the veneer of calm he had tried to maintain cracking under the pressure of the confrontation. He stepped closer again, his voice dropping to an almost conspiratorial tone. "You don't understand the kind of power I wield. I have connections, influence. You're out of your depth, Claire."

At that moment, the realization struck her like lightning. His intimidation was fueled by fear—not only of exposure but also of the unraveling of the control he had maintained for so long. It was a fleeting glimpse into his psyche, and she seized it with both hands.

"Power maintained through manipulation is the weakest kind of power, Dr. Harrow," Claire countered, feeling her heart race. "You think that your connections can save you when this community stands united against you? The truth is stronger than your influence; it's a force that can withstand even your greatest efforts to suppress it."

He glared at her, his eyes hardening as he calculated his next move. "Be careful, Claire. You're playing with fire, and that can burn more than just you."

With those words hanging ominously in the air, Harrow turned abruptly and walked toward the exit. The crowd shifted, some murmuring among themselves, their expressions painted with uncertainty. It felt as though the room had been holding its breath, caught between the fraught silence and the anticipation of what might come next.

Claire watched Harrow leave, her chest tightened with an uneasy mixture of emotion. The confrontation had revealed the gaping cracks in his facade, but it also left lingering questions regarding the lengths Harrow might go to protect himself.

"Everyone, let's regroup!" Claire called, feeling urgency swell within her. "We need to stay vigilant. Harrow won't take this lying down. It's time we prepare for any backlash."

The families nodded, newly fueled by Claire's passion as they contemplated the risk that lay ahead. They began to share their thoughts about the confrontation, voicing their concerns and reinforcing their unity.

Mary stepped forward. "We can't let him intimidate us." She held Claire's gaze with trust. "We're all in this together, and that means we support each other and remain strong, no matter how he tries to manipulate us."

With renewed determination, the families began to strategize on how they could reinforce their voices and prepare for any fallout from Dr. Harrow. It was clear that while they had gained ground, they were also stepping into a volatile confrontation with a man now backed into a corner.

As shadows lengthened outside the community center, Claire felt a mix of anticipation and dread. They were caught in a precarious balance, and the confrontation with Harrow loomed closer than ever, a reality that could either solidify their fight for justice or force them back into the depths of fear he had perpetuated.

Determined to face whatever lay ahead, Claire gathered her materials and locked eyes with the families. "We'll weather whatever storm he brings. Together, we will shine a light on the truth and reclaim our community."

With voices strengthened by their unity, the families stood tall, ready to confront the darkness that had threatened to consume them.

CHAPTER 25
THE CONFESSION

The evening of the community forum arrived with palpable tension hanging heavy in the air. Claire stood at the front of the packed community center, her heart racing as she prepared to confront Dr. Harrow in front of the families who had been so bravely sharing their stories. It was time to reveal the truth behind his manipulative facade—a moment she had been preparing for since this investigation began.

As attendees filed into their seats, Claire glanced around the room, catching the anxious looks exchanged among the families. Each person carried their own burden of fear and hope, a tidal wave of emotion building toward the confrontation that lay ahead.

"The importance of tonight cannot be overstated," Claire began, addressing the room. "We are here to share our experiences and seek justice against the manipulations and negligence we have suffered under Dr. Harrow. Together, we can hold him accountable."

At that moment, the door swung open, and Dr. Harrow stepped inside, his customary confidence radiating through the crowd. Pressing his lips into a thin smile, he quickly scanned the room before fixing his gaze on Claire.

"Detective Avery," he called out, his tone dripping with condescension. "I see you've assembled quite the audience. How quaint."

"Dr. Harrow," Claire replied, fighting against the unease that began to coil in the pit of her stomach. "We need to talk about your practices and the allegations against you."

"Oh, we're going to talk, alright," he retorted, stepping closer, his facade of charm slipping ever so slightly. "But let's not pretend this is anything more than a witch hunt instigated by a rogue detective looking to bolster her career at my expense."

Claire held her ground, refusing to let his intimidation tactics take hold. "This is about the lives that have been affected under your care—families that have lost loved ones due to your negligence. We will not back down."

With a simmering anger, Harrow seemed to lose some of his veneer. "You think you can rally these people against me and expect to come out unscathed? They are misguided, Claire. Trust me. Today, you will regret targeting me."

Claire noticed the glances exchanged among the families present, their expressions shifting from fear to resolve. "The time for standing idly by has ended, Harrow. This community is coming together—stronger than ever—and they're ready to face the truth."

Harrow's expression hardened. "What truth? That you're operating on hearsay? I dedicate my life to these patients, while you're simply throwing them under the bus for your own ambition."

Claire stepped forward, refusing to be intimidated. "I've gathered evidence, testimonies from families who are ready to speak out. We will unveil the truth about your negligence and advocate for those who cannot defend themselves."

An unsettling flicker crossed Harrow's face, the certainty that had marked his demeanor beginning to unravel. "You think you hold all the cards, don't you?" he said, his voice lowering menacingly. "People like you only see half the picture. The truth can be manipulated in more ways than one."

The tension in the room sharpened as Claire drew closer, determination fueling her. "And the lives you've neglected are the consequences of your control. You can try to spin this narrative, but there's no disguising the pain you've caused."

Glimpses of doubt sprung to Harrow's brow as Claire continued to press. "You have something to lose, don't you? Your reputation, the trust you've built. You can't hide behind your false persona any longer."

Caught off-guard, Harrow's bravado faltered momentarily. In that instant, the floodgates began to open, and Claire pressed forward, sensing victory within reach. "The people of this community deserve transparency—not manipulation. If you care so much, why have you dismissed their concerns? Why have you surrounded yourself with deceit?"

Just then, Claire saw the rage simmering within him reach a boiling point. "You have no idea what I've sacrificed to earn this position!" he shouted, his voice laced with a raw intensity. "I've had to make hard decisions—decisions you wouldn't understand! If these patients suffered, it was simply part of a greater good!"

"That's not how medicine works, Harrow!" Claire exclaimed, her voice rising above his. "Your responsibility is to care for your patients, not to play God based on your twisted perception of what's 'for their own good'! Those lives were not just pawns in a game; they were people! You failed them!"

With each word, Claire could feel the tension swell in the room, a storm gathering as the families began to nod, echoing her sentiments. Harrow's facade was crumbling as desperation clawed at his composure.

"Enough!" he shouted, voice wild. "You don't know what real sacrifice is! I've risked everything for these patients! You think you come in here and criticize me without understanding the pressures I face in this profession? The lives I've saved outweigh the few who might have suffered under my care!"

His outburst sent a ripple of unease through the gathered families, but Claire stood firm, refusing to let his words sway her. "You speak of sacrifice, but every life you've put at risk is a testament to your negligence. You wield your power over those who trust you, and for that, you must be held accountable."

Harrow's expression shifted, a storm of emotions flickering across his face. Anger, fear, and—was it guilt? Claire seized the opportunity, pressing on. "You've created an illusion of care, yet underneath that charming facade lies a reckless disregard for your patients' well-being. Today you stand exposed."

"I am not exposed," he hissed, stepping closer, his voice low and intimidating. "You think you can unravel me in front of all these people? You think they will believe your lies over my years of dedicated service? You will regret this, Claire. I have connections, people who will ensure you pay for your insubordination!"

Just then, a large crowd outside began to murmur, their voices rising as they expressed confusion about the tension brewing within the community center. Officers stationed at the entrance shifted their positioning, aware of the fragility of the situation unfolding.

Claire's heart raced, fueled by a mix of fear and resolve. "This isn't just about me, Harrow. It's about the families gathered here, those who've suffered while you circumvented responsibility. You may think you have power, but the truth has a way of cutting through deception!"

Out of the corner of her eye, Claire noticed Mary standing beside Mrs. Mills, each watching the confrontation unfold with anxious determination. The families began to murmur their agreement, their voices rising in unison, fueled by Claire's passion.

"Enough of your games, Harrow!" Mary shouted, stepping forward to join Claire. "You won't silence us anymore! We will fight for the truth!"

"You think numbers will protect you?" Harrow responded, frustration bubbling beneath his calm facade as he looked around at the gathering crowd. His confidence began to falter, the walls he had built up now starting to crack under the pressure of the collective force that stood against him.

"This is exactly what you do, isn't it?" Claire said, infusing her voice with conviction. "You try to twist the narrative, to gaslight these families into silence. But now they see through you, and you're losing your grip."

Harrow sneered, attempting to regain control over the situation. "Just remember, once the truth comes to light, you may find yourself faced with consequences that you never anticipated."

At that moment, Claire sensed a final, desperate attempt to manipulate the narrative. Harrow's eyes darted, calculating how to turn the situation to his advantage.

"You think you're the hero?" he spat, the ire reflecting in his voice, each word laced with venom. "You're digging your own grave."

"I know who I am, and I know what I'm fighting for," Claire shot back, unwavering and fierce. "I stand with the families you've deceived, and together, our voices will not falter."

As she spoke, the tension in the room shifted, and hope began to swell among the gathered families. The desire for justice blazed bright, even in the face of Harrow's threats. They were ready to confront the darkness he had tried to cultivate, and they would not be intimidated.

Harrow's composure finally slipped, revealing the desperate man hidden beneath the polished exterior. He stepped back, his hands clenched into fists at his sides, anger flickering in his eyes as he left the gathering. "You'll all regret this," he warned, his voice chilling as he retreated toward the exit.

The families erupted into a chorus of whispers, and Claire knew they had reached a pivotal moment. "We've drawn the line!" she exclaimed, raising her voice above the murmurs. "This is our moment to stand strong together, to ensure Dr. Harrow is held accountable for his actions."

As the meeting concluded, Claire felt the weight of victory swelling within her. Harrow's true nature had been revealed, and though the path ahead would not be easy, they had taken a significant step toward justice.

United, the families began to work together, ready to face whatever Harrow might throw at them next. Claire knew there would be fallout from this confrontation, but their voices were now fortifying the foundation of safety and integrity they had been striving to regain.

As night fell, Claire looked around at the faces of those who had gathered. The glow of determination illuminated the room, and she could feel the strength of their conviction. They would rise together, weaving a collective tapestry of resistance that would not be easily unraveled.

But even as hope coursed through her veins, a gnawing sense of caution reminded Claire that Harrow would not retreat quietly. He was a skilled manipulator who would likely counter their momentum with colorful rhetoric or worse. The unease that had settled in her gut whispered warnings that echoed the same fears she had voiced to the families.

"Thank you all for standing strong," Claire said, her voice resolute, as she addressed the group once more. "Our next step is crucial. We must prepare to present our testimonies not just for ourselves but for those who have been silenced too long. Transparency is our weapon against the darkness."

The families nodded, their resolve shining brightly despite the challenges ahead. "We'll support one another," Mrs. Mills spoke up. "We can create a network, ensuring that everyone feels safe and knows they're not alone in this fight."

As the families began discussing strategies, Claire took a moment to step aside, pulling out her phone to check for any messages. She realized that the remnants of her earlier confrontation with Harrow had left her with a low simmer of anxiety. Her instincts told her to remain vigilant.

Just as she was about to message Officer Daniels, her phone buzzed with an incoming call. It was an unknown number, and Claire's heart raced. "Hello?" she answered cautiously.

"Detective Avery," came Dr. Harrow's unmistakable voice, calm yet chilling. "I see you've gathered quite the following. But it won't save you, you know. You're meddling in affairs that don't concern you, and the ramifications could be... catastrophic."

Claire took a steadying breath, pushing down the dread that threatened to cloud her resolve. "You think intimidation will work on me, Harrow? Your days of manipulating this community are over."

"Oh, but Claire, this isn't just about manipulation," he replied, his tone shifting to one of chilling sincerity. "This is about loyalty and trust. Those families? They trust me. They come to me for help. You? You're an outsider who wants to tear them apart."

"I'm protecting them from you," Claire retorted, feeling her pulse quicken. "Your actions have consequences, and it's time for you to face them."

"What an admirable stance," he said, the undertone of his voice darkening. "But you may find that the truth isn't quite as clear-cut as you imagine it to be. I have connections that ensure I'll remain unscathed, regardless of your efforts."

Claire felt a surge of anger rise within her. "And you think that intimidation and threats will secure your position? Your arrogance is a weakness, Harrow. People are beginning to see through your charming exterior."

"They may be seeing what you want them to see," Harrow countered, his voice almost conspiratorial. "But what happens when the dust settles, and they realize you've led them to believe things that are baseless? You're not their champion, Claire. You're a misguided detective chasing shadows."

With that, he hung up, leaving Claire staring into the silence of her apartment, the walls closing in around her. Each breath felt heavier, suffused with the weight of his manipulative threat. But she refused to let him undermine her resolve.

Gathering her materials, Claire steeled herself for the fight ahead. She needed to ensure the families stayed connected and fortified against Harrow's tactics of intimidation. With each step she took toward the community center, she vowed to be the face of truth—a guiding force illuminating the darkness.

When she arrived, the families were waiting, their expressions a mix of anxiety and determination. She stepped to the front of the room, a sense of purpose pooling within her.

"I know we are facing immense pressure as we confront Dr. Harrow, but we must remain united," Claire began, capturing their attention. "Harrow will try to manipulate our fears, trying to push us apart. But we will stand together, and we will expose the truth."

The families nodded, their eyes reflecting a newfound courage. Together, they began to share their experiences, recounting the manipulations and the culture of fear that had shadowed their lives.

As voices filled the room, resolute and vibrant, Claire felt the energy shift. This was a moment of clarity in the midst of chaos—a revelation igniting strength where once there had been doubt.

The darkness Harrow had cast was beginning to lift, and as Claire listened to the families speak, she recognized the power of their unified front— one capable of withstanding intimidation. They would reclaim their narrative and rise against the shadows that had haunted them for far too long.

But in the back of her mind, she couldn't silence the whisper of fear. Harrow's threats were real, and his temperament was increasingly volatile. Claire knew that there was an imminent confrontation on the horizon—a clash that had the potential to escalate drastically.

As families continued to share their stories and rally behind each other, Claire remained vigilant, noting every expression of determination as well as the flickers of anxiety that crept into some faces. Each shared experience tightened the bond among them, but she remained acutely aware that Harrow would not let this go unchallenged.

"Before we conclude, I want to address the risks we may face," Claire said, raising her voice to capture the crowd's attention, her heart pounding. "Harrow may attempt to intimidate you, either directly or through his supporters. I need each of you to remain on high alert. If you notice anything strange or encounter any threats, contact an officer immediately."

A chorus of murmurs filled the room, and one of the fathers, his voice slightly shaky but resolute, spoke up. "We will not be silenced. We will come together against him. But the fear he spreads runs deep; we need to remain strong."

"Yes, we need to rely on one another," Claire affirmed, her heart swelling with pride. "This community has the right to reclaim their voices. For too long, we've allowed manipulation to dictate our lives. We are fighting for justice, for accountability, and for every life impacted by Dr. Harrow."

As the forum concluded, Claire felt a renewed sense of hope. They were forging ahead, constructing a united front that would shine a light on the darkness. Yet, as she walked to her car, the reality of the situation weighed on her.

The glowing streetlights formed long shadows on the pavement, and as she drove home, Claire's eyes darted to every passing vehicle. A sense of unease settled in her chest, an instinct that something was lurking just beyond her view, waiting for the opportune moment to strike.

When she finally arrived home, she took a moment to gather her thoughts. As she stepped inside, her phone buzzed with a new message. It was from Lucy, her voice trembling through the text: "Claire, I think Harrow is keeping tabs on me. I've seen a car parked outside my place for the last few nights."

Claire's heart raced as she read the message. She quickly dialed Lucy. "Lucy, you need to be careful. Are you sure it's Harrow?"

"I can't see the driver clearly, but they keep lingering," Lucy said, her voice laced with fear. "I don't know what he wants, but it makes me uneasy."

"Stay inside; lock your doors, and I'll send someone to check on you," Claire instructed, her mind spinning. The paranoia surrounding Harrow was reaching a boiling point, and Lucy was now in the crosshairs.

As Claire hung up, she felt the weight of guilt wash over her. "This has to stop," she murmured to herself, determination igniting once again. "I won't let him intimidate anyone else."

Claire contacted Officer Daniels, briefing him on the situation and insisting they check on Lucy immediately. She knew the risks were high, but it was vital to keep Lucy safe and provide reassurance to the families.

Just as she finished her call, her phone pinged again—another alert from the precinct. Frowning, Claire opened the notification to read about an increase in reported sightings of Harrow near residences of known patients. The shadow he cast was growing.

Fueled by resolve, Claire decided to take immediate action. She grabbed her notebook and began jotting down names of other patients she had spoken to during the investigation. They needed to consolidate their findings and push forward before Harrow could retaliate.

But then, a chilling thought struck her. Harrow had been pushing back, and it was only a matter of time before he took a drastic step to protect his interests. A plan was forming in Claire's mind—one that involved confronting Harrow head-on, armed with the truth.

Just as she prepared to leave, Claire heard a noise outside her window. Peering through the curtain, her breath caught in her throat—the same dark vehicle was parked across the street, its silhouette lurking ominously in the shadows.

Her pulse raced as the realization sunk in. Harrow had made his move, and he was watching her. Terra was shifting beneath her, and the stakes of this confrontation heightened exponentially. She would not cower; she would take the fight to him.

Fueled by adrenaline, Claire grabbed her jacket and prepared to head back out, ready to face Harrow's threats head-on. The risk of exposure was great, but the safety of the families and Lucy depended on her acting decisively against the manipulator lurking in the shadows.

CHAPTER 26
AFTERMATH

The dawn of a new day broke over Elderwood, but the light felt cold and unwelcoming. Claire stood outside the community center, feeling the weight of the past few days pressing down on her. The air was thick with tension, palpable reminders of the confrontation with Dr. Harrow still lingering in everyone's minds. The fallout from their efforts to expose him was unfolding, and the community was grappling with the aftermath.

As families began to arrive, Claire could sense the mix of anxiety and determination simmering among them. Some looked shaken, while others wore expressions of defiance. They had rallied together to confront their fears, but now the reality of Harrow's retaliatory nature loomed like a shadow over the gathering.

"Thank you all for being here," Claire said as the families trickled into the community center, their faces reflecting a spectrum of emotions. "I know things have become overwhelming after yesterday, but today we need to focus on each other and support one another."

Mrs. Mills stepped forward, her voice steady but tinged with concern. "What happens now, Claire? We faced Harrow, but I can feel the fear still settling in. His influence runs deep."

"We need to remember that we are not alone in this," Claire replied, feeling a swell of pride for the families who had defied Harrow. "We've built a network of support here, and together we will be stronger than his manipulation."

As stories began to surface once more, the atmosphere shifted; each family shared their feelings, their apprehensions, and their experiences

240

since the confrontation. Claire listened closely, offering words of encouragement and understanding. The emotional currents flowed freely, a mixture of fear and hope that filled the room, creating a supportive bubble around them.

Then, suddenly, the door opened, and Officer Daniels stepped inside, his expression serious. "I've got news about Dr. Harrow. He's been brought in for questioning, but there are families who need to be on alert."

Claire's heart raced as she processed what he was saying. "Questioning? About what?"

"There's been a significant amount of evidence compiled against him from the testimonies you gathered," Daniels explained. "But some families have reported harassment. We need to ensure everyone is safe and feels secure in their homes."

The realization sent ripples of anxiety through the group, and Claire felt a wave of resolve wash over her. "Let's not allow fear to spread. We can't let Harrow manipulate us anymore. Stand strong, everyone. We will face this together."

Over the next few hours, Claire and the officers coordinated security measures for the families who had spoken out. They worked tirelessly, making patrols around the residences, ensuring that everyone felt safe while they began to process the emotional impact of their experiences.

Claire made visits to a few families' homes to provide direct support, comforting them through the anxiety and uncertainty they faced. One such family was the Thompsons, who were still grappling with the aftershocks of their previous experiences.

"I don't know if I can go back to normalcy, Claire," Mrs. Thompson admitted, her voice breaking as she clutched a photo of her husband. "Every time I close my eyes, I see the way he talked to me. I was petrified."

"That's understandable, Mrs. Thompson," Claire said softly, kneeling beside her. "What you experienced was traumatic. It will take time to process—but acknowledging what you've been through is the first step toward healing. You are not alone in this."

As the day wore on, more families reached out to Claire, seeking support and reassurance. The community had begun to embrace open dialogue, allowing vulnerability to foster connection; it was a transformation unfolding right before her eyes.

As evening descended, Claire felt profound gratitude swell within her, but also a familiar knot of worry. The community had taken massive strides, but Harrow was still lurking, watching every move they made.

Later that night, Claire returned home exhausted but resolute. As she prepared for bed, her phone rang, startling her. The number displayed on the screen was unfamiliar.

"Hello?" she answered, slightly apprehensive.

"Is this Detective Claire Avery?" came a voice on the other end—a voice she didn't recognize but felt laden with significance.

"Yes, who is this?" Claire asked, trying to conceal her unease.

"I have information about Dr. Harrow," the voice said, revealing an urgent tremor. "But we need to meet. It's critical."

"Who are you?" Claire pressed, sensing that this could be the breakthrough they needed.

A pause hung in the air, and then the voice said, "I'll explain everything when we meet. Just know that this could change everything."

Claire's mind raced with the implications. "Where and when?"

"Tomorrow, at the diner by the highway at noon. Don't tell anyone, and make sure you come alone."

Before Claire could respond, the line went dead. She stared at her phone, a mix of excitement and trepidation swirling within her. This could be the lead she needed, the information that would turn the tide against Harrow once and for all. But it also sent a ripple of anxiety through her; what kind of information was this stranger offering, and could it be trusted?

With a deep breath, Claire vowed to approach the meeting with caution. She understood the risks that lay ahead—Harrow was not just a man; he was a master manipulator who wouldn't hesitate to silence anyone threatening his control. If this person had information, they were likely aware of the danger involved in coming forward.

The following day arrived with the sun hanging low in the sky, casting shadows that seemed to creep ominously along the streets of Elderwood. As Claire prepared to meet the mysterious caller, her heart raced with anticipation. She felt a mixture of fear and determination coursing through her veins; the stakes had never been higher.

Arriving at the diner just off the highway, Claire parked her car and stepped out, scanning the area for any sign of danger. The diner's neon sign flickered in the early morning light, a familiar sight that seemed to mock the gravity of her mission.

Walking inside, she was instantly greeted by the warm aroma of coffee and the comforting sounds of sizzling bacon. The friendly waitress gave her a nod as she took her seat in a booth at the back, her eyes scanning the room for any sign of the promised informant.

Minutes ticked by, and just as doubts began to creep in, the bell above the door jingled. A figure entered, a hooded sweatshirt pulled tightly around their face, casting a shadow over their features. Claire's heart raced as the figure moved with purpose toward her booth.

"Are you Claire Avery?" the figure asked, their voice low and cautious as they slid into the seat across from her.

"Yes," Claire replied, feeling a rush of adrenaline course through her. "You reached out to me about Dr. Harrow. What do you know?"

The figure leaned in closer, glancing around to ensure no one was eavesdropping. "I used to work at the clinic, in administration. I know things—things that you need to hear."

"Please, tell me everything," Claire urged, leaning forward, her sense of urgency growing.

"Dr. Harrow has been altering patient records," the figure revealed, lowering their voice even more. "He's been covering up adverse reactions and, in some cases, changing diagnoses to suit his needs. If someone spoke out against him, he would manipulate their records, sometimes even making it look as though they had fabricated their experiences."

Claire felt her heart race. This was significant evidence that could expose Harrow's deceitful practices and potentially link his manipulations to the growing list of suspicious deaths. "How do you know this?" she pressed, trying to wrangle the details.

"I've seen the files," they said, glancing nervously around the diner again. "I accessed them regularly, and when I saw the discrepancies, I tried to speak up. But instead of support, I was silenced. Harrow has the backing of powerful people in this town, and anyone who threatens him faces the consequences."

Claire listened intently, processing every word. "What exactly should I be looking for?" she asked, knowing they needed concrete evidence to fortify their claims against Harrow.

"I can help you access the records, but I can't go back there," the figure admitted. "I'm terrified of what he'll do if he finds out I've reached out. But I believe you can bring him down."

"Thank you for coming forward," Claire said sincerely, her heart filling with a blend of hope and resolve. "This could be the evidence we need. I promise to protect your identity and ensure you're safe. Together, we can expose him."

As they exchanged contact information and made plans to meet again, Claire felt the tide beginning to shift, but the shadows of paranoia still hovered. She knew the risk involved in confronting Harrow's power, but she also understood that the truth had a way of revealing itself, especially when fueled by a collective desire for justice.

After their meeting, Claire's mind buzzed with excitement and urgency. This was the breakthrough they had been waiting for—a chance to unveil Harrow's manipulative tactics and hold him accountable for the suffering he had caused in the community.

With renewed momentum, she made her way back to the precinct, ready to share the information with Officer Daniels and the families. They would turn these revelations into actionable evidence and push back against the darkness that had engulfed their lives for too long.

Claire could feel the storm stirring, but now, with the support of the community and the new evidence in hand, she was more determined than ever to illuminate the truth and confront Harrow once and for all.

CHAPTER 27
REVEALING THE TRUTH

The day of reckoning had arrived, and the community center was filled to the brim with families ready to confront the truth about Dr. Harrow. Claire stood at the front of the room, her heart racing with both anxiety and hope. Today marked a significant turning point in their fight for justice—a chance to expose the darkness that had lingered in the shadows for far too long.

As the families gathered, Claire felt a sense of solidarity enveloping the room. There was an undeniable energy in the air, fueled by a shared purpose. Each family member had come forth to not only tell their stories but to reclaim their power from the manipulation that Harrow had wielded.

"Thank you all for coming today," Claire began, taking a deep breath to steady herself. "Today is not just about confronting Dr. Harrow; it's about giving voice to the pain and suffering many of you have endured. Your stories matter!"

The crowd murmured in agreement, exchanging supportive glances while the weight of emotion hung heavily in the air. Claire focused her gaze on Lucy, who stood alongside her, visibly nervous but resolute. Lucy had courageously agreed to share her experience working closely with Harrow—and her testimony would play a pivotal role in revealing the truth.

"Today, I want to invite Lucy to share her experience," Claire said, stepping aside to allow her colleague the spotlight. "Her insights as a nurse in Dr. Harrow's practice are crucial to understanding the manipulation that has taken place."

With a shaky breath, Lucy stepped forward, her expression a blend of determination and trepidation. "Thank you, everyone," she began, her voice trembling slightly. "I've worked with Dr. Harrow for several years, and during that time, I saw many things that made me uncomfortable. The way he dismissed patient concerns became increasingly troubling."

As Lucy recounted her experiences working alongside Harrow, the gravity of her words resonated throughout the room. "I witnessed patients express fear and uncertainty about their medications, yet he would laugh it off and insist they were simply overreacting. It felt as though he was more interested in maintaining his authority than providing genuine care."

Claire watched as the families exchanged glances, the sincerity in Lucy's voice striking a chord. They could sense the truth beneath her words and felt empowered by her willingness to stand up to Harrow.

"I remember one patient, Mrs. Collins, who was anxious about her treatment. Instead of addressing her fears, Dr. Harrow became irritated, telling her she needed to trust him or it would hurt her health," Lucy continued, her voice strong with emotion. "That moment was pivotal for me—I realized then that he was prioritizing his ego over patient safety."

Tears threatened to spill from her eyes, but Lucy pressed on, determined to ensure her story would resonate. "When I saw the families affected by these practices, I couldn't just stand by. I knew I had to do something."

As Lucy spoke, Claire could see raw emotions surfacing among the families—anger, grief, but above all, a shared conviction to fight back against the injustices they had suffered.

"I know many of you have been scared," Lucy paused, glancing at the crowd, her voice filled with compassion. "But coming forward is the first step toward healing. We can no longer let fear dictate our actions."

The crowd erupted with murmurs of agreement, voices rising as their collective strength began to amplify. Claire felt a rush of pride and determination, watching as Lucy's bravery inspired others to share their stories, one after another.

Families began recounting their experiences, detailing the neglect and manipulation they had endured in Harrow's care. Each version of the truth was a powerful thread woven into the fabric of their movement—a movement that sought to expose the darkness that had clouded their lives for too long.

As the testimonies continued, Claire noticed a gray cloud moving in just outside the room—the ominous reminder of Harrow and the influence he still wielded. She knew the emotional toll on each of the families was steep, but so was the importance of holding him accountable.

When the meeting finally drew to a close, Claire stood at the front, gazing at the families gathered before her. "Today we've taken an enormous step toward reclaiming our narrative. Harrow may try to push back, but we are united. Together, we can reveal the truth and ensure that this community is protected."

Tears shimmered in Mrs. Thompson's eyes, her voice thick with emotion. "Thank you for giving us a voice, Claire. We couldn't have done this without you."

As families began to file out of the center, Claire felt a mix of relief and exhaustion wash over her. They had faced their fears, and now the truth was out there. But she also knew this was only one part of the long journey ahead.

Before she left, Claire gathered her notes, already contemplating the next steps. They had to prepare for whatever retaliation Dr. Harrow might unleash. The emotional toll on the families was immense, and she knew their courage had stirred the proverbial hornet's nest.

As she made her way to her car, Claire noticed Lucy waiting by the entrance, a worried look etched on her face. "Claire, are you alright?" she asked, concern deepening her expression.

"I'm fine," Claire reassured her, though she could feel the weight of the situation pressing down. "We're making progress, but we need to stay vigilant. Harrow will likely retaliate, and we have to be prepared for his defensive tactics."

Lucy nodded, still looking uneasy. "What if he tries to come after me again? I can't shake the feeling that he's watching my every move."

"Then we'll make sure you stay safe," Claire replied warmly, placing a hand on Lucy's shoulder. "You're part of this fight, and we won't let his intimidation tactics cause any more harm. I'll speak to Daniels about increased patrols around your apartment. We can't let fear dictate how we move forward."

"Thank you, Claire." Lucy stepped back, a flicker of gratitude lighting her eyes. "I just want to make sure our families are safe, especially after today."

Claire's heart swelled with appreciation for Lucy's commitment. "We'll do this together, and you won't be alone. Remember, we're building a support system to protect one another. That's what this fight is all about."

When they reached the precinct, Claire felt the atmosphere buzzing with urgency. Officers were discussing their steps to ensure the safety of the families who had come forward. She quickly moved to join Officer Daniels.

"Have you heard anything from Harrow's supporters?" Claire asked, scanning the bustling precinct.

"Nothing concrete, but I've caught wind that he's been making rounds, trying to sway public opinion back in his favor," Daniels replied, crossing his arms thoughtfully. "He might be trying to rally enough people to isolate the families you've been working with. We must be ready for any potential fallout."

"Let's bolster the patrols around the families tonight," Claire suggested, her determination sparking anew. "Keep an eye on Harrow's movements, and if he makes a move, we'll be prepared to respond."

As they laid out their plans, the evening felt heavy with impending confrontation. Claire couldn't shake the creeping sense of paranoia, knowing that the stakes were rising. If Harrow resorted to desperation, who knew what lengths he might go to protect himself?

Hours later, as Claire returned home, she flipped through her notes, reviewing the families' statements and trying to map out a strategy. But all her thoughts seemed to circle back to Harrow's threats and the growing climate of fear.

That night, sleep eluded her, her mind racing with scenarios and possibilities. The darkness of the night felt suffocating, and with every creak of the house, her heart raced. She was acutely aware of the danger lurking beyond the edges of her consciousness.

The next morning, as she prepared to leave for the precinct, Claire caught sight of a shadow lingering outside her window—one that felt strangely familiar. Tension coiling within, she hurried toward the window and pulled back the curtains slightly, peering outside.

But the street was empty, the unease returning as she tried to shake off the ominous feeling. It had been days since she had first encountered Harrow's unpredictable presence. Was he truly watching her now, or was the weight of fear playing tricks on her mind?

Once at the precinct, Claire brought her newfound vigilance and energy, ready to face whatever lay ahead. She called for an emergency meeting with Officer Daniels and the local team to ensure all families were protected and apart from the chaos Harrow had set loose.

"Together, we'll face Harrow," Claire stated, determined to shield the families from the potential fallout. "But we need robust strategies," she continued. "He's going to try to manipulate us again; that we can count on."

As the officers rallied around her, Claire felt the collective resolve from the community seep into her spirit. They would no longer stand in the shadows, but would confront Harrow with unwavering strength, exposing the truth behind his fearful facade. The tides were turning, but the fight was far from over.

CHAPTER 28
HEALING WOUNDS

As dawn broke over Elderwood, its warmth rejected the cold uncertainty that had lingered in the wake of their recent confrontation with Dr. Harrow. Claire stood at her kitchen window, gazing out at the sunlit streets, still reeling from the whirlwind of emotions that had rippled through the community. The rally had proven to be a pivotal moment, but it had also left its scars, and healing would take time.

Lucy called just as Claire was pouring her morning coffee. "Hey, Claire. Can we talk?"

"Of course," Claire replied, a sense of relief washing over her. "I was just thinking about you. Come over when you can."

Within a short time, Lucy arrived, her expression a mix of determination and introspection. "I've been reflecting on everything—what we've done and the choices we've made," she began, taking a seat at the table, her tone serious.

Claire nodded, feeling the weight of their shared journey settle in the air. "It's been a lot to process. I think we all need some time to reflect on what we've faced."

"I realize how much trust played a role in our actions," Lucy continued, her voice tinged with uncertainty. "Trust in each other and trust in the families. But I can't shake the feeling that maybe I put myself in danger by coming forward."

Claire leaned in, her heart heavy with understanding. "You weren't in this alone, Lucy. Trust is a double-edged sword; while it brings us together, it can also expose us to risks—especially when confronting someone as dangerous as Harrow."

Lucy looked down, swirling the remnants of her coffee in her cup. "I feel torn. I wanted to support the families, but I also cared for Harrow. I didn't want to believe he was capable of causing harm."

"That's a natural feeling," Claire reassured her gently. "We invest in people, and it can be devastating to realize that someone we trusted has betrayed that trust. But your choice to come forward was brave. You've stood up for what's right, and that speaks to your character."

"Thank you, Claire," Lucy said, looking up, her gaze steady. "I just hope the families feel safe moving forward. I hate knowing that my decisions might have put them at risk."

"They'll be okay," Claire assured her, remembering the resilience she had seen among the families. "We've built a supportive network, and we're taking precautions to ensure everyone feels secure. We have to allow ourselves to heal, too. The emotional toll of this fight is heavy, but that doesn't mean it was in vain."

The conversation took an introspective turn as they reflected on the impact of their choices. Lucy began to share her concerns about the emotional scars left behind by the confrontation with Harrow, each word weighted with the realization of how deeply trust had been breached within their community.

"It's hard to rebuild that trust after experiencing manipulation," Lucy reflected, her voice thoughtful. "I just hope the families can find peace again."

"They will," Claire said firmly. "But it will require open communication and support from all of us. Healing doesn't happen overnight; it's a process. Just as we're fighting to expose the truth, we need to find ways to support one another in moving forward."

Lucy smiled faintly, a sense of reassurance seeping into her expression. "You're right. I can see how strong the community has grown despite the fear Harrow instilled. They're ready to reclaim their narratives."

"Exactly," Claire echoed, the warmth of their shared resolve drawing her closer to Lucy. "And we're in this together. The journey ahead may be challenging, but we'll face it united."

As they continued their conversation, the sun crested higher, spilling golden light into the kitchen, illuminating their shared commitment to healing wounds—both within themselves and within their community.

Driving home the point of resilience, Claire leaned back in her chair, an idea sparking in her mind. "Let's organize support groups for those directly affected. Creating a safe space for discussion can help everyone process their feelings."

Lucy's eyes sparkled with enthusiasm. "That would be fantastic! Encouragement and open dialogue could go a long way toward rebuilding trust."

With renewed hope and purpose, they finalized plans for the support groups, aiming to create an environment where families could share experiences, process their emotions, and begin to heal together. Claire felt a wave of relief, knowing that each step they took brought the community a little closer to recovery.

As the conversation wound down, Claire realized that their struggle had driven them deeper into empathy and understanding, as they collectively navigated the shadows that Harrow had cast. They had committed to fighting back against manipulation, but they were also prioritizing the emotional well-being of those they sought to protect.

With a sense of purpose anchoring her as the sun dipped low on the horizon, Claire felt a powerful truth settling in her heart: healing would come not only from confronting the darkness but also from fostering connection and trust among the families affected by Dr. Harrow's manipulations.

Returning to the precinct later that evening, Claire found the energy charged with anticipation. Officers were gathering around, discussing the latest developments as they prepared for the next day's rally to further confront Harrow and amplify the families' voices. The resolve seemed palpable, a rotating sphere of unity swirling around her.

"Hey, Claire!" Daniels called, waving her over from the corner of the room. "We're getting reports about Harrow trying to contact patients again. There's a growing concern he might attempt to discredit everything we're doing."

Claire felt a knot of frustration tighten inside her. "He's still trying to control the narrative. We have to ensure that families feel supported, just as we planned."

"Absolutely," Daniels agreed, urgency clear in his voice. "We've set up increased patrols around the homes of the families who've come forward. But we should also prepare for any potential backlash from Harrow. If he feels threatened, he could lash out in unexpected ways."

Once again, the weight of their fight settled heavily on Claire's shoulders, but instead of succumbing to the pressure, she felt invigorated by the challenge. "Every patient who's come forward is a step toward justice. We won't let fear dictate this community's path any longer. We must empower these families, ensuring they know they're not alone."

As the meeting continued, Claire noticed a sense of collective determination. The conversations turned to coordinating efforts for the rally, drawing on their shared emotions and experiences to create a powerful collective voice against Harrow.

That night, Claire stayed late, working to finalize statements for the rally. The echoes of the families' voices filled her mind, and she felt every word deepen her resolve. They were more than testimonies—they were testimonies filled with hope and a collective fight for justice.

Just as she started reviewing her notes for the hundredth time, her phone buzzed with an incoming message from Lucy: Any updates? I'm feeling anxious about the rally tomorrow.

Claire quickly typed back: We're all feeling it. Just remember—the strength of our voices matters. We stand together.

With the message sent, Claire leaned back in her chair and sighed deeply. She didn't want to admit it to herself, but she was feeling anxious, too. The tension surrounding Harrow's growing paranoia haunted her thoughts. He was a formidable opponent, and she could not overshadow that fact as they approached the rally.

As she prepared to leave the precinct, Claire felt a sudden urge to check her surroundings. The shadows lingered, and the quiet of the night felt heavy with apprehension. With a quick glance outside, she noticed unnatural movement near the entrance of the parking lot—possibly cars with unknown faces watching closely.

She steeled herself as she walked toward her car, determined to forge ahead despite the undercurrent of fear tugging at her. Salvation was within reach, but only if she could outmaneuver Harrow's attempts at intimidation.

Checking her phone one last time, Claire dialed Daniels, her tone serious. "We need to remain vigilant. I just noticed some possibly suspicious activity outside. Harrow may be lurking somewhere near."

"We'll have officers stationed nearby during the rally," he reassured her, his voice calm. "No one will get through without our knowledge."

"Thanks, Daniels. I don't want to put anyone in danger," Claire replied, grateful for his support. As the call ended, she felt a fleeting sense of comfort wash over her amidst the gathering storm.

The next day would be the pivotal moment in their fight for justice—the crucial confrontation that could either uphold the dignity of their community or leave them vulnerable to Harrow's manipulations. With each step she took, Claire felt the weight of the truth propelling her forward, ready to embrace whatever came next.

As night fell over Elderwood, Claire resolved herself to face the challenges ahead with unwavering strength. Together with the families who had entrusted her with their stories, she would strip away Harrow's facade and fight for the justice they all deserved.

CHAPTER 29
ALONE IN PAIN

The day of the rally arrived, and Elderwood was cloaked in an expectant hush as families congregated at the community center. The sun rose brightly, but beneath that warmth lay an undercurrent of anxiety. Claire stood by the entrance, taking in the sights of families arriving—some with eyes filled with trepidation and others shining with a sense of purpose. The emotional weight felt palpable, thickening the air with the unspoken bonds of shared experience.

"Claire," Mary approached, her face a mix of resolve and fear. "Today is it, isn't it? We're really doing this."

"Yes," Claire replied, her voice steady, though her heart fluttered with apprehension. "This is a critical moment for all our voices to come together and face the truth. We're here to support each other. Remember, you're not alone in this."

As they entered the crowded hall, Claire felt the mingling emotions swirl around her—a tapestry of anxiety, hope, and camaraderie inherent in shared pain. The energy in the room buzzed as families gathered, exchanging uneasy glances while clutching one another's hands. They were bound not only by the grievances they shared but also by the trust they had built during this tumultuous journey.

Claire stood at the front of the room, poised to share her thoughts, when whispers of uncertainty swept through the crowd. "What if Harrow tries to sabotage this?" one woman murmured, her voice filled with worry.

"He's desperate, yes," Claire acknowledged, trying to calm their fears. "But we've gathered strength together, and that unity can't be broken. We've all come too far to let someone intimidate us now."

As the meeting commenced, families began recounting their experiences, stitching together a narrative rich with both sadness and resilience. Claire listened as the shared stories illuminated the themes of isolation and betrayal that had seeped into their lives. The pain etched on their faces was all too familiar; they had grappled with trust and uncertainty as Harrow manipulated their vulnerabilities.

"After my husband's passing, I felt so alone," Mrs. Thompson shared, her voice shaking with emotion. "It was as if no one else in the world understood the depth of my pain. I kept it to myself, thinking maybe I was overreacting, that no one would believe me if I spoke out."

"Exactly," Lucy chimed in, her voice steadying as she joined the conversation. "I worried that my doubts about Harrow would make me look ungrateful for his care. Yet it was that very silence that allowed the erosion of trust to go unchallenged."

With each testimony, Claire could sense the walls of isolation beginning to crack, replaced by a unified chorus of shared experiences. It became clear that their pain stemmed not just from Harrow's negligence but also from the growing fear that had silenced them.

"Today, we are breaking that silence," Claire said, stepping back forward to address the gathering crowd. "We are healing by coming together, acknowledging that what we've each faced is valid, and vowing to stand united against the shadows of doubt Dr. Harrow has cast."

The families responded with murmurs of support, their collective energies ignited by Claire's passionate declaration. They began to share more openly, standing shoulder to shoulder, their bond strengthening through each shared story. Claire could see the walls of isolation crumbling, replaced by an embrace of understanding and fortitude.

As the rally continued, Claire felt a wave of emotions whisk over her. The stories of pain interwoven with moments of healing felt like fresh stitches on a wound anew—a community was emerging from its isolation, ready to reclaim its narrative.

But just as hope began to crest, Claire felt a familiar chill creep in—the notion that while healing together was powerful, there were still threats lurking in the shadows. Harrow's influence wasn't entirely extinguished, and the potential fallout from today remained acutely present.

As Claire wrapped up the rally, a palpable sense of hope flowed through the families. It was a moment of triumph; they had begun the process of healing and were no longer alone in their pain. Yet the journey ahead would require them to remain vigilant and resolute.

That night as Claire returned to her apartment, a wave of exhaustion washed over her, mingled with the lingering ache of concern. She knew this battle was far from over; they still had to confront the ramifications of their collective courage.

The process of healing would take time, and while the community had found strength in unity, the specter of Harrow still loomed on the horizon, waiting for its chance to strike back. Claire resolved to guard against that darkness, prepared to support the community as they navigated this new path toward justice and healing.

CHAPTER 30
AN ECHO OF SILENCE

As the first light of a new day broke over Elderwood, Claire stood at her window, gazing out at the stillness of the morning. The community felt different, a once-vibrant town now cloaked in a palpable tension that pushed against the fragile hope they had worked so hard to establish. The sun's rays illuminated the streets, casting long shadows that reminded her of the darkness they had fought against—a darkness that had tried to suffocate them all.

The fallout from the rally had sent ripples through the community. Dr. Harrow had been apprehended, but the haunting impact of his actions lingered like a specter, a reminder of how easily trust could be manipulated. The faces of the families who had stood together still haunted her; their pain etched into her memory like scars that wouldn't easily fade.

Claire gathered her notes one last time, mindful of the journey that had led them to this point. While they had succeeded in exposing Harrow, the scars left behind were undeniable—a tapestry of grief and betrayal tied intricately to the very fabric of Elderwood.

As she made her way to the community center for a debriefing, Claire felt the weight of solitude pressing against her. The hustle of the town had transformed into a cautious awareness, where whispers still echoed in the corners of coffee shops and local gatherings, and trust had frayed.

Upon arriving, Claire was greeted by familiar faces—families who had once felt isolated but now remained connected through shared experiences. Yet within that connection, Claire could see the remnants of doubt, the lingering effects of how easily someone could exploit trust.

"Thank you for coming," Claire said as she glanced around the room, her heart heavy with the knowledge of what they had collectively endured. "Today, as we discuss our next steps, I want us to take a moment to acknowledge the impact Dr. Harrow had on our lives, but also the strength that has emerged from our unity."

The families nodded, their expressions a blend of gratitude and lingering hurt. "It's been a long road, but we're together in this," said Mrs. Mills, her voice steady yet filled with bittersweet emotion.

Claire felt the connection radiate through the room, woven tightly by collective narratives, and it emboldened her spirit. "We've fought against manipulation and deception, and together we'll work to heal—not just the wounds Harrow inflicted, but also the fractures within our community. We must remember that healing doesn't happen overnight; it requires patience and understanding."

Just as Claire began to outline their future steps, the door creaked open and Officer Daniels entered with a solemn expression. "I have an important update regarding Dr. Harrow," he announced, pausing for a moment before continuing. "The investigation is ongoing, but we've discovered he's made connections to certain community members who are still loyal to him. The potential for backlash remains."

The families exchanged worried glances, unease rippling through the group like a wave. "Will he try to come after us again?" one father asked, his voice tinged with concern.

"We must remain vigilant," Daniels replied, his tone firm. "But this is also an opportunity for us to educate the community about the signs of manipulation and the dangers of misplaced trust."

Claire nodded, feeling the weight of responsibility settle heavily on her shoulders. "Absolutely. We can't let fear dictate our actions. We will work to create awareness and encourage open dialogue within our community to prevent future situations like this from arising."

As the meeting continued, plans to foster education and communication began to take shape, the tension in the room slowly dissolving as the families focused on healing.

But that evening, after the meeting concluded, Claire returned home, the fatigue of the day hanging heavily on her. She sat at her kitchen table, staring out into the night, her heart heavy with reflection. The battle against Harrow had stirred the community awake, yet the aftermath left plenty of unanswered questions.

The realization struck her—while they had pushed against the darkness, every community has its shadows, and healing takes time. Even amidst connectedness, solitude can linger within the hearts of those who have suffered. With each echo of silence in her apartment, Claire felt the reminder of their shared pain linger in the depths of her soul.

In that stillness, Claire reflected on how appearances can deceive, how trust can be built and broken, and how the journey toward healing is just as necessary as the fight for justice. And even though the path ahead was uncertain, she knew one thing for certain: the community had found their strength together, and in unity lay the resilience necessary to face whatever challenges may arise.

As she closed her eyes, she felt the whispers of hope surround her, the acknowledgment that while solitude may always attempt to creep in, the bonds forged through shared experiences would illuminate the way forward, reminding them all that they were never truly alone.

ABOUT THE AUTHOR

Jamar Berry is a former British soldier who served under HM King Charles III. With a strong foundation in law, Jamar holds a Diploma in Police Foundations and Criminal Law, as well as a Diploma in Paralegal Studies. Currently pursuing a Bachelor's degree in Law, he combines his military experience with academic knowledge to craft compelling narratives that explore the intricacies of justice and morality. Jamar's passion for storytelling reflects his commitment to raising awareness of the complexities of human experience within the realms of law, conflict, and community.